JAYNE EVERARD

The Loved & The Lost

This book was professionally typeset on Reedsy.
Find out more at reedsy.com

For Simon, Oscar and Harvey

Contents

1

Babette

The chisel hit the wall with the resounding clang of metal on flint and fell to the floor. Letting loose a barrage of profanities, Julius slumped back down in the chair and ran a dusty hand through his mop of thick grey hair.

He was wood turning in his workshed at the top of the garden. His intention was to make a spindle to replace the one that had splintered on the back of the kitchen chair that Elisabeth had been swinging on and had subsequently fallen off of.

"All four legs on the floor, Elisabeth!" she was often told, but of course she forgot. The chair crashed to the tiled floor with her full weight landing on top of the already split and loosened back that had been glued and re-glued several times over the years. How Elisabeth had screamed! But this was from the fright rather than any pain or injury, and then she'd stood up quite suddenly and kicked the fallen chair three times. When her mother had rushed to her and examined her there was not a mark nor a bruise to be found.

The treadle of the lathe was causing Julius much vexation;

it had become loose and no matter how much force he used on it, it made very little impetus and the piece of wood he was working on still failed to rotate. He went to the bench and checked the spindle gauge; he had been thinking it was time to buy a new lathe, something considerably more modern, run on electric. Reluctant to part with the money, he wondered if he could make a replacement Pitman rod so that the treadle would work properly; that was certainly the problem, and no wonder - he'd bought the lathe second hand over 20 years ago so it had seen a lot of use.

He scratched his head and looked about his workshop; stuff everywhere. Rough sketches littered the corner by the lathe, cracked and dusty plastic goggles hung from rusty nails knocked into the mortar between stones, tools of all sorts and sizes were strewn on the workbench along the back wall, and next to it was a lopsided shelf holding blocks of wood, heavy logs, and tree stumps. Above this, irregular planks of wood served as more shelves that were cluttered with jam jars full of nails and screws, plastic tubs holding lengths of various sized wire, and pots of varnish, brushes and glue. In the centre of the workshop on a chipped concrete plinth was a pot-bellied stove, long redundant and years since parted from the flue pipe that was now hanging in mid-air from the corrugated tin roof. Worm eaten, cobwebbed ladders leaned against the wall behind the door, hiding brooms and shovels that were clearly unused, as everywhere was sawdust and piles of wood shavings. Ivy crept in where it could; in the gaps at the top of the walls and around the rotting window frames long tendrils took hold in dogged determination to claim the shambolic old barn.

The resonating beat of punk music reached Julius' ears,

vocals shouted rather than sung; Babette was home, which meant it was gone half past four. He looked out of the window and saw the French doors fly open; the music seemed to charge up through the garden like some unruly mob let out of custody. Ah Babette, Babette! At times she had been like a whirling dervish, bringing chaos to the home with some minor crisis in her personal life; it would take light in her mind like a flicker in the depths of a bonfire, racing this way, that way, twisting round and round, spiralling higher and higher until it blazed irrationally out of control, sparks crackling out into the household, bringing a tense and unsettled air until, after the passing of a few days whatever it was had subsided, dissipated, and calm was restored. With age, she had become more imperturbable, as if the passing of the years had soothed her, though her nature, at the core, remained vivacious and lively; some would say gregarious.

Julius supposed Babette would never change and that part of her would always be highly charged emotionally, after all, she'd been this way for as long as he could remember, even though she was little more than five years old when he first knew her. His brother married her mother having met her at a festival and lived with her for a few months in a commune in the New Forest. The 'wedding' took place on a prehistoric hill fort where they were married by a young man with a very long beard who was dressed in druids clothing. Apparently, he was a priest of some sort, so he officiated at the ancient hand fastening ceremony. That day Babette was pale and almost ghoulish, a ragamuffin bridesmaid in a once white dress that was tattered at the hem. She wore a makeshift headband of lavender, rosemary and sage, possibly an attempt to tame her dishevelled hair.

3

Oh that day! So awkward! Julius shook his head at the thought of it, even now. Louisa had said it was a sham and that the marriage would never last; Nathan, she said, was either bewitched or had taken leave of his senses.

Julius did not want to be there. He remembered the long climb to the top of the hill, in the blazing afternoon sun; it was as if some mischievous imp had run among them brandishing a flaming torch, weaving in and out of the weary throng, snarling and laughing, a gruff and malevolent laughter. Patches of perspiration spread across the back of Nathan's thin lilac shirt as they all trooped up over tussocks of mat-grass with the baskets of flowers they had been asked to bring, wondering 'Why? What are we to do with these flowers? What are they for?'

The flowers were to be laid on the ground at the summit, to form a circle into which the bride and groom were called to take their antediluvian vows, whilst the bewildered onlookers were requested by the self-claimed druid to repeat '*And so we mote ye*' each time he spoke the words himself.

"*And so we mote ye. And so we mote ye.*" Again, and again, like some monastic chant to drive them mad under the unbearable heat of the hottest day of the year.

Bored and irritated, Julius had wandered off alone to the edge of the hill to contemplate. It occurred to him that it was of course, a superb vantage point and that in its former use as an Iron Age camp it would have fulfilled its purpose well; a 360 degree panorama and the steep ramparts allowed plenty of time to fend off any impending attack from enemies, but that day, the day of Nathan's wedding, the views out over miles and miles of a usually spectacular landscape felt dreamlike, obscured by a penetrating, other-worldly fog.

When the ceremony was finished and the druid speak done with, the guests were invited into the circle of flowers to share refreshments. Far from the usual wedding breakfast, a stoneware goblet of non-alcoholic wine was passed from person to person as each took a sip and handed it to the next. Then a piece of fruit cake, likewise, was passed from hand to hand. Julius was thirsty and found this ritual uncomfortably tiresome; he wondered why his brother had chosen this course, and why this woman - why her of all people? Surely he could have chosen someone better suited to him?

He struggled to remember his own children being there, his only recollection being that Fabia was still in nappies and crawling, and that unattended for a moment, she had sat on the cake which had been left in opened foil on the grass. Where was Caspian? Why couldn't he remember Caspian being there? He would have been about seven, in shorts, with his first glasses on, but Julius could not remember. Louisa was there of course, increasingly hot and grumpy, and complaining, her primrose yellow dress smeared with chocolate from Fabia's grubby hands.

* * *

Julius closed the window of his shed and sighed. He had noticed that he sighed more lately and he wondered why. 'Why am I sighing now?' he'd question, tracing his thoughts back, but there was never any real reason to be found. He supposed it was just something that you did more as you got older, although the ensuing thought came that it couldn't be so – imagine if everyone over the age of 56 sighed as much as he did! There would be millions of people, shuffling and sighing as they went about their days, pushing trolleys around supermarkets, sighing; walking dogs in the fields and parks, sighing; driving to work sighing. The world would rise and fall with the frequency of a colossal universal sigh!

"Julius! Julius!" came Babette's urgent voice as she burst into the workshop. "I've got the kettle on for tea. Would you like a cup?"

He peered over the top of his glasses at her and back at the sketch he was studying, "Yes please Babette, I would, thank you. How are you? Did you have a pleasant day at work?"

"Same as usual really. I typed a few letters, answered the phone, made coffee for everyone, went to the bank. The same as usual, nothing exciting."

"Well, I suppose that's how it is for a lot of people. It's an income though, isn't it?" he gently reminded her. "It all helps."

"Well, yes, of course. I couldn't manage without it, that's for sure. It's just that sometimes it gets a bit, well… monotonous." She paused, folded her arms across her chest, and looked around the workshop.

"This place is a bloody mess Julius. I don't know how you can work up here, with all this dust, and cobwebs and spiders everywhere. Why don't you have a good tidy up and get things organised a bit better? Why don't you sweep some of this sawdust up?"

"It's not that bad, and besides, I know where things are. I'm quite happy with it like this. It's been like it for years. It seems to work alright for me."

"It doesn't look like these ladders work, nor those brushes up there! And," she said, pointing to the dangling stove pipe, "that thing certainly doesn't work! Honestly Julius, it's a mess!

6

You should ask Caspian to help you sort it all out one weekend."

Julius continued to study the sketch, allowing Babette's words to tumble around the room, drift up, up into the ivy and away through all the little cracks in the walls.

"I'll be down for tea shortly," he muttered, quite sternly without looking at her. He brushed wood shavings from his sleeve. Babette refolded her arms, turned on her heel and left, leaving the door wide open, the click-clack of her shoes on the garden path growing fainter as she neared the house.

* * *

Almost seven minutes later, Julius locked up the shed and started on his customary amble down through the garden to the house where tea, made by Babette and now going tepid, awaited him. It was late March and after three or four days of gales and squalls typical of the time of year, the skies were calmer now, with a weak sun trying desperately to break through the clouds, and the temperature had noticeably risen. The birds had become quite vocal and were busily going about their business, chirruping from the dense laurel hedging running along from the garage to the top of the garden. Three cock blackbirds let loose a light trilling song from the fruit trees close to the hedge that bordered the field, as they laid claim to their territory. Julius had watched them from the conservatory that morning, hopping across the lawn, stopping now and then, as if frozen by some unearthly magic, cocking their heads to one side, entranced by an unseen bird charmer; but of course they were only listening for the movement of worms beneath the soil. They froze stock still at the slightest sign of possible danger, mostly in the form of the big tabby from the house next door, who had a habit of prowling the garden at certain times of the day. Every so often the blackbirds would squabble and fly at one another, wings spread, squawking; witches fighting over the eye of a bat, the toe of a shrew.

Nearing the house, Julius could see Babette and Caspian in the kitchen, talking and laughing above the music; Caspian was home early after dropping his client off at the railway station in time for the 4.38 train to London.

"Where is Elisabeth?" Julius asked.

"She's gone to Anna's," Babette said, lifting the teapot. "She's having tea there, she'll be home around seven. It was all very last minute, the girls planned it at breaktime. A bit annoying because I could have worked later if I'd known, but never mind." She poured fresh tea into a mug and handed it to Julius.

"I thought I could have some time to myself," she continued. "A nice cup of tea and a piece of fruit cake, put my feet up and read the paper, but Caspian's come home early and spoilt my plans."

"Charming, Babette!" was Caspian's sarcastic riposte. He was sat at the table, the television guide spread out in front of him, hoping to find something of interest for the evening's viewing.

"I thought you liked my company, but I can see when I'm not wanted! I take the hint, I take the hint!" he said dramatically.

Babette laughed. "Oh Caspian! You know I don't mean it, of course I like your company, it's lovely to have you home early! It means you'll have time to fix the dripping tap in the bathroom!"

Standing behind him, she put her hands over his ears and planted an audible kiss right on the top of his head.

Julius shook his head as he carried his tea outside. 'She'll be a mad old bat one day,' he thought. He sat on the bench by the back door, took a tobacco tin from his pocket and rolled a cigarette, the fourth of the afternoon. He crossed his legs and sat and smoked, watched the blackbirds, and thought of little else.

Caspian gave Babette's arm a playful twist as she pulled away from him, "What's for dinner tonight?"

"I have no idea! You can have whatever you want, I'm not cooking tonight. I'm just going to have cheese on toast or something before Elisabeth comes home and when she's gone to bed I'm planning on having a nice long soak in the bath."

Caspian feigned disappointment, "Oh, Babette!" he wailed. "How very selfish of you! I've had such a hard day at work and I was hoping you'd be cooking one of your wonderful Shepherd's Pies tonight! I've thought of little else all day, I've barely eaten a thing! I've been saving myself for it and now I'm so hungry! What will I do? What will I eat?"

"If you want a Shepherd's Pie you'll have to go to the shop and buy a frozen one and cook it yourself. You know how the oven works, don't you?" With a self-satisfied smile Babette turned her head and left the room, a mug of tea in one hand and her work bag in the other.

"Babette!" Caspian called after her, his tone more serious, "What's everyone else having?"

"I don't know," she said, glancing over her shoulder. "I expect Fabia's poking about a few lettuce leaves and Julius is having something he found in his beard from yesterday's roast." She grinned and winked at Caspian; her scathing wit never failed to amuse him. "There's leftover chicken in the fridge, you could do something with that if you fancy it. There are a few potatoes too, we didn't eat them all yesterday. Don't worry, you won't starve!"

After Louisa had left, Babette had stepped into the role of household cook; this was without discussion, but neither was it assumed that because she was now the oldest woman in the house it was her duty. More, it was something she wanted to do; she had to feed her daughter so she may as well cook something they could all eat together. So she made a hot dinner almost every evening and with the exception of Julius, who was often out, they all sat down at the same time and chatted over a meal which included pudding, usually a homemade fruit crumble or tart. It was not an entirely conventional household, but this held them together as a family, and it was good for Elisabeth who functioned better with routines and structure.

"I'm going to the woods," Julius announced, pulling on his old corduroy jacket. "We could do with more logs and there's just about enough light if I go now. It's still very chilly in the evenings, isn't it? I think we'll need to light the fires for a while yet."

"Do you want help with the trailer?" Caspian stretched his arms up high, above his head, and out to the sides. Suppressing a yawn, he got to his feet, expecting to help his father.

"I'll just put the seats down and fill the boot up for tonight I think, that will be enough for now." Julius was already rummaging for his car keys in the wooden bowl on the hall table, a receptacle for all sorts of odds and ends that were dropped into it without thought; rubber bands that held letters together in the post, a few pairs of sunglasses, not in cases so mostly scratched, coupons from the supermarket, one of Elisabeth's red woollen mittens, and several of her plastic beads and small toys that came free in cereal packets.

"We need milk, Julius!" Babette yelled down the stairs as he closed the side door behind him. "Do you think he heard that? I really can't be bothered to go out and get milk now. Can we manage 'til tomorrow if he doesn't get any?"

Caspian went back into the kitchen, opened the fridge door and peered in, lifting the milk carton to see how much was left in it. "Just about enough for tea in the morning," he concluded. "Maybe I'll go for a stroll later, and get some, just in case."

"That would be very helpful, thank you!" said Babette as she quickly vanished back up the stairs.

In the sanctuary of her bedroom Babette started to tidy away a few things; jewellery she'd worn over the last week or so that she'd left in a coruscating heap on the green glass tray on her dressing table, rich pickings for a magpie. Lipsticks, face powder and nail varnish were all put away in their rightful places. She draped strings of beads; amber, pearls, jet and jade over the corner of the mirror; placed peridot stud earrings and silver and tourmaline drops in the bottom of her jewellery box, ornately carved ebony lined with rose red satin. She gathered together more make-up, pots of cream and tubes of lotions, and put them all in a drawer, and then she picked up clothes from the low chair in the corner of the room. She quietly sang to herself as she folded jumpers and buttoned cardigans, before putting them neatly in the mahogany chest of drawers. She hung blouses and dresses in the matching wardrobe.

Catching sight of one of her favourite dresses she pulled it out, held it against her and admired her reflection in the full-length mirror. How she loved this dress, how she loved to wear it! So exquisite! Of darkest maroon velvet (the same colour as the polish on her long fingernails), a sweetheart neckline, and intricate black lace that formed short sleeves

11

and a deep hem. She remembered the last time she'd worn it, at a party just before Christmas in the White Hart on George Street. She'd gone with Caspian and a small group of friends to drink and watch bands play; the perfume she'd worn that night still clung faintly to the fabric. The memory stirred her, evoked a smile, and she held the dress for a few moments more until she broke her reverie, put it back in the wardrobe, and closed the door. Then she stood in front of the mirror, raised her hands to the back of her head and loosened the clip that held her hair piled high, the way she wore it for work most days. With careful fingers she slowly ruffled her thick tresses, dark, dark as chocolate, and let them fall down over her shoulders and her back. Such beautiful long hair, often wild and tousled, as if she belonged in the pages of a melodramatic Gothic novel.

She lay down on her bed with a contented sigh, and for several moments thought of nothing in particular, though parts of the day floated in and out of her mind; they did not trouble her. Then taking a well-thumbed leather-bound volume of Coleridge's poems from her bedside table, she turned on to her front, and propped up on her elbows she started to read. Outside the occasional car passed the house as they always did, the streetlights came on, and a soft rain began to fall.

2

Fabia

As usual, Fabia had left the table without clearing anything away. The remains of, or rather, most of, her late lunch, was still on a tray on the kitchen table; a bowl of hummus, scooped away on one side with thin strips of vegetables; peppers, celery and carrot. Those uneaten were left on a plate next to the tray, and exposed to the air, were already beginning to dry, the edges starting to shrivel. A blue Moroccan tea tumbler with gold motif decoration was still more than half full of apple juice.

How Fabia flitted about as she did, staying up until the early hours of the morning was something of a mystery considering how little she ate. Some days she seemed to get by on little more than an apple and a slice of wholemeal toast, though this was nothing new. She had never had a healthy appetite and even as a young child her eyes had not widened at the sight of sweets and cakes. At birthday parties she sat quietly picking at the crust of a sandwich until the other children had finished their tea and were ready to play again. Unsurprisingly, there was not much of her. She was very thin and slight, with an almost ethereal quality, as if she might suddenly spin round and disappear without a sound; her light, quick movements added to this spritely aura.

Fabia had always been happy with her own company; she liked to be on her own and even when she had just started at infants school she would often take herself off to a corner of the playground and inhabit whatever realms her imagination created for her. She talked to herself, or to imagined others, in a low and quiet, almost whispering voice, as if in another language – that of a world that no-one but she could ever be part of. 'Fabia is prone to daydreaming and can be rather fanciful at times,' a teacher had commented on her report one year. Yet as she grew, her work did not suffer, she showed a creative and inquiring mind far beyond her years, leaving adults open-mouthed with the questions she asked, the stories she wrote and her juvenile drawings. People presumed she had inherited this artistic bent from Louisa, but even she jokingly referred to Fabia as her changeling, left by fairies who had snatched away the human baby and tucked a strange little elfin child in its place. Her daughter appeared fey but her quiet nature belied a mind that considered carefully and gave great thought to matters big and small, and an imagination that soared high and wide. Physically, Fabia was beautiful, though not in a classical way; her beauty was entirely her own, yet it didn't go unnoticed and was often remarked upon. The effect was one of unusual delicateness; skin that was pale and clear, with an alabaster quality, a small snub nose and thin mouth, and piercing grey-blue eyes, the colour of Angelite; her fair hair fell in long, fine wisps over her shoulders.

"Such a pretty little thing, your sister," Caspian's friends remarked, with smirks of roguishness, yet none of them attempted to seduce her, such was the air of higher-being that she emanated.

* * *

Julius was standing in the dining room next to the kitchen, reading the front page of the local newspaper, when Fabia darted down the stairs to the hall.

"Oh, hi Dad!" she called, glancing over her shoulder at him. She wound a voluminous scarf around her neck, squares of dark green, ochre and black velvet, her hair tucked in at the back.

"I'm just going into town to meet Polly and Jenna, they're back from uni so we're meeting for coffee and then going back to Polly's. Tell Babette not to worry about dinner for me, I'll find something when I get back if I'm hungry."

"Yes, of course Fabia. Have a nice time with your friends. See you later," muttered Julius. The front door slammed shut and she was gone, leaving behind a faint scent of the rose absolute oil she wore. "You smell like the garden," Elisabeth had once remarked.

Unlike her father, Fabia was not completely solitary though she was also not overly sociable. For one so young she was very discerning about the company she kept and the number of solid friendships she had could be counted on one hand. These girls, Polly and Jenna, she saw the most of. The three of them had met in their first few days at secondary school and formed a lasting mutual attachment. They shared a curiosity for the natural world and for art and literature.

Fabia had left school at 18, after taking A' Levels in art,

history and English literature. She had decided not to go to university straightaway and had instead taken a part time job in an art gallery in the town. Three years later she was still there, outwardly happy with her lot. Any plans she'd had for higher education seemed to have fallen by the wayside during this time and it was a subject that was never raised by her or by anyone else in the house.

The owners of the gallery were a middle-aged couple who had moved to the town from London several years ago when their children were young, believing that this small community, these fields and these hills, offered a better upbringing for their offspring. They were kind and deeply intelligent people, and Fabia kept good relations with them at work, and sometimes socially when she was invited to parties or smaller gatherings at their home. She'd met two of their children, twin girls who had left for university around the time that Fabia started working at the gallery; she had even had a few nights out with them during holidays, though they did not come back much as they both found part-time work in the cities where they studied. They had since completed their degree courses and found full time jobs miles away so their visits home were now reduced to Christmas and the occasional weekend when they could spare the time.

The family home was a commodious Georgian property just off the main street, with a long drive to one side. The two front reception rooms had been altered to form the gallery, and spare bedrooms on the first floor were converted to living quarters. At the back of the house was a stable block which was used as a workshop and occasionally for art classes and talks given by visiting artists. It was a successful business and Fabia's job there was very enjoyable, but although she could not wish for better employers she knew that she did not envisage herself still being in this town in twenty years' time. Most of her associates had moved away in recent years and there never seemed to be anyone new to meet. Fabia had little in common with anyone else from her school year, and besides, a lot of them had settled down and were starting families; doing so at such a young age seemed to be par for the course among those whose families had lived in the locality for generations.

Jenna relished her life at drama college and the excitement of living in London; Polly was soon to start the final year of her zoology course in Cornwall. They both came home to their families during the holidays and they always spent time with Fabia, picking up where they had left off, but neither of them had any intention of moving back for good. Fabia could see that they now had a life elsewhere that made them happy and she envisaged herself in a similar situation one day, though she did not yet feel brave enough to break away from her roots.

She had briefly entertained thoughts of going to live in France with her mother but quickly realised that nothing was to be gained from such a move, no advancement or progression in her life. It would be a very idyllic existence but in effect it was just uprooting from a small town to an isolated village with far less in the way of employment and no social life or young people to mix with. And besides, she had not entirely taken to her mother's friend Dana who owned the rambling chateau where they lived. She did not dislike Dana, but she often found her frosty or intimidating and she sometimes felt quite awkward in her company.

Fabia considered applying to art school and moving away to live in a city, but it remained at that, nothing more than castles in the air, and so she carried on with her work at the gallery, working extra hours when she could, and putting away as much money as possible in her savings account.

Fabia did not wish to discuss her future or anything else with her father; she simply did not like talking to him. She generally found him monosyllabic and difficult to converse with, as though he was disinterested and only half listening to what was being said. She thought him uncaring and could not remember him ever expressing any type of emotion; not anger, not remorse, nor joy.

She also thought him quite a repulsive man, which in part stemmed from her childhood memories of him with food in his beard and sawdust on his clothes, and a stale unwashed odour that emanated from him. She had, when seven or eight years old, likened him to a slovenly and mean-spirited character in a book she had read, and somehow it had stuck with her ever since. She was disgusted by his snoring which she heard at night when she tiptoed past his door on her way to the bathroom, and she wondered why he spent so much time in his woods. What did he do up there for hours at a time, on his own? Was he on his own? She suspected that he was having a clandestine relationship with someone – a woman, or even a man, and that it had been going on for some years and was the reason why her mother had left.

It was unfortunate that Fabia had no idea of the real motives for Louisa's departure, but even so she was sure that Julius had too easily allowed her to go. She thought this unnatural, that he could not have truly loved her mother, and she laid the blame for their separation entirely at his door, believing it to be completely his fault. She felt that if she too, walked away from him tomorrow or the next day or the day after, he would simply let her go and all contact would be lost.

In short, she thought her father cold and selfish and unlovable. Deep beneath this, unable to be seen or felt was the stark truth that she loved him and that equally, her father loved her.

* * *

The town was busy for a Wednesday afternoon. There was more traffic than usual, partly because it was the time of day when school was almost over, and with the long Easter weekend ahead, people were heading to the supermarket to buy provisions for imminent visits from friends and family; lamb and vegetables, Hot Cross Buns, Simnel cakes and chocolate eggs; enough to feed a platoon.

The streets were bustling; matronly women striding purposely with wicker shopping baskets gripped in dry knuckled hands, old men bent stoically over their walking sticks, returning from their habitual lunchtime pint of beer and game of darts in the Masons Arms, and tired mothers dashing into shops to buy odds and ends before collecting their children from school. Those not in a flurry were gossiping and eating cake in the busy cafes, heads nodding, eyes widening, oh-yes that and oh-yes this, as they exchanged idle tittle-tattle. Within the hour their seats would be vacated and filled again by pupils from the secondary school stopping off for a milkshake and a doughnut on their way home, their laughter and screeches resounding in the streets as they milled along, scuffing their shoes along the pavement, hands half hidden up blazer sleeves, rucksacks slipping down their backs. Their excitement at school breaking up for the holiday would be evidenced by their voices, louder than usual, shouting out to their peers as they passed.

'Everything Half Price' said a sign in the window of the discount clothing outlet at the bottom of the High Street. '10% Off' said another advertising the latest sale in the cookware section of the family run department store. Office juniors ran to the banks, to pay in business cheques before the doors were closed; the portly traffic warden paced resolutely round the car park in the square and up and down the hill, hoping to find an expired parking ticket, or better still, none at all. A group of women, mostly in their sixties, strolling from the town hall signalled that the afternoon yoga class had finished.

In the churchyard preparations were under way for the Friday and Sunday services, a colossal wooden cross had been erected, to be illuminated at night. Head high, the vicar scuttled up the path and into the side door of the church, his cassock billowing in the early spring breeze, a rook about to take flight. The strong sense of community the town had always fostered remained unchanged and had in fact improved, as the town grew and attracted incomers wishing to escape the larger cities but still enjoy the spoils of urban life – art centres, restaurants, galleries, and bars with live music, jazz and blues, acoustic nights.

As a conurbation the town was visually attractive; a 16th century Ham stone market house used as a bus stop and for small markets stood in the square. Off this a mix of mainly Tudor and Georgian style buildings ran along both sides of the main parade which tapered to narrower streets of small cottages and Victorian red brick terraces. Further on were the modern housing estates where Sunday mornings were spent mowing lawns and washing cars, a cacophony of strimmers, leaf blowers and pressure washers drowning the peel of bells calling the few worshippers at the Anglican church half a mile away. Birds sat puffed up, like indignant dinner ladies, in rows on telegraph wires that stretched out, and on and on, over the fields where families walked their dogs, to the new business park where warehouses and workshops stood with contemporary glass fronted offices which became a shimmering mirage of clouds and blue skies on brighter days.

The office where Caspian worked was the last to be built and occupied a corner position at the edge of the park, where the buildings suddenly stopped and wasteland took over; irregular mounds of earth and rock, shallow puddles of murky water, roughly laid tracks of hardcore. Coils of water pipes, stacks of concrete blocks and iron girders lay ready for the next phase of development, often delayed for months. Brambles spilled out from the hedge, sending coarse arching stems earthward where they set down new roots amidst chickweed, groundsel and pineapple weed. Bright pink fronds of rosebay willow herb reached skyward, the occasional buddleia established itself, attracting peacock butterflies, small tortoiseshells and acid yellow brimstones. The papery scarlet petals of field poppies fluttered, their seeds blown from the field margins where in the spring, buttercups, campions, stitchwort and common vetch jostled for space amidst cow parsley, cleavers and nettles; some were carried on the feet of birds, mice and foxes to the wasteland, there to flaunt their flamboyant beauty amidst the desolate industrial jetsam.

Caspian worked as an architect for Tompkins and Parker, partners for over 25 years, and had done so since graduating from university. From his office on the first floor the view stretched over the wasteland and the fields beyond, to a farm on the edge of the next hamlet; in the far distance hills blurred where they met the sky. He had recently been promoted to the position of senior architect, having first joined the company as an architectural assistant. He had shown exceptional design prowess and an applaudable work ethic, so when a major client had offered him a job, rather than let him go, Messrs Tompkins and Parker made him a counteroffer of a promotion, along with a substantial increase in salary. He now had not only his own office, but also a part-time secretary and an engraved silver plaque on his door: Caspian Mortimer, RIBA.

As the architects behind the design of the new offices on the business park, Tompkins and Parker had negotiated a good contract with the landlord to take a fifteen year tenancy of the premises on completion of the project. Their offices were completed to their exact requirements and enabled the business to move from a small and somewhat claustrophobic workplace above a pharmacy in the town, to a larger, contemporary space where daylight flooded in through floor to ceiling windows. The theme carried throughout with interior glass partitions, and with the exception of the partners' and Caspian's offices, the layout was largely open plan. Caspian's office was carpeted in a muted grey tone, with white walls. Block shelving on one side neatly housed red and black box files, each labelled in the same printed font, along with an assortment of books on influential architecture and photographic tomes of inspiring building design. A dark grey ergonomic L-shaped desk dominated the opposite side of the room, six feet in front of the window. Beneath each end were wheeled drawer units and behind the desk was Caspian's chair; adjustable lime green leather, in mid-century style. A large monitor stood on the corner of the L-shape, a white anglepoise lamp to the left edge, and little else; Caspian advocated an uncluttered work space, believing that it aided clear focus and efficiency, and this was the overall effect. His secretary came in two days each week to type reports, and he shared a full time administrative assistant with the partners, a young newly married woman called Rachel whose time was divided between reception and working with the office junior in the wide central space between the offices and the staircase. Downstairs on the ground floor was the reception area, and beyond, a glass walled studio where two junior architects worked.

* * *

Each morning after his shower, Caspian dressed and went downstairs to eat breakfast at the kitchen table with Babette and Elisabeth, whilst Fabia stood by the sink sipping black coffee. Julius was seldom around at this time of day; sometimes the whirring and banging of his tools signified that he was busy in his workshop, otherwise the empty drive at the side of the house meant that he had either gone early to his woods or had not returned the previous night, having slept in his hut beneath the trees.

They shared the usual early morning exchanges of how they had all slept, and what the day held in store for each of them; Babette's lively ramblings floated about Caspian's head like a pleasant aroma or a happy song. Then he took from the fridge the lunch that she had made for him, said goodbye, and listening to the local news on the radio, drove to the office in the small silver Peugeot that he parked on the wasteland at the edge of the business park. Usually, on Tuesdays and Thursdays, when Fabia was working at the gallery he gave her a lift, concentrating amidst the rush hour traffic whilst she fumbled in her bag, checking that she had all that she needed for the day, telling him how tired she felt after staying up half the night reading, recalling a line from a novel or poem that had stuck in her mind and made her think: 'Why has no one said that before; why did that not come to me?'

She kept notebooks to scribble down any words of wisdom or descriptions that she thought perfect, of people, countryside, or paintings. Often these veered towards the philosophical and she liked to read these to her brother or discuss them as he drove; Fabia had never really been one for small talk though this would have been enough for Caspian on his drive to work.

It was in this manner that he moved into each working day.

3

Julius

The fog had not lifted all morning. Julius stood at his bedroom window looking out over the garden, or what little he could see of it. He could just about make out what he thought was someone standing by the gate in the hedge that led onto the field, but it was difficult to be sure, so he dismissed it as a trick of the light; in any case it was probably one of the regular dog walkers pausing as his dog went about its business. The fruit trees at the side of his workshop were just visible if he strained his eyes, spectral shapes with ghostly fingers pointing skyward, desperately trying to reach above the greyness that had rolled in unexpectedly, silent and ominous, from the hills and fallen like a blanket, smothering the town in a dense and dank mist.

He had been watching on and off, since after breakfast, hoping the fog would soon clear. He wanted to go to the woods to walk, and to gather his thoughts, alone in the hut, away from the house, away from Babette's music that she sang along to, out of tune. Away from the clatter of her doing the

25

household chores, washing the saucepans from last night's supper, the knocking of the broom against the skirting boards, the incessant whirr of the washing machine.

Julius looked at his watch; it was now a few minutes to eleven, though the alarm clock on his bedside cupboard said it was almost ten past. It was always set ten minutes fast, a habit Julius got into several years ago when he taught evening classes in woodwork at the local secondary school. He found it gave him enough time to prepare for the lesson, before the door burst open and his students came with their chatter, their questions and examples of projects they had been working on.

He decided at last, that he would go out anyhow, and picking up a dark green sweater that was draped on the back of the chair in the corner of his room, he went quickly downstairs, put on his boots and a thin coat, and left the house.

* * *

He drove slowly up the hill that led out of town. He could not see very far in front of the car and to make matters worse, the fan wasn't working properly so he had to keep leaning forward to clear the condensation from the windscreen, wiping it with his sleeve. Where the valley widened, the fog swirled about, a huge and menacing beast that skulked, at any moment about to roar and pounce, lifting the car up in a moment to whorl it high in the thick grey air and drop it into the dense hawthorn hedge at the side of the road, or worse, into the fields at the edge of the steep drop down into the valley.

Julius turned from the road onto a narrow lane and then after a short distance, on to the potholed track that led to

26

the woods, where he parked on bare earth beside a row of towering fir trees. The track led up the hill to his own plot of woodland, part of a bigger parcel that had been split up and auctioned off in smaller lots when the estate it belonged to was bought by a prosperous hotel chain who wanted to redevelop the substantial country house that dominated a vast open expanse in the valley. Whatley Hall had passed down through five generations of the same family and was believed to have foundations dating back to the 12th century, and associations with the English Civil War. The last generation to live in the Hall had struggled to maintain such a rambling pile, eventually closing off the central part and living only in the west wing. Much of the house had fallen into disuse long before Major Portman, at the age of 87, passed away in a private nursing home 24 miles away.

The rule of primogeniture dictated that Whatley Hall estate should pass to the Major's eldest son who, having moved to New Zealand over 30 years ago was living very happily on a considerable sized ranch and had no intention of returning to the UK, so he decided to sell off his inheritance.

The Hall was converted to an upmarket 42 bedroomed hotel, the magnificent façade and tall chimneys were restored to their former glory. The interior became an opulent blend of centuries old features and swish modern furniture; the conservatory was now a restaurant, the saloon a lounge and bar. The grounds had been cleared and landscaped, working from old black and white photographs. Follies were reinstated following the discovery in one of the attics, of the original architect's plans. A once thatched tennis pavilion was now used for wedding receptions, a huge marquee, big enough for dancing and for a band to play, extended onto the lawn to make

27

room for a bigger crowd. The ornamental lake, overspread with a thick, tangled mat of pond weed for years, was dredged, arousing much excitement when the local newspaper reported 'macabre findings' which the townspeople took to mean the body of a former lord of the manor who had disappeared in strange circumstances had been found. There was much gossiping in the streets, and it became the hottest topic of conversation in the pubs for a while. People suddenly took to walking on the estate hoping to get a glimpse of whatever was going on, their interest heightening and then quickly subsiding when it was revealed that from the silt at the bottom of the lake a horse drawn coach had been raised, well preserved, along with the skeletons of two horses.

Older people in the parish had recollection of a rumour that the grounds of the house were haunted by a phantom coach that glided across the lake on All Hallows Eve; a few had even claimed to have seen it or said that their forefathers had.

Theories flew about as to how the coach had ended up in the lake, but mostly conjecture, they quickly dissipated like puffs of hot air. The most believable story was told by the butcher, whose great-grandfather had delivered meat to the Hall around the turn of the century. One night in late October, the horses were being harnessed by the stable boy in the yard at the bottom of the drive to take guests home from a party thrown at the house by the sons of the absent squire. The revelries got out of hand and one of the sons had unlocked the gun room cupboard and fired a pistol into the night. The shot rang out, echoing around the barns and outhouses on the estate like a loud thunderclap, spooking the horses and causing them to bolt, terrified, across the lawns and into the lake where the carriage quickly filled with water and submerged, pulling

28

the two horses down with it.

The cobbled yard was now a Japanese garden, and the former coach houses, stables and blacksmith's workshop around it had been converted into a gymnasium and spa treatment rooms.

The estate in its entirety had totalled almost 950 acres. The farms and cottages were sold off in lots set out by the land agent, along with the pasture and woodland. Julius had snapped up his 15 acres in an auction held at the Bull Hotel in town. These were the woods he had played in as a child, with his brother and visiting cousins who had long since moved away to distant cities to follow careers hacked out for them in law and medicine. Just a mile away down the hill was the tiny cottage where Julius and Louisa had made their home not long after they married. On Sunday afternoons and lighter evenings when they'd eaten early, they strolled up to the woods, stopping to watch badger cubs play, or to gather chestnuts in the autumn. Julius had remonstrated with Louisa many times for picking bluebells, maintaining that wild flowers were precisely that – wild, and should be left to grow and multiply; they were not there to be picked and taken indoors.

"Julius, there are hundreds of them, what difference will it make if I pick a few now and then?" Louisa expostulated, and Julius had replied that if everyone shared such a careless notion, there would not be any wild flowers at all.

* * *

He wandered slowly up the track, aware of an ache in his knees. He opened the gate into his woods and walked through a holly thicket into a clearing; ash, wild cherry, birch and oak trees grew at the perimeter, tall and straight, as if standing on guard.

When the children were very young, he and Louisa had brought them here to play or to picnic, and much later, after Julius had bought the woods, Caspian and his friends had built a den in the coppiced branches of the wild cherry; most of the structure stayed there for years before being finally pulled down one night in a storm that felled several younger pine trees in the depths of the wood. From the clearing, Julius had made three paths; one of the outer ones ran alongside a stream, and the other lead along a dense hedge of conifers. The middle path went, as suggested, more or less straight up through the middle of the woods, through hazel and ash saplings to where in early May, a carpet of bluebells grew beneath enormous ancient beech trees.

By a thicket where the ground levelled out below the beech trees Julius had built a hut just big enough for a chair and a folding table, and an old camp bed. A makeshift set of shelves housed a collection of all sorts of things useful for the constant maintenance of the woodland – saws and axes, a bill hook, secateurs, balls of twine, reels of wire, work gloves and plastic goggles; hurricane lamps, a dented tin kettle, a couple of camping stoves, and a red faded washing up bowl containing enamel crockery and old cutlery. There was a lidded tin trunk, full of cushions and woollen blankets, ragged and moth eaten, but they served their purpose well on the nights that Julius slept there.

Just outside of the hut, Julius had cleared a small area where he made a campfire, with two sturdy tree stumps for seating, and a small pile of logs and twigs which he kept replenished to keep the fire going. He spent a lot of time just sitting there, watching the flames, brooding over his past, and shirking the responsibilities of his household which he found to be an annoyance, offering him little sanctuary. This is where he loved to be; he enjoyed watching the birds and wild animals that flitted and wandered through his woods – rodents, badgers, foxes and sometimes, deer that became nervous when they noticed him and swiftly disappeared into the dark of the conifers.

Several years ago, Julius had reluctantly bought Caspian and Fabia to the woods on what was intended to be one of his solitary excursions. Louisa had been suffering with a heavy cold for a few days and had not felt like getting up that day.

"Would you please take the children with you?" she had asked of Julius when he said that he was going out to gather firewood for the house. Despite his mild protesting, Louisa had pleaded, almost weeping when she repeated how dreadful she felt and that all she wanted was a few hours of sleep. "Oh, for some peace and quiet!" she'd cried. And so Caspian and Fabia had been made to put on their old coats and wellington boots; they clambered into the car, already complaining that they would be bored, that there was nothing to do in the woods and that it was going to rain, so what was the point in them going, why couldn't they stay home, they'd be quiet, they promised.

On the short journey to the woods Caspian was quiet and sullen, Fabia tearful; she was seven, her brother, thirteen. The age gap between them had been too wide for them to be close but they had generally got along well enough, though Fabia was more inclined to spend time with her mother, or alone, playing in her room or in the garden.

"I'm staying here, I'm not getting out," Caspian announced when Julius pulled up on the track and turned the engine off.

"So am I," said Fabia. "It's boring in the woods. I'm staying here too." They sat in the car, arms folded, chins resting petulantly on anoraked chests.

"Get out! Both of you! NOW!" their father had ordered. "The fresh air will do you good, and if you do as you're told, we'll go to the bakers on the way home and I'll buy you iced buns." He'd held the car door open for a full five minutes, glowering at them whilst he waited for them to get out.

After ten minutes in the woods, their sulkiness had passed and they were soon chasing each other about, dashing in and out of the trees in the shadowy gloom of the conifers, throwing armfuls of leaves at each other out in the open where the beech trees stood. Fabia's screeches carried around the woods, she clung on to her rag doll as Caspian ran after her, tormenting and yelling. Julius glanced up from his arduous task of splitting logs and saw them disappearing into the thicket and down to the streamside path. He worked on and got into a pattern of splitting and stacking, splitting and stacking, moving the logs nearer to his hut where it would be easier to carry them to the car. The thoughts that came and went in his head were only practical ones, of how big the logs should be in order to burn well, of how deep the bowl he was turning should be, and of things he must remember – to oil the vice in the workshop, to cut the ivy that had crept through the garage window.

The children had been gone about half an hour or more, their shouts grown quiet. Julius felt relieved; he did not like their noise, especially not their teasing and squabbling. He set the fire and lit it with a match from the box in his pocket. It took well, despite the dampness in the air, and it was soon roaring as he tidied inside the shed and filled the kettle with water from a container he'd brought from home. He put the kettle on a rough metal stand over the fire and waited whilst it boiled, then he made himself a drink in a chipped enamel mug; strong, dark coffee, which he sipped sitting in the doorway of the hut. After a while he went back to his work, splitting and stacking, splitting and stacking, his back turned to the fire.

A sudden commotion made him jump as the children came running back, shouting and hollering, both at the same time, though with different words. Caspian was in front, brandishing Fabia's rag doll high above his head, his sister not far behind him, crying and yelling breathlessly, her face red and snot streaked.

"Give her back to me! Give her back! I hate you, I hate you!" she screamed as Caspian leapt over stumps and bracken. Fabia stumbled in her desperation to catch up with him and have her doll back. Panting, he leapt into the clearing, with his sister still some way behind him.

"Want your doll, you stupid girl?" he shouted, and he laughed menacingly as he turned and glared at her.

"Well, get her then!" and with that he threw the doll high into the air and on to the fire. The woodland echoed with Fabia's screams, "DAD! DAD! MY DOLL! DAD! DAD! GET HER! HELP DADDY, HELP!" Never in her life had she made such a noise; no-one would have thought it possible.

Julius looked up; he had not seen the doll thrown onto the fire and missing the moment did not understand the full scale of his daughter's horror, of what her brother - his son - had done.

"DAD! DAD!" she screamed between sobs, and as Julius realised what had happened, he dropped his axe and rushed to the fire, but it was far too late. Fabia's favourite toy was beyond rescue, already barely recognisable; the flames devoured the rags and stuffing as Caspian ran off into the fir trees at full pelt.

This was unusual behaviour for Caspian, quite out of char-acter. He was not an unruly child nor an unkind one, in fact both children had, like their mother, a quite gentle nature, but at the cusp of his teenage years, Caspian had for a short while become sullen. He was disobedient and impertinent, often answering back, and for a few months, the stamping of his feet on the stairs, and the slamming of doors became commonplace. Fortunately, it was a phase that did not last long.

* * *

Behind the bracken in front of the top hedge, Julius had built a latrine within the slope. From there he had a good command of most of his land and though not part of his plan, it gave him an excellent vantage point for watching the deer that came through the woods on their way into the field to feed. Recently, rather embarrassingly, he had been sitting there when he'd seen a woman walking a dog in the woods. She'd passed the front of the hut and carried on along the edge of the conifers, a tall woman with shoulder length blonde hair, wearing a red coat. He did not recognise her and was thankful that there was no possibility of her spotting him. He'd watched her, looking about as she walked, calling now and then to her dog, a small wiry terrier, a Border Terrier, Julius thought at first glance.

He remembered how years ago, when they were first married, he and Louisa had owned a Border Terrier, an adorable scruffy little thing that they bought from the village pub when the landlord's bitch had her first litter. Louisa had been so taken with the smallest pup, with his appealing expression, and the way he had scampered about with his mother. They took him home and he slept each night in a basket at the foot of their bed. On cold winter evenings he dozed contentedly by the fire, and on summer morning walks bounded excitedly through the long grass in the fields. Sadly, the dog suffered most of its life from prolonged epileptic-like fits, a condition common in the breed though little was known about it. There were occasions when Julius had come down in the morning to find Louisa in her dressing gown, sitting on the tiled floor in the kitchen, holding the dog; a fit having started in the small hours of the morning, she'd quietly carried him downstairs and stayed with him until it passed. His short life ended abruptly one autumn morning when Louisa had left him under observation at the vets following a longer episode. Just after lunch the vet had called to say that sadly, the dog's heart had given out under the strain and he had not recovered. Louisa was heartbroken and had sobbed uncontrollably when they buried him in the little garden at the back of the cottage. Julius offered what little comfort he knew how to give.

It was not an easy time for Louisa she missed her little dog desperately, especially when he was no longer there to greet her when she came home from work. The following spring she discovered that she was pregnant with her first child, and as the evenings became longer and the days brighter, she moved out of the shadows into a lighter world and looked forward to the baby's arrival.

* * *

The woman in the red coat who walked in the woods had moved to the Old Rectory in the village just six months ago. Her husband was a consultant in a hospital over an hour away and it was his work that had forced a relocation, but his shifts were long and she had found it difficult to make new friends as most of the women in the village were considerably older than her. Their time was taken up with WI meetings, visits to garden centres and the pursuits of those who have such time; jam making, cross stitch, and voluntary work for local charities. Helena Craig was lonely and spent her days talking on the phone with friends that she missed from the Yorkshire village where they used to live. She tidied the sprawling old house that was her new home and wandered from room to room looking at the peeling paint and the windows that didn't shut properly, and she wondered how they would ever find the time to redecorate. She took to exploring the immediate area with her dog, discovering walks around the fields and recently, through the woods, and though it was all very nice, it wasn't enough. In short, Helena was bored and in need of a new hobby or a distraction.

4

Elisabeth

Julius had nodded off again. On the arm of the chair was a small plate with the remains of his meal; a few crumbs of oat biscuits, the papery skin of a piece of Spanish sausage and the hard, brown rind of a hunk of Manchego cheese.

Fabia tiptoed across the room and removed the plate. She put it onto the side table, in case Julius should move in his sleep and nudge it to the floor. As she leaned over him, she noticed there were crumbs in his beard and she felt her stomach turn and quickly looked away. She had an aversion to beards; finding it creepy and disgusting the way bearded men's mouths moved amid the hair when they talked, like some ugly parasitic creature attempting to break out of a body of fur it had unwelcomely inhabited.

She looked out of the window onto the street. It was starting to get dark, the streetlamps would soon be on and a few people would pass unhurried, in front of the house, on their way to church, or on their habitual evening dog walk. Now that the clocks had gone forward the evenings were noticeably lighter;

thoughts of being in the garden late on balmy nights flitted through her mind. A quite scruffy young man walked past and glanced in, probably not expecting to see someone standing there, though this did not deter him from continuing to look as he walked on.

Suddenly, Fabia noticed little coloured shapes falling past the window, at first just three or four, then more, and then a glittery ball, followed by something that shattered as it hit the paving stones in the front garden. Fabia rushed out of the room and taking the stairs two at a time, burst into Elisabeth's bedroom above the sitting room where her father was asleep.

"Elisabeth! What are you doing? What are you throwing out of the window? We've told you not to do it!"

Elisabeth was sitting cross-legged on the bed in her night-dress, fidgeting with her bare toes, her head held down in embarrassment.

After a while she spoke. "It wasn't me," she said very seriously, and turned her head aside.

"Well, who was it then?" demanded Fabia, hands on hips.

"It was NOT me!" replied Elisabeth sullenly, continuing to look away.

"But, of course it was you Elisabeth! There's no one else here!"

Elisabeth picked at her toenails, pushing her fingers between the toes of her right foot. She furtively glanced at Fabia from beneath her fringe.

"Stop picking your feet, it's disgusting!" Fabia folded her arms.

"It was Marsha," Elizabeth mumbled.

"Not her again! Well, she's very naughty! I don't know what we're going to do about her!" Fabia shook her head in disbelief, threw her arms up in exasperation, and turned to leave the room, unsure of what else to say. Hand on the doorknob, she looked back at Elisabeth,

"Tell Marsha she must not throw things out of the window. If she does it again, I will glue the lid on her teapot!" She left the room, just catching the look of horror on Elisabeth's face.

It had quickly become dark; all the bedroom doors were closed and the only light was from the streetlamp outside. The dim orangey glow crept in through the uncurtained window at the far end of the landing, above the stairwell that overlooked the drive at the side of the house. Opposite was the wall of the neighbouring house, so even during the day the landing had only a little natural light.

"It was Marsha! It's always Marsha!" Fabia muttered as she headed down the stairs. Babette had gone to see a film with Caspian, and they would probably go for a drink on the way home, but she would tell her of this in the morning.

Marsha was Elisabeth's imaginary friend. The teapot Fabia had threatened to glue the lid on was where Marsha lived, or where Elisabeth imagined she lived. Did she imagine she lived there, or did she actually believe she lived there? Whichever it was, Marsha had a lot to answer for and was often held to blame for various misdemeanours; it was Marsha who ate the last slice of cake, who took Fabia's red velvet shoes without asking, wore them in the garden and made them dirty, then hid them under Elisabeth's bed. It was Marsha who took the Georgian sugar bowl from the hallway, one of only two pieces of silver in the house of any value, and left it in the garden, filled with mud and daisies.

'What a funny little thing she is,' mused Fabia (who actually thought the world of Elisabeth). 'She lives in a world of her

39

own most of the time.'

Fabia wondered if this was due to her mother's irrational nature, and whether this had some early influence upon Elisabeth, making her retreat into a private world where Babette's fears could not be projected on to her. Babette's procrastinating gave rise to anxiety and Fabia found it tiresome that whatever was worrying her at any particular time seemed to grow entirely out of context and consume her every thought. She became grossly preoccupied and distracted, and was almost impossible to have any type of conversation with; she'd barely eat and would survive for a few days at a time on nothing but cups of tea and cigarettes, with the occasional biscuit for sustenance. They had all become quite used to her erratic behaviour and had different ways of dealing with it, except Julius who didn't seem to notice, but then he was never about much. If he wasn't in his sitting room snoring, or in his workshop, he was up at the woods chopping logs, unblocking the stream, and doing whatever else it was that made it necessary to spend so much time there.

It was Caspian who tended to offer the comfort and reassurance, both physical and emotional, that Babette needed at these times and she habitually sought her solace in him, tapping lightly on his door in the middle of the night because she had been unable to sleep and rather than lie there tossing and turning, she would go and pour her worries out to him. So self-effacing was Caspian that he never seemed to mind, even though he usually had to be up at an early hour in the morning for work. He was always patient and accepting, being one of those fortunate people who could get by quite easily on just a few hours' sleep, yet still retain a contented countenance. This was fortunate for Babette, as they would whisper long into the early hours before she tiptoed back to her room, feeling lighter of heart and mind, and then she'd sleep soundly until her alarm went off.

Caspian's resilience suited Babette entirely, because it also meant that there was someone to stay up late with at weekends, or on the rare occasion when she'd been out for the night and returned not yet ready for sleep. Fabia thought that though Caspian was only a couple of years older than Babette, he was markedly more mature and so quietly self-assured. He was, Fabia supposed, the one constant in Babette's life, always dependable and always to be found in the same untroubled frame of mind which happily took whatever course Babette needed.

Fabia enjoyed analysing the reasons why people behaved as they did, and in this case, she concluded that most likely, Babette's ups and downs were a result of being abandoned by her mother at such a young age; some might say she was emotionally unbalanced. As almost everyone had predicted, her mother's marriage to Nathan didn't last; within eight months she had run off with the drummer of a folk band she'd been hanging around with. The band had come to play at a weekend party in the grounds of the commune; a rambling former rectory on the outskirts of a typically picturesque Hampshire village. Inhabited by the well-to-do, the wives stayed at home baking cakes in the Aga whilst their husbands commuted to managerial jobs in London, mostly in finance, and their offspring studied at public schools and leading universities. The band stayed on for a couple of months and when they returned to their native Ireland, Martha, Babette's mother, went with them, following the new love of her life, and leaving Babette in the care of her relatively new stepfather.

Louisa, like Fabia, certainly believed this was the basis of Babette's troubled character - that sense of abandonment that had never left her. Louisa indicated that even before that, Babette had been subject to maternal neglect; Martha was no earth mother, far from it, she was a flibbertigibbet, a fly by night.

Babette, though very young, had at first cried ceaselessly when her mother left, and then took to moping and sitting in dark corners hugging her knees tight to her chest; she became withdrawn and sullen for a while and would hardly speak. After a year, a sudden wildness took hold of her and though still very young, she unfurled into a huge beacon of anger, some tempestuous storm raging inside her, as she clattered and banged about the cottage where she lived with Nathan, hurling ornaments and crockery at the walls at the slightest provocation, kicking over furniture, and screaming obscenities. The maelstrom subsided and though she retained a detached feral quality for a while, Babette accepted her stepfather as the one guiding light in her life. Gradually, he calmed her, he cared for her, and with his counsel she progressed well at school. One dismal autumn day, Nathan was fatally injured in a motorbike accident; such a devastating time for all of them, but mostly for Babette, who now, at the age of eleven, was utterly alone in the world. Her mother had never kept in touch and despite efforts to trace her, she could not be found, so there was little alternative but for Julius and Louisa to give Babette a home; after all, she was in many ways a part of their family. She had spent a lot of time with them all, coming to stay during long summer holidays, at Christmas and at Easter. A part of Louisa was initially concerned about the difficulties this presented, but they had the room and besides, the only other option was for Babette to go into care. Julius persuaded Louisa that this was the right thing to do, that they could offer stability for the girl, who got along well with their own children, that in time she would settle down and that only they could give her a good future.

There was also Babette's failed relationship with Elisabeth's father to consider; Babette met Luke at a festival where he was working on a stall serving farmhouse cider in gallon containers. Within two months she had moved in with him, in the tiny red brick cottage he rented on his Uncle's farm in Shropshire. Eighteen months later she came back, with seven month old Elisabeth, after Luke left her to go travelling with a fire juggler he'd met at Glastonbury Festival. The parting had been very bitter, even though Babette and Luke had not been getting along very well for some time. Babette had become increasingly unhappy at his refusal to take responsibility for his baby daughter, with his immature attitude and the constant lack of money due to his inherent laziness.

Fabia remembered the phone ringing late one night, not long before midnight. Julius answered it in his sitting room, appearing ten minutes later looking for his coat and car keys.

"Where are you going Dad? What's happened?" Fabia had asked him. It was unusual for Julius to go out once he was home, especially so late at night.

"That was Babette," he replied. "I'm going to fetch her. Luke has left her and she's very upset so she's coming back here to live for now."

"Is she bringing the baby?" Fabia asked. She had no idea of the intricacies of Babette and Luke's relationship and was shocked at the unexpected turn of events, especially considering that Babette had only sporadically kept in touch with them since she left.

"Yes, of course she is," replied Julius. "Luke has gone, he's gone for good. He's left her. She can't stay with the baby in that house – it's cold and damp, it's in the middle of nowhere and she has no money. She was crying so much that she could hardly speak. She must come back here. They can both live with us."

Fabia stood on the stairs and fiddled nervously with her necklace, "Shall I come too? I could help with the baby. It's a pity Mum's in France, she'd know what to do."

"No, don't worry, I'll go on my own. I need to leave straightaway, it's late and I want to get them back here as soon as possible. It would be better if you stay here and make a bed up in Babette's old room; they can both sleep in there for now."

"But it's miles away Dad, couldn't you get her in the morning? I could come then, I don't have any lessons until the afternoon."

"No Fabia, I don't want to leave it 'til the morning. She's so upset, I'd rather go and get her now."

"How long will she be here for? Will Mum mind?"

"I don't know, I'm not really worried about that." He pulled on a warm coat, "She can stay as long as she likes. Until she sorts herself out, it doesn't matter, we have plenty of room. I'll explain to your mother when she gets back – or if she calls before then."

He paused and looked at his daughter, standing on the bottom step, unable to meet his eye.

"Elisabeth has a cold, neither of them have been sleeping well for a couple of weeks. I must fetch them tonight, do you see?"

"Of course. I understand. I'm just offering to help."

Julius hesitated for a moment, "I wish Caspian was here then he could come with me. He gets on well with Babette and he'd know what to do, he's much better than me in these situations. But there we are, he's not here and she's in a mess so I must go and get her."

"Dad, I could come with you, honestly. Sometimes another woman is a help. It can be comforting."

Julius had already unlocked the side door; he turned back to where Fabia stood in the dim light of the hall, her arms folded, wrapping her cardigan tight around her.

"There won't be much room in the car with Elisabeth's things; there's the cot and the pram and her toys. If I leave now we'll be back in a few hours. They can sleep in the car on the way home. I'd like you to stay here and get the bedroom ready for them. Put the radiator on; that's what they need, a nice warm room."

* * *

"I was thinking, Julius, about Elisabeth's birthday."

Babette was in the kitchen, preparing lunches for herself and Caspian to take to work; for Caspian she had made egg mayonnaise to go in soft white rolls, the dark leaves of watercress poking out at the sides. For herself, a wholemeal sandwich of peanut butter, sliced green pepper and grated carrot.

"I wondered if we could have a party for her, in the woods. What do you think? Me and Casp were talking about it last night. We think it's a lovely idea, and I know Elisabeth will love it! We were talking about cooking sausages on a campfire, toasting marshmallows, having a nature trail to keep them all

45

amused... don't you think it's a good idea?"

"It is, it's a wonderful idea," Julius replied. He was long used to Babette's morning conversations starting before he'd actually entered the room; it was almost a ritual they took part in before he left for the woods and the rest of the household descended upon the kitchen for coffee, cereal or toast.

He was in the dining room, or what they called the dining room, even though it was too small to hold a table big enough for them all to sit at comfortably. It was a sort of anteroom through to the kitchen, and more than anything, was used as a dumping ground for letters and whatever else came in the post, the weekend newspapers, and Elisabeth's school things. It was a very untidy room; the windowsill hadn't been cleaned or dusted for months and was piled with an assortment of wool, twigs, stones, beech masts, acorns and various other oddments that had been collected by Elisabeth and Fabia. The intention was that they would make things out of these bits and pieces, though so far, the only evidence of this was a few smaller twigs, crusted with lichen, strung onto green twine and interspersed with colourful beads and seed heads from the poppies that burst extravagantly into flower each year behind the garden pond.

A bookcase beside the window had over the years, become home mostly to Babette's ever-increasing collection of vegetarian cookbooks and antiquarian poetry volumes. In front of the rows of books were more of Elisabeth's finds; empty snail shells, a bird's egg, trinkets from Christmas crackers, and the teapot where Marsha lived, although today Marsha would have found herself pushed out of her home by a knitted red beret which had been jammed into the teapot as much as possible, much like the dormouse at the Mad Hatter's tea party.

46

"Have you said anything to her about it?" he asked, peering over the top of his glasses at Babette.

"Not yet. I wanted to check with you first, but if you're okay with it I'll talk to her about it on the way to school. I thought we could hang lollipops from one of the trees in the clearing, then at the end of the party her friends can choose one to take home – we'll call it the lollipop tree! Isn't that sweet? And we can hang bunting between the trees, so it all looks lovely, and magical, and I thought about putting the gazebo up by the hedge, with old rugs and cushions for them to sit on."

"It all sounds very enchanting Babette! A proper birthday party!"

"We can take the gramophone up there and play some of the old 78s," she enthused, standing in the doorway with Caspian's lunchbox in her hands.

Babette was wearing a short-sleeved dress, the colour of the fuchsias that grew beside the garage; a huge silver butterfly was embroidered across the chest, and over her shoulders she wore a black knitted bolero. Several silver bangles jangled on her arms as she moved them when she talked, and silver butterflies dangled from her ears. Her hair was piled in its usual style, very loosely on top of her head, like an unruly bird's nest; stray wisps fell down around her shoulders. She looked radiant with the bright sunlight in the kitchen behind her and for a moment Julius thought her beautiful.

"Casp said we should ask Fabia's friend to come up with the pony and cart and give the children rides around the woods. They'd love that, wouldn't they? Elisabeth will be so happy! Oh, thank you Julius, it'll be brilliant, the whole thing! She's never had a party before. I'm really looking forward to it, I'm going to make it absolutely perfect for her!"

"I'm sure you will," smiled Julius. "It will be a very special day for her."

He was looking for the latest newsletter from the wood turning group he belonged to, whose meetings he never went to; he'd seen something in it about rustic bowls made from spalted beech and he wanted to read it. Although he hadn't made a bowl for years it had interested him; it was something he thought he'd like to try again.

* * *

Caspian parked at the edge of the wasteland as he always did. He turned off the engine, got out and put his jacket on. Then he took his work bag from the back seat and locked the car.

"Do we have the back to work blues this morning?" Babette had teased him as she rushed around the kitchen, busy with Elisabeth's breakfast and the school things.

He did indeed have the back to work blues; in the last week of the Easter holidays he'd gone to Cheltenham to visit an old university friend for two days and then spent the rest of the week going out and about with Babette and Elisabeth. They'd taken a steam train to the beach and even though it was far from warm, they'd splashed about in the sea, made sandcastles and ate fish and chips. They'd had a trip to the zoo and a picnic at a nature reserve where Elisabeth paddled in the stream looking for minnows. Caspian had reached down and turned over a stone to show her the beginnings of the gritty case of a caddis fly nymph.

"See his little house, Elisabeth?" he makes it himself from all the bits and pieces he's collected from the bottom of the stream," he explained.

"What are those bits and pieces?" she'd asked, closely inspecting it with the magnifying glass she was wearing around her neck.

"These are little tiny stones and bits of sticks and plants that he finds in the stream. He carefully sticks them all together and makes this little house around himself. It keeps him safe whilst he grows, so the fish can't eat him."

"Oh wow, that's incredible!" Can we take him home and put him in the pond?"

"I'm afraid that's not possible because in our pond the water is still, it doesn't move. This little fellow likes to live in water that moves, what we call running water."

"Mummy!" Elisabeth called, turning around. "You should see what Caspian's found! This little fellow likes to live in running water!"

She turned back to Caspian, "Can he fly?" she asked. "Does he fly under the water?"

"Ah, well that's the amazing thing about caddis flies. At the moment he's like a little worm, but while he's in his house he grows wings and then one day he'll crawl out of his house and fly away and live in the trees."

"A bit like a butterfly!" said Elisabeth. She put one hand on Caspian's shoulder and lifted one leg, then the other as she studied the caddis fly case again. "How do you know it's a he?"

Caspian smiled and ruffled her hair. "You've got me there," he chuckled. "I'm just guessing. I haven't a clue how to tell if caddis flies are girls or boys!"

Babette was watching from the bank at the edge of the stream, taking photographs of the two of them, heads together, chattering away.

The three of them had also gone shopping in the nearest

city, to buy sandals for Elisabeth for the coming summer. Though the streets were far busier than they'd imagined, they made a day of it. They went to the cathedral and to a café for lunch, where Caspian had remarked that Elisabeth's burger was almost as big as her head and that she wouldn't be able to eat it all, but of course, she did.

* * *

"Morning Caspian," smiled Rachel, in the same cheerful way she greeted everyone who walked into the reception of Tompkins and Parker.

"Good morning Rachel. How are you?"

"I'm very well, thank you. Did you enjoy your week off?"

"I did, I enjoyed it very much, but back to the grindstone now!" he winked and took the stairs to his office.

"Ah, Caspian," waved one of the senior partners. "Meet Laura, she's from the agency and will be helping us here whilst we have the big project on. She'll mainly be in reception so that Rachel can help us with the reports. Laura, this is Caspian Mortimer, our senior architect, his office is just around the corner."

"Hello Laura," They shook hands.

"Hello Mr. Mortimer."

"Please, – Caspian," he smiled. "All first names here. If you'll excuse me, I must get in and have a refresh of the plans before I start work." He smiled to them both.

"Well, he's rather handsome," thought Laura and she made a mental note to herself to get to know more about Caspian Mortimer as soon as the opportunity arose.

5

Julius and Louisa

As Julius left the woods and drove down the hill to the main road, he began to wonder who would be in when he got home. He wished that he would be returning to an empty house, where he could wander freely through all rooms, instead of staying in his sitting room, which was usually the only place where he could be alone.

He remembered the house as it had been in previous years, how it had changed from when he and Louisa had first moved in with the children still so young, Caspian a little boy and Fabia just starting to walk. They knew when they bought it that it was in need of updating; the plumbing system was old fashioned and inefficient, pipes that clanked and clanged as the water got hotter, a loud rumbling whoosh when the boiler came on. The electrics were out of date and largely unsafe, the kitchen was tired and shabby, but they knew that houses in this part of town didn't come up for sale very often and to find one that they could afford to buy was a rare opportunity. Of course, it was a relatively low price because of all the work required to bring it up to scratch but despite their initial anxieties, Julius and Louisa were happy to put up with this, to move in and do what renovations they could piecemeal. What they had instantly loved about the house was the character; many of the original features were still there, including the wooden panelling in the hall and the main sitting room, and the Victorian tiles in the kitchen and scullery. The barn at the back of the house was a bonus; it was in relatively good repair then and would be more than sufficient for Julius to use as a workshop for his new hobby of woodturning.

It was five to seven; the sun was already setting, a glorious blazing sky of gold, pink and pale purple, trees perfectly silhouetted, a foretelling of a good weekend. It had been a brighter day, the weather much better than it had been for a while. It felt to Julius as though spring was truly on its way, as though despite the false promises, this was it at last. Now the plants would burst into life and each morning would be heralded by a sun that climbed high in a sky the colour of forget-me-nots.

The darkness had crept into the woods just as he had begun to pack up and it soon grew too gloomy for him to see further than the dim light of the oil lamp hanging at the threshold of his hut. He tidied away his tools in the gloaming, emptying the kettle and dampening down the fire, pushing the lid down firmly on the tin trunk when he put the cushions away. On leaving the woods it was a surprise to see that it was in fact still light and his eyes took a moment or two to adjust.

Julius pulled into the drive at the side of the house and carried a sack of kindling wood round to the garage where it would dry out. He noticed that the mice had been busy again and going by the scraps and shreds on the floor, were busy making nests. He picked up a sponge from the bench and it almost fell apart in his hands; little bits of yellow honeycomb drifted down to the floor. The wretched mice got everywhere and were a nuisance. Casting his eye around to make sure there was nothing of any use or value that might be chewed he made a mental note to remember to put traps out in the morning.

Entering the house through the back door he found the lights on in the kitchen though no-one was there. It was very tidy; the table had been cleared after dinner, which must have been rather good judging by the welcoming aroma in the room. He went over to the cooker and lifted the lid of the saucepan; Babette had cooked a stew and to his delight, there was more than enough left for him. He was ravenously hungry, having eaten nothing since scrambled egg at breakfast time. He set the stew to warm and washed his hands at the sink, drying them on a tea towel that was draped over the back of a chair.

Babette and Caspian were in the sitting room watching television. The curtains were not yet drawn so the orange glow of the streetlamp crept in and cast warm shadows about the walls and furniture.

"Hello, you two," Julius almost made them jump. "What are you watching?"

"Nothing much," replied Caspian. "There's nothing on really. We were just going to turn it off and play Scrabble. Good day up the woods?"

"Yes, thank you. I brought some kindling home. I noticed we were getting low."

"Nice one Dad, I meant to tell you that this morning, but you'd gone by the time I got up."

"Yes, I thought I'd make an early start. Where's Elisabeth? Is she in bed?"

"She is," nodded Babette. "She went to bed early tonight. I think she's a bit under the weather, she didn't seem herself at all. She didn't eat much at teatime and she said her tummy hurt. I hope she's not going down with a bug or something."

"Ah, so that's why there's so much stew left!"

"Well, I made plenty anyway, I thought you'd like some. Help yourself, clear it up, otherwise I'll put it in the freezer for another day. There's half a crusty loaf in the bread bin, have some of that with it."

"I've already got it warming up! I'm looking forward to it, I haven't eaten much all day. It smelt wonderful when I came in."

Julius paused in the doorway, "I'll leave you to it then. I expect I'll turn in after I've eaten."

He went back to the kitchen, spooned a generous helping of stew into a dish, cut a thick slice of bread, buttered it, and took his meal to his sitting room where he sat in the chair in the corner and ate his supper with only the light of the lamps in the street outside to see by.

* * *

Julius awoke with a start. He had a feeling of panic and noticed a tightening sensation in his chest as he gradually became aware of his surroundings and his consciousness shifted from his dream world to reality. He fumbled for the switch on the bedside lamp and pushed it. The light immediately brought a sense of security to another night during which Julius had been disturbed by frightening dreams. He re-arranged his pillows and pulling himself upright leaned against them and drew measured deep breaths in an attempt to calm his racing heartbeat. He glanced at the alarm clock on the bedside table, a small, round thing with angled rectangular feet, slightly art deco in style, with very faintly illuminated hands. He tried to recall, though he didn't know why, where he had got it, where it had come from. He had owned it ever since he remembered and concluded that it was something given to him as a child as he had a recollection, an image in his mind, of this same clock, on the scratched pine table beside his bed in the house where he'd grown up.

It was almost 4.00am; the time when oxygen levels in the human body are at their lowest. He'd been told this by an old friend who had trained and worked as a nurse. Julius assumed she knew what she was talking about, although he had sometimes questioned whether that rule applied to everyone. What about night workers, he wondered? Surely, if you worked by night and slept by day your body would develop circadian rhythms that differed to conventional patterns?

It was always about this time of morning that Julius awoke and he briefly wondered if there was an underlying medical reason for this, then dismissed this thought knowing that it was without doubt the recurring dreams that disturbed his sleep.

What did it mean, this dream? Did it have some latent meaning? Was it some manifestation of his subconscious, some unresolved feelings for which he had no other outlet? In this dream, he was being pursued or watched by a cloaked figure, a faceless being he felt was laughing at him, mocking him, and it appeared in various places – his workshed, the house, in the street, and the woods. He tried to think why tonight's dream had been particularly disturbing to him, and he remembered that the figure had actually touched him this time. In the dream he had been in his work shed making a bowl from spalted beech; out of a crack in the pattern, a bright green beetle had emerged and was scurrying round and round in the bowl, as though its life had no purpose but to repeatedly run around the shallow interior. He was fixedly watching the beetle, his eyebrows knitted together in intense concentration, when he became aware that he was not the only observer. In the corner of the shed, in the shadows where thick stems of ivy hung down, stood the figure. It was cloaked and mysterious, unknown and ominous.

"Look at this beetle," Julius said to it in his dream. "Is it an emerald or a beetle? I am not sure which it is." The figure made no reply and Julius carried on watching the insect scuttling around in the bowl, which had become wider and shallower. The figure stepped forward and touched him, tapped his arm twice, just above the wrist. He couldn't remember seeing a hand or fingers touching him, but he knew that he felt it, a light and very gentle tap-tap on his arm. Strangely, it was not frightening; that was not what had made him wake with a start. He remembered now; it wasn't that at all, it was when the figure spoke. It was not even what it had said, absurd as it was: "Sing it a song, you silly man." That was not what had terrified him, penetrated deeply into his consciousness like an electric shock; it was something else.

"Sing it a song, you silly man," it had said. What had disturbed him, and truly frightened him was that the voice was Louisa's.

Now that he was awake, sitting in bed with the light on, Julius found this puzzling. He was at once confused and perturbed. He acknowledged that it was perfectly acceptable to dream about one's ex-spouse, or indeed spouse, as technically, he and

Louisa were still married though they had not lived together as man and wife. At Louisa's request they had not even had any contact for a few years.

He thought about it and realised that it wasn't only the fact that it was so clearly Louisa's voice that unsettled him, it was the way the words were spoken, as if she too, were deriding him. Did this abstruse dream figure represent her then? Perhaps he harboured notions that she thought him pathetic and hated him, and that was really why she had left. They had never talked about it to the point where there could be repair; Louisa had quietly and clearly explained that she was leaving and where she was going, and Julius, in his resigned manner of acceptance had not tried to persuade her otherwise, he had metaphorically shrugged and lived through his days as usual.

Theirs had not always been a conventional relationship in the way that most marriages are, though it had worked for many years and had built its foundations around a detached co-existence, with the common ground of the children at its core.

"We're like two whole oranges that have come together, me and you, Julius," Louisa had said in the early days of their marriage, when they were happy. "Two wholes when they come together, that's good, that's really strong, not like two halves." A simple analogy, Julius thought. She had read it somewhere years ago, some pearl of wisdom about how two strong people form a better alliance than two weaker people, two halves. But was it true? His friend, the nurse, speaking of her new husband on their return from honeymoon had said: "I was only half a person until I met Stefan, it's like I've met the other half of me now and we have this wonderful, synchronistic whole." But Louisa maintained that if you are not a whole person yourself, you have little to offer; a whole or entire person is self-assured, complete and happy within themselves, and could quite happily exist outside of a relationship, without a partner. Two whole people therefore have more to offer one another.

His nurse friend and her husband were one of those couples who always hold hands, or touch each other in some way, a gentle pat on the knee, a caring hand at the elbow. They did everything together, went everywhere together and would feel a pronounced sense of loss if one were without the other. If Stefan was ill or had to be away on business, the nurse would politely decline any social invitations, feeling that it would not be the same without her husband by her side – without, as Louisa said, her quite literal other half.

Julius and Louisa had never been like that. Julius was to the greater extent a strange and outwardly emotionless creature. He was not entirely without feeling, but he seemed incapable of expression, as if to ostensibly show emotion was an unfamiliar concept to him, something he had never done. Even when his children were born, he acted out of duty rather than out of feeling; he did what he thought he should do in the circumstances. He visited Louisa in hospital, took flowers to her, gave gifts to mark the occasions; he cradled the babies in his arms, awkwardly cooed to them, but retained an element of detachment, always that element of detachment. He never held them up, metaphorically raised his progeny for all to see and said: "Look! See what I have created. This is my son, my daughter, and I am so proud." It was as if he could not find a natural or correct way to present or express the pride of fatherhood. He did not delight in them as most fathers do their offspring; he had always loved them, that was without dispute, though he did not think about or question it as such, and he acted as a decent and responsible father to them. He talked to them, more so as they grew older, and he made them toys out of wood; a doll's house and a tricycle for Fabia, a go-cart and a bow and quiver of arrows for Caspian. It was Louisa who had done most of the parenting, the nurturing, spending time with them, reading to them, playing games, baking and painting, or making things out of odds and ends. Despite this, she was no earth mother and sometimes freely confessed what she saw as her failings, whilst carrying a relaxed reassurance that her children would be 'alright'.

Had Julius loved his wife? Truly loved her, in a way that meant he would be desolate without her? Again, it was something that he had not questioned; he never imagined what life would be like without her. He knew, or took it for granted that he had a certain depth of feeling for her, that he was very fond of her, and to him, that was adequate, otherwise he would not have asked her to marry him, he would not have chosen her as his life partner. When she left, he missed her very much at first, but he chose to carry on without her, accepting that she had wanted to leave, acknowledging her reasons for doing so, and later, that she did not wish to maintain contact with him. He did not believe it was right to stop someone from doing what they reasonably wanted to do.

In fact, Louisa had a part of her that was perpetually irritated by Julius and as her friendship with Dana re-established itself she felt that the only way to stop that gall from spreading was to remove him from her life and to cease all communication with him. She was angry at him for not ever doing anything to improve their relationship, for not making any attempt to make things better, and she knew that there were things he had done that she could not forgive him for. Even when she told him she was leaving, his passive deference, though it had made things easier for her, had enraged her. "What is wrong with this man?" she thought. "Has he no feeling at all?"

"I'm sorry Julius, I don't want to live here anymore. Last time I went to France, Dana and I had a very long chat about everything, and she asked me if I would consider living there with her in her house. I've thought about it a lot and I've decided that's what I want to do. I'm going to live with Dana and I'm sure I'll be happy there; the way things are there, it's more the kind of life that I want. Maybe it's my age, a sort of midlife crisis, but I feel that I can be myself there; I feel that now the children no longer need me, that I must allow myself to be happy." She stopped, suddenly aware that what she had wanted to say for some time was now pouring out of her. It felt liberating and she continued, "You see, I feel as though I must do what I really want to before my life is gone. I haven't told you before but besides the issues we have, I've actually been quite wretched and miserable for years. I've felt that I've just been living my life around others and now it's time I lived for myself. That's what it's like when I go to France, I feel so truly myself, I feel like I am really alive; here it feels... well, I don't know... it's like I'm just existing or something." She ran her hands through her hair and then folded her arms, "It's been like that for years, just trundling on, day after day, not going anywhere or doing anything, just a flat, invisible existence where I'm expected to go along with what everyone else wants even though there are things that I don't agree with. It's like I've been living in the shadows, just Julius' wife, Caspian and Fabia's mother, a mother figure or auntie to Babette, a grandmother to Elisabeth. I know it

60

sounds clichéd but now I feel like it's time for me to move into the sun."

Julius listened to every word that she spoke but did not interject.

"I'm leaving Julius. Do you understand? I'm going to go and live in France with Dana." She took a handkerchief from the pocket of her smock and wiped her eyes. Her husband had not even looked at her since she began her speech, he just stared straight ahead, unblinking. She had no idea what he was thinking.

'This is the woman I married. This is my wife, for better and for worse, and she is leaving me because I have failed her,' is what he thought but could not speak.

"I understand," he at last solemnly said. His hands were clasped together on the table in front of him, "I understand Louisa. I'm very, very sorry that you've been unhappy for so long and that I didn't notice. I realise how I've failed you, the terrible mistakes I've made, and I am truly sorry, you must know that." He hesitated and for a moment Louisa thought she might see a rare outburst of emotion from him, but he continued in the same flat and unemphatic tone, "I don't know the reason why, but I'm not the sort of person who can make others happy, perhaps I'm too selfish. I've done what I thought was my duty over the years. I know I haven't been the best husband in the world, or the best father and for that, I can only apologise again, as I have before, many times. I'm truly sorry that I've let you down and I understand why you want to leave."

"So you're happy for me to go? There really is nothing you're prepared to do to make things better?" Louisa blew her nose, incredulous and incensed that he could be so dismissive. "I

61

won't be coming back Julius, not ever."

"Louisa, we've talked about this before. How would it make things better?" He sighed, "It would only make things worse, so yes, if it's what you really want, you must go. It may be hard for you to believe it, but I want you to be happy. You *must* be happy, you deserve to be and that's obviously something I can't do; I cannot make you happy. You've said yourself that you've been miserable for years, nothing I can say or do will change that. If I begged you to stay it wouldn't be right, especially when no matter how much I try I know that I'll never change. I don't believe I have the capacity to change, you see. I might for a very short time, but I'd soon go back to my old ways. I'm inherently selfish I suppose, maybe that's what it is." Louisa was surprised to hear him admit this and she let him continue, "Then you'd just be miserable again and I honestly don't want that, I don't want to make you any more unhappy. I don't want to stop you from going to live with Dana if you'll be happier there. Louisa, you must be happy; it is me, not you, who is only existing."

Five days later Louisa had gone, taking only her personal belongings – clothes, books, trinkets. Dana's chateau in France was well furnished and had all that they needed, and Louisa had no desire to rob the household of the furniture that had become part of its character. Caspian and Babette were not surprised and had resigned themselves to the reality of Louisa's departure; they understood and would come to terms with it. There had been conciliatory hugs and tears, but they had accepted it and acknowledged her reasons for leaving.

For Louisa, hardest of all was leaving Fabia; she was still at school and would soon be sitting exams. Not wishing to prolong her mother's unhappiness she adopted a mature stance and decided that she would finish her education, and then apply to university. She told Louisa to go to France with her blessing; she would go over to visit at the end of term and she knew that she would be welcome to live there if she wished to. But when it came to Louisa's departure Fabia astounded them all by becoming dreadfully upset and clinging to her mother, begging her not to go.

6

Helena

Fabia was crouched in the small thicket at the top corner of the woods. It was easy for her to creep within Julius' boundary as, unlike the owners of the neighbouring parcels of woodland, her father had not bothered to put up stock proof fencing. He liked the thought of deer roaming free, unimpeded by harsh barbed wire barriers that they could not jump.

That morning she'd borrowed Caspian's car and driven to the tumbledown cottage that had long ago been claimed by nettles and briars as it slowly fell into ruin. She'd parked along the disused track to the side of the cottage, where she tucked the car in tight beneath the conifers out of sight and then, rucksack on her back, walked half a mile up the lane, and joined a footpath. To one side a large tract of Douglas Fir sloped downhill to a stream and to the other stood her father's woods. To enter them she had to step over a shallow ditch and up into the hedge that was largely supported by the roots of ancient beech trees, now coming into leaf.

Once in the woods, Fabia slipped almost soundlessly along

the line of the hedge and into the thicket where she took her rucksack from her back, unzipped it and pulled out a long grey cloak. She shook it loose and slipped it over her shoulders, tying the ribbon drawstring at the neck and pulling the hood up over her head, enough to conceal her face from a distance but not to obscure her visibility.

She now had an almost unhindered view of Julius' hut, down over the slope beneath the elder tree, the back of it virtually hidden by holly and buckthorn. When she was a little girl and Louisa had brought her for walks in these woods, they stopped by the spinney to watch her father building the hut. Her mother told her how the berries of buckthorn had a laxative effect and so the proper name for the tree was purging buckthorn; a memory that had, for some reason, stayed with Fabia. Julius would be in the hut now, brewing mid-morning coffee on his tiny camping stove. Fabia had watched him long enough to know his habits, she knew which parts of the wood he preferred, and she'd worked out the best positions where she could spy on him unseen. Julius had put seats in his favourite spots; one was by the badgers' sett, where she'd seen him sitting one evening, drinking from an enamel mug. She wondered what was in it; was it tea, or more likely, red wine or whiskey? She knew that her father had taken to drinking in the woods as she'd seen the evidence in his shed; bottles of spirits, empty wine bottles and beer cans. The shed was kept tightly padlocked when Julius wasn't there, but she had stood on tiptoe and peered through the window, curious to know what was inside. The answer was nothing much, certainly nothing of any interest, just the bits and pieces that would be expected from a man who liked his own company and cared little for the material trappings that others yearned for or cosseted.

There was another seat in front of the huge clump of brambles, almost directly in line with the enormous beech tree which stood almost central in the woods where the ground was level. It was surrounded by several other trees that were not as substantial, and in May the floor beneath the newly forming canopy was carpeted with bluebells; a mass of purple-blue and a delicate scent carried on the late spring air.

Fabia had often seen Julius sat on the floor beneath the huge beech, his back against the broad trunk. She wondered if he liked to sit there because he felt it offered security or protection; most likely not, it was simply somewhere to sit that gave him a favoured outlook over the woods. She likened the vast spreading branches to the rafters of an old house, or even an ancient church: 'I have no walls, but beneath my roof you will find shelter.' Where did she remember this from, this offering, this phrase that gave personality to a building, like some saintly being who gave sanctuary to those who found themselves tempted to come beneath its roof?

It may of course, have been pure fancy. Fabia had often felt on entering the woods as though she were stepping into a world of sanctitude, like the stillness and quiet felt upon going into a church or cathedral; the entire separateness from any other place, that pervading, protective, otherworldliness. And there in the centre of it stood this prodigious tree, towering and magnificent, as if it were the crux beam that, should it fall, would cause the whole woodland to collapse: 'Come unto me; sit at my roots, rest against my trunk, my body. Climb into my branches, my arms. I will keep you safe.'

Fabia narrowed her eyes, glimpsing a movement within the hut. Was he coming out? She had been scanning the broader aspect of the woods as it was possible, though unlikely, that

Julius had veered from his routine and she needed to keep her wits about her to remain unseen. That sudden movement brought her attention back to the hut; the door had been closed and Fabia was surprised when it opened wide and a woman emerged. Until now she'd seen no suggestion of a secret liaison, nothing that confirmed her suspicions; this perhaps, could be a revelation.

Fabia judged, quite rightly, that the woman was middle aged; from an observable distance she could see that she was tall and slim, fair haired, dressed in dark trousers and a sky-blue T-shirt. She moved with graceful, long limbed movements as women of such physique often do.

"Maggie! Maggie! Mag-gie!" the woman called. A wiry haired terrier came scampering to her from the lower side of the hut.

"Chasing squirrels again!" roared Julius, laughing as he stepped out of the hut behind the woman. They walked together along the track leading from the hut to the lower boundary, along the stream and down to the gate. The dog, Maggie, scampered ahead, snuffling in and out of the under-growth, nose to the ground, tail in the air, with the same hurried excitement as a child on a hunt for Easter eggs.

Fabia thought that she recognised the woman, though she could not think who she could be or where she may have seen her. Their heads were bowed, deep in conversation, as they walked on, soon out of sight beyond the lower tree line as they headed down the incline. The temptation to creep out and follow them was strong but Fabia resisted; it had not occurred to her that there may be a dog about and she was already anxious that it may have picked up her scent and might suddenly turn and dart up to the corner of the woods, revealing her hiding place. If that were to happen she would quickly throw off her cloak and step out of the thicket before her father or the woman saw her, then if she met them she could casually say that she had been out walking and fancied a stroll in the woods. Julius would introduce the woman to her, and she would then know who she was and would realise where she had seen her before. Though this would not be such a dreadful course of events and she felt sure that she could carry it off, Fabia hoped the dog would not discover her. She preferred to remain unnoticed, where she could merge into the shadows, as she had been doing for the past six months or so that she had been furtively watching her father.

In spite of her tendency to question other people's motives for their actions, it was odd that Fabia never deeply questioned why she did this. Had anyone asked her she would have told them that she needed to know him better and that because he was impossibly difficult to talk to, this was the only way. She needed to know what he did, why he spent so much time in the woods, and why some nights he did not come home. Why would he prefer this basic rough sleeping to a warm and comfortable bed? Did he really sleep in the hut or did he, as she thought, slink off to some lover's cottage? Fabia wanted to know; to her this was the only way of finding anything out and she did not think it unreasonable.

Julius and Helena had met in the woods two or three times in the past month, not by any design or arrangement, but because since moving to the village Helena had discovered a footpath that led from the field at the back of her house, along an old holloway and into the woods. It was not a walk she took daily, but once, when she'd been all around the perimeter of the woods and was heading back down through the middle to the lane, she'd met Julius, sitting on the bench near the beech tree. She had at first been startled to see him because she was not expecting to see anyone else; though new to the area she'd been this way several times and had not seen a soul. She didn't know if the path was a permitted one; although it seemed to lead quite naturally from the lane into the wood, it was obviously used very little, if at all. For that reason, it had quickly become one of her favourite walks with the dog; she saw no-one and it gave her opportunity to be alone and close to nature where she found it easier to reflect and organise in her head her daily chores. More often than not she would end up thinking about what she and Andrew would do to the house, if they would replace the old roll top bath, how they would hide the old fashioned serving hatch between the kitchen and the dining room, or if they might instead make a feature of it. That was the sort of things she thought about on her walks.

When she saw Julius, she was at first taken aback. He looked pensive, possibly brooding, and for a moment or two, from his unkempt appearance, she'd wondered if perhaps he lived in the woods, or was a vagrant who travelled the country on foot, had unexpectedly ended up there and found the perfect spot to sit and think for a while. She wondered whether to continue past him or to turn and find a different way back.

Something made him turn in her direction; it could have been a twig that snapped beneath her foot as she moved, or the rustle of the dog scampering along beside her in the ivy and dog's mercury.

Julius was equally surprised to see another person in the woods. In all the years he had been spending time up there he could count on one hand the number of other people he had seen, so he had grown to presume he was always alone.

69

He mustered up a smile and said hello, "Nice morning. Warming up a bit, perhaps spring is on its way at last."

"Hello. Yes, it is a bit warmer today. It's lovely up here, isn't it? So peaceful. I often walk the dog here; I don't usually see anyone else."

"Neither do I! I thought no-one came up here, except me! I've hardly seen anyone else here in all the years since I bought the woods."

"Oh, I'm so sorry, do forgive me! I should have thought to find out if it was private property! I didn't see any signs so I presumed it would be alright to walk here. I come in from the lane over there, it seems to lead here so I thought it might be a footpath."

"Please, don't worry," interrupted Julius. "I don't mind at all. It's nice to know that you appreciate the woods. Honestly, please don't worry. I don't really mind people coming here as long as they don't leave litter, or trample the flowers, and I wouldn't want the wildlife disturbed."

"Oh, I quite agree! That's one of the things I like about it. I saw a deer up here the other day, it must have been a young one, it was quite small. It was feeding under the trees over there, such a wonderful sight, I felt really privileged. I just kept still and watched it for a couple of minutes, then it looked at me for a moment and suddenly took off. I've seen a fox up here a couple of times too. I saw it last week, about ten in the morning, up the top by the hedge. It stood there looking at me, bold as brass for a minute or two, then it ran off over that way." She gestured in the direction of the top boundary, aware that she was talking a lot because she was nervous, not because she felt afraid of Julius, but rather that she felt awkward at being caught trespassing.

"Oh, they come out all times of the day when they have young to feed. Bold as brass, like you say. I love watching them, it's something I've enjoyed doing for years, since I was a boy." He paused and looked around, over to the beech trees.

"The bluebells will be out soon, there'll be a carpet of blue beneath the beech trees. You should come and see it, it's such a beautiful sight."

Helena smiled; she was pleased that he had extended this invitation to her and accepted her as a welcome visitor on his private land. She'd noticed that he was polite and articulate, quite softly spoken, and she suspected that he was probably very intelligent, perhaps a little eccentric, which explained his dishevelled look.

"Thank you, I'd like to see that, I imagine it'll be quite a picture!" She looked around the woods then glanced back at him and saw that he was looking not at her but up at the trees.

"Do you live nearby?" she asked, not knowing what else to say.

"Not far. I live in the town, right at the end of Victoria Road, getting on for a couple of miles from here. I used to play in these woods with my brother when I was a boy. We lived in the village, so I've always spent a lot of time here. When they came up for sale, I thought I must buy them, I had to. I'd just inherited some money, not much, but enough for this, so I went along to the auction and fortunately there weren't many other people bidding so I got them for a good price." He paused for a moment and chuckled.

"This bit doesn't appeal to many people, you see, because it's on the hillside and it slopes quite steeply down there, but I don't mind that. It's nice and level here, this middle bit, so the slope doesn't bother me. It helps with drainage too, the water runs down into the stream, so the rest of the woods don't get too boggy, especially not up here, it's always dry here."

"It's not that steep, is it? Only down by the stream, like you say. I love it here, it's so peaceful. I love hearing the birds sing. Bird song always sounds so different in the woods, more clear I suppose, because there's no other noise to drain it out. Oh, I'm sorry," she exclaimed, offering her hand, "Helena Craig."

"How do you do Helena?" smiled Julius, lightly shaking her hand. "Julius Mortimer."

"Maggie, come back here!" called Helena, a slight panic in her eyes as the terrier bounded off into the undergrowth.

"Excuse me," she apologised to Julius. "Maggie! Maggie! Maggie! Come here, come back here! I'm sorry!" she offered again, turning to Julius. "Named after Margaret Thatcher. Or from the Rod Stewart song, whichever you prefer! I must go and find her, you know what terriers are like, minds of their own! She was gone for four hours once! It's good to meet you Julius. I'm sure I'll see you again. I'd like to come when the bluebells are out, if you don't mind. Thank you for letting me walk here."

"You're welcome. Walk here whenever you like. The middle of May is best for the bluebells, don't miss that."

Helena was slightly embarrassed to be rushing off so abruptly. She muttered further thank yous and called to her dog.

'Well that was nice,' thought Julius. 'She seemed a very agreeable woman. I don't suppose I mind her walking here at all.'

In fact, he was quite looking forward to meeting her again; female company, for Julius, was very thin on the ground, as it had been for years. It wasn't that he was an unattractive man; he still retained the bare bones of the charm and good looks of his youth, though his hair had been in need of a cut for some months and his usually short and tidy beard had grown bushier. He had not particularly cared for nor thought about women since Louisa had left. Some of their then close friends would have said that he had not particularly cared for nor thought about Louisa much throughout their marriage, appearing so unemotional and completely without passion, or even compassion. They would have said he was unaware of her needs, and that instead of spending time with her he whiled away the hours alone in his shed, making things out of wood; bowls, platters and lamp bases, most of which sold at exhibitions or in the local art gallery and gift shops. A few still lurked, dusty and forgotten, in boxes in the corner of the loft above the garage.

He and Louisa had been quite an odd couple. They would have been regarded as a good looking pair in their younger days, though somewhat mismatched; he with his olive skin and thick dark hair, a genetic throwback from a faint Indian heritage on his great grandmother's side, and his curious, almost shuffling stance. Beside him Louisa seemed slightly frail, despite a quite wholesome appearance. She was small in stature, with a frame that would be considered petite; she was fair haired and her skin so pale that in some lights it took on an almost transparent quality so that veins could easily be noticed on her forehead and her thin white limbs, mapping out roads to unknown territories, like decades old cracks on fragile china cups.

They'd met at university as art history students, and five years later they'd married, setting up home in the rented cottage in the village which lay in the shadow of the woods. Julius, when he reflected, thought of those times as his happiest days with Louisa; he knew that he was content and as was his way, never bothered to question anything. He never thought about whether or not he was happy, sad, or fulfilled. Without thinking he just 'got on with it', accepted everything – not a blind acceptance, more an acknowledgement of all that was, all that happened. As a consequence it was rare for him to be angry, which should be regarded as a good trait, but the truth was that nothing really stirred him, not joy, not pain, nor passion, and that is why those who knew him well, who shared his life as much as he allowed, they were the ones who said: "Julius has a heart that is made of wood, one day he'll pluck it out and make a bowl out of it."

In that tiny cottage, prone to damp, with no central heating, Julius and Louisa were happy. He was content enough with his job in the timber yard on the outskirts of town, by the station. Louisa had made more use of her degree and was teaching at a grammar school 17 miles away. At first, she'd had to endure a bus journey of an hour and a half to get to work and back, which some would see as a nuisance, but Louisa saw it as time to herself, a transitional time between two elements of her day where she had no choice but to use that time to daydream or read, so she did both. After a few months, a new deputy head started at the school and as he lived fairly close to Julius and Louisa, she shared his car journey to work and back, which in turn made her happier because the commute was much quicker. Unlike the bus, they didn't have to stop off at every village along the way, so she could stay in bed longer in the morning and was less tired, and she arrived home earlier each afternoon, with more time to prepare dinner and to relax with Julius in the evenings. Sometimes, during the spring and summer, they'd leave the plates and dishes on the table after their meal and go for a stroll around the village, from one end to the other, admiring the bigger houses. They often walked along the mill path and up the hill into the woods where Julius told her of the times when he and Nathan played there.

'So long ago,' thought Julius when these memories drifted into his consciousness. 'So long ago,' and he brushed off his thoughts, sent them floating far, far away until they dissolved into the ether.

7

The Birthday Party

On the morning of the party Babette awoke later than she'd intended to. During the night Elisabeth had been into her room and woken her four times, such was her excitement. Is it time to get up yet?" she asked; Who was going to blow the balloons up? What was on top of her birthday cake? What game were they playing first? On waking, Babette was not surprised to find Elisabeth still sleeping soundly beside her; curled on her side, with her head tilted back and her mouth open so that a small wet patch had formed on the pillow.

Babette lay still for a while; all she could hear was her daughter's breathing and the sound of passing traffic in the road outside. She thought about the day ahead, how much she was looking forward to it. She hoped that the rain that had been forecast would hold off until the evening, or better still, until tomorrow. There was so much to be done and really, she should be getting up and getting on with things, though physically doing so was not easy when she was so content and snug in those early waking moments with Elisabeth beside her.

She remembered the strange dream she'd had. She was in a shopping centre with Elisabeth whilst elsewhere in the city there was some sort of disturbance or riot going on. Despite the clamour and panic in the streets, the shopping centre was calm and quiet, and strangely, quite empty. The few people that were there moved about silently; somewhere a music box was playing, a barely audible tinkle, like water trickling over a shallow and stony riverbed. Though faint, the tune was just about discernible as one that played in a jewellery box Babette had as a child; the lid opened to reveal pink satin lining and a mirror, the music played as a small plastic ballerina in a white dress twirled slowly round.

Elisabeth held her hand slackly, every so often squeezing it tightly, as they went in and out of the shops. The child's hands were dirty and felt sweaty. In part of the dream she pointed to a dish piled high with fudge on a glass counter, "Can I have some of that please Mummy? I need some of that." Then they were in a shoe shop standing in front of rows and rows of red party shoes, some sparkly, others shiny patent leather, and Elisabeth was asking, "Please can I have those? Are those my size? That's just what I need." The next minute they were in a toy shop and she was reaching for a little toy house; inside a family of mice sat cosily in a country cottage living room with flowery armchairs, a grandfather clock and a Welsh dresser. "I want this, I really, really want this," Elisabeth said. "Mummy, please will you buy this for me?"

Babette was aware that someone was standing uncomfortably close behind her, laughing at Elisabeth's demands. She suddenly realised it was Luke. Out of his pocket he pulled a brown envelope, stuffed with twenty pound notes, which he gave to Babette with a sneer of satisfaction. "Buy her everything she wants," he said. "I have to go to Germany tomorrow. I don't expect I'll be back till she's grown up, so this money is for her."

The dream disturbed Babette. She wished that she did not dream about Luke, she wanted to completely forget him, as if he had never existed, like he'd done with her. She hadn't heard from him since he left her and sometimes, when she thought about it long enough, the anger that she tried to keep suppressed rose to the surface and cracked and snapped like lightening. She was outraged that he had never made contact, not the slightest enquiry after his daughter, and that he was not interested in her upbringing. She dreaded that there would be a time in the future when Elisabeth would want to know who her father was and might want to meet him, and she was thankful that as yet she had asked no questions. Babette supposed that Elisabeth thought Caspian was her father; it was a subject that was never mentioned within the household and she felt that for the time being, things were better left unsaid. She was not inclined to fix what was not broken.

Babette quietly got out of bed, pulled back the curtain and opened the window. Across the road, Mr. Elliott was tending his small front garden, the clip-clip-clip of the shears as he snipped at the box hedge drowned out by the occasional passing car. He glanced up at Babette's window, catching the momentary movement from the corner of his eye, hearing the scrape of the catch; it being of no significance to him, he continued with his tasks. His fat ginger cat sat on the wall, watching him, narrowing its eyes.

Elisabeth stirred and rubbed her eyes, then remembering what day it was she sat bolt upright, eyes wide open and excitedly sang: "Happy birthday to me! Happy birthday to me!"

She clapped her hands then leapt out of bed and eagerly tugged at her mother's dressing gown.

"We'd better get dressed and have our breakfast, hadn't we Mummy? We've got to get everything ready for the party! Come on, there's so much to do, we'd better get our skates on!"

"Happy birthday darling!" exclaimed Babette. "Yes, we have got lots to do! We've got a busy morning ahead of us, but we don't need to rush too much. First, we'll have breakfast and then you can open your presents, and then we'll get on with things. Caspian and Fabia will help so we'll all be busy bees together!"

They were showered and dressed in no time at all and together they went downstairs and through to the kitchen. The radio was on, though no one was about, outmoded middle-of-the-road songs the only sound in the empty room, other than the quiet hum of the fridge. On the table a book lay open at a page of intricately illustrated moths: Rosy Marsh Moth, Cousin German, Autumnal Rustic, True Lover's Knot, Plain Clay, Pearly Underwing. Babette paused to look at it and smiled at the names.

"Where can they be? I hope they'll be back soon!" Elisabeth went to the cupboard, took out a saucepan and handed it to her mother, and in the way that children's minds trip from one thing to the next she declared, "We'll have boiled eggs today, runny ones to dip our soldiers in," and she dragged a chair across to the fridge so that she could reach to find the eggs.

She turned and shrieked with delight as Fabia and Caspian came in from the garden, full of happy birthdays, and the merriment that rang around the kitchen was enormous as

Caspian picked the little girl up and spun round with her in his arms.

"Let's all have eggs and soldiers!" she squealed; her excitement was far beyond measure.

"Then after breakfast I'll open my presents, or maybe just some of them, I'll save the rest for later!" She flung her arms around Caspian's neck and buried her face in his hair. How joyful they all were in that moment, how contagious this child's excitement, how jubilant the air on this happiest of mornings.

"Any idea where Julius is?" One by one, Babette carefully slipped eggs into the pan of boiling water.

"I'm not sure," replied Caspian, putting Elisabeth down onto a wide carver chair that stood at the end of the table. "He went out in his car early this morning, I heard him leave when I was getting up. He didn't mention anything about going out last night. He's probably just gone to the supermarket or something, I'm sure he'll be back soon."

"He said something about going to pick up a new lathe," interjected Fabia.

"Well, I hope he hasn't! He can't have forgotten it's Elisabeth's birthday!" Babette was rather surprised at Julius' absence and felt disappointed. It was true that he had an aversion to small children, finding them noisy and irksome, but this was Elisabeth's birthday! He knew that she was having a party and how excited she was; surely he hadn't forgotten or had gone off to pick up a lathe, without even seeing her? He could pick his lathe up any day!

Elisabeth had run out into the garden and was skipping about on the lawn, singing and waving her arms about above her head.

"Don't worry, Babette, I'm sure he'll be back soon," Caspian put a reassuring hand on her shoulder. Dejected, she stared into the pan where the eggs were boiling, rattling against one another.

"Was he up the woods?" she asked, lifting her face to Caspian.

Fabia was setting down placemats and spoons, salt and pepper, the butter dish. "No, he wasn't," she answered. "Well, we didn't see him, but we only went as far as the clearing so he could have been further up, but his car wasn't there. Don't worry Babette, he won't miss the party. I'm sure he'll be back soon."

* * *

A couple of hours before Elisabeth's birthday breakfast Fabia and Caspian had driven up to the woods and between them carried the tent to the edge of the clearing where they'd put it up, spread blankets inside, and arranged cushions for the children to sit on. The day before they'd dragged the same tent from the back of the garage, brushed off the cobwebs and the spiders that had taken up residence in its folds, and Fabia had done a hasty repair on a long tear along one of the seams.

"Remember this old thing Caspian?" she asked her brother as she threaded the darning needle. "How many holidays did we sleep in this?"

"Ha! I just remember it being freezing cold in the morning," he said. "Mum always gave us extra blankets because our sleeping bags were so thin!"

"That's what they were like then! What about that time you trod in cow shit and brought it in the tent on your wellies!"

And so they went on, the day before, reminiscing and laughing about their childhood holidays, whilst Fabia mended the tear.

In the middle of the clearing Caspian had set a fire and arranged logs for the children to sit on when they cooked sausages. He'd cut sticks, sharpened at one end, for marsh-mallows to be toasted and he'd blown balloons for his sister to hang in bunches from the trees. They'd left trestle tables unfolded, leaning against the cherry tree and Fabia had tied bunting from tree to tree, and hung lollipops from the lowest branches of a young ash.

A tenor of gleeful anticipation had been running through the household all week, such was the effect that Elisabeth had upon them all, this dark-haired sprite with her mischievous nature and her strange ways, her fruitful imagination. She amused them and she gave them all the gift of calmness, of coming to her as a child themselves, to talk with her and to play, to be part of her world where the responsibilities of work and the house could fall from their shoulders as they temporarily eased themselves into her province. How they loved her, each one of them; Julius especially.

* * *

Caspian parked the car at the field gate, honked the horn three times just for fun, and then they all clambered out to unload the boot; boxes of food, bottles of fruit juice, the gramophone, preparations for games, little boxes gift wrapped for the winners. Fabia, helped by Elisabeth, set up the tables, spread them with gingham cloths and began organising food; bread rolls to slice, sausages to be cooked, cheese straws and fairy cakes, bags of marshmallows to toast, and in a round white tin, the birthday cake, iced and decorated with tiny flowers and hundreds and thousands, and seven little candles. Caspian lit the fire, putting a metal sheet on top once it had got going, ready to cook upon. It was to be an adventure; Babette had organised a nature trail, the children would set off in teams to find a list of things in the woods: a fir cone, a feather, seeds, three different leaves, an acorn, pine needles and a little piece of moss. They would eat together round the fire, then they'd play pass the parcel and a game where the children had to sit on a balloon until it burst. Inside was a forfeit they must act out: bark like a dog, cluck like a chicken, cry like a baby, act like a monkey. There would be an egg and spoon race with hard boiled eggs and then it would be time for the birthday cake and Elisabeth's friends would sing 'Happy Birthday' to her, then with all her might, she'd blow out the candles and they'd all cheer.

Soon came the girls and the boys, Anna and Harriet, Charlotte and Rosie, Alice and Meryl, Jack and Thomas, Daniel and Ben. They ran excitedly into the woods, screeching and laughing, arms full of presents, their mothers or fathers behind them, with smiles and compliments.

"This is gorgeous!" exclaimed Susie, Harriet's mother, looking around the clearing. "It looks so magical! And what a lovely day! The sun shines on the righteous, as they say!" She kissed Babette lightly, once on each cheek.

"Wonderful!" agreed Charlotte's father. "What a brilliant idea! Charlotte's been so excited, she was up with the lark this morning!"

"So was Ben!"

"Jack must have forgotten, I had to wake him up at 8.30!"

The children were desperate to play and explore so parents

gave them kisses, told them to behave and have fun, and off they went, with orders to collect them at four o'clock. Susie and Emma, Daniel's mother, stayed to help.

Susie bent down and took two bottles of wine from her basket. "I've brought grown-up fruit juice!" she winked. "I thought you might need it Babette!"

"I'm sure I will!" laughed Babette. "I bought some too, it's under the table! Plastic glasses though I'm afraid, but at least I remembered to bring a corkscrew!"

The children had gone up into the woods on the nature trail, their laughter and exuberant chatter carried back down to the clearing; soon they would come tearing back eager to show their finds. The adults sat on the logs around the fire and slipped easily into conversation, a peaceful interlude that was suddenly interrupted by screaming and shouting as Daniel, Charlotte and Jack came at full pelt down the middle path into the clearing. Shaking with fear they ran into the grown ups' arms, crying and shrieking all at once, noses running, unable to take a breath to say what was wrong. The adults looked at the children, at each other, back at the children, confused and dismayed. What on earth had happened? Why were the children so frightened?

Fabia, with her gentle way, managed to calm Jack down, enough for him to speak. "There's a man in the woods, he's really scary! I think he's a tramp or something," he stuttered between tears. "He chased us, so we ran away from him!"

"He came out of that old shed and tried to talk to us, but we ran away! He's a tramp, he smells, I've seen one before in the town, they stink. He won't come down here, will he? Can you get rid of him if he does? We should tell the police!" Charlotte gulped. This set all three of them off again, snivelling and gasping, all trying to speak at once, wiping noses and faces with hands and sleeves.

Then Elisabeth and the rest of the children came running into the clearing, breathless, and they crowded round. "You silly cow!" shouted Elisabeth, "That's Julius, he's not a tramp, he lives in our house, you idiot!"

"Elisabeth! Don't talk to your friends like that!" scolded Babette.

Elisabeth kicked a log and scowled at the three children who were crying, "Well she is a silly cow! They're all silly cows, they're all stupid! It's only Julius, isn't it!"

"But he's really scruffy! He said something to us and he chased us!" Jack shouted at her, between sobs. "Who's Julius anyway?"

"It's Julius!" Elisabeth turned to her mother. "Mummy, they saw Julius in his hut. He came out to talk to them, that's all! He did not chase them one bit, he was being friendly," she protested. Babette was shocked; she did not know what to make of this turn of events and was worried that the party was now ruined.

Elisabeth turned to the children who had arrived back in the clearing with her, "Is he a scary man or not? Does he look like a tramp or just like an ordinary man?"

Her friends looked from one to the other, with some confusion. "No, he's just a normal man, but with a beard," responded Alice, shaking her head.

"Well, he looks a bit scary. I mean when you first see him," said Ben.

Anna interrupted, "Don't be stupid Ben! He's Elisabeth's grandpa! I've seen him hundreds of times at her house. He's not scary, he's nice sometimes."

Then Julius came down through the middle path, noticeably stumbling and short of breath as he reached the clearing. Between breaths he slowly apologised, as his eyes moved from Babette to her friends, to Caspian and to Fabia; the children looked away. A silence, gauche and uncomfortable hung over the small group of children and adults.

"I must apologise," he said, addressing everyone there. "I must have startled Elisabeth's friends. I don't suppose they were expecting anyone to be in the hut, I must have given them a fright." He bent over slightly, coughed and thumped his chest. All the while he kept his left hand behind his back, an observation of Babette's that served as a reminder for Julius when he noticed her watching him.

He coughed again and stood up, as straight as he could considering that he had drunk half a bottle of whiskey and was a little off balance, "I'm sorry if I frightened you, I'm very sorry, all of you." He coughed again.

"Elisabeth," he said quietly. "Come here, I have something to say to you."

Elisabeth stepped forward and stood in front of Julius who then stooped to talk to her. She clasped her hands behind her back coyly and shuffled her feet.

"Elisabeth, I understand that today is a very special day. Is that right?"

"Yes, Julius, that's right. It's my birthday!"

"Ah, I thought so! And on birthdays it's customary to give presents, isn't it? So I have something for you. Will you hold out your hand please?"

Elisabeth smiled and looking up at Julius, she held out her right hand. He extended the arm he had kept behind his back and as everyone watched, he slowly unfurled his fingers. In his hand was a perfectly beautiful wooden apple; in actual fact a trinket box with a lid that was lifted by holding the stalk. Elisabeth gasped as he put it onto her open palm.

"Happy Birthday Elisabeth," turning away he began to walk slowly back up through the woods.

Elisabeth called after him, "Thank you Julius!" She held the apple in her hand, stroked it with her fingers and felt how smooth it was. She turned it over and round and round, as if she were examining every part of it. The children watched as Elisabeth continued to study the apple; the mothers stared, open mouthed, all were quiet. None of them knew that Julius had made the apple himself, though of course, it occurred to Babette, Caspian and Fabia that he had done so, and they were astonished.

The apple was made from a single block of yew that had been on the bottom shelf in his workshop for several years, so long that he had forgotten exactly where it came from, although he knew that it was from one of the local churchyards. He had noticed it lying there recently and thought perhaps he should make a small bowl with it; it was seasoned well by now so it shouldn't split as yew often did. Then only two weeks ago he saw on the table in the anteroom a leaflet that Fabia had brought home from the gallery, advertising a forthcoming show; on the front of it was a photograph of a wooden apple with a little lid. 'Elisabeth will like that,' he thought, and he decided he would make one, at first from a block of holly that he had, but the holly was badly split so instead he came to the yew. Julius had turned countless wooden fruit before, usually apples and pears, but he did not find it so easy now and he had to make a screw chuck to hold the fruit on the lathe. He shaped the stalk from a silver birch twig and with much patience he'd glued it into place.

Considering there were five adults and eight children stand-ing around, the silence in the woods was remarkable. One of the children gave a small cough, a twig snapped beneath a foot, but the clearest sound was the birdsong. Although it was gone mid-afternoon, somewhere in the tree tops, the trill voices of chiffchaff and nuthatch could be heard, the occasional call of a jay, and in the hedge where the woods met the field, blackbirds were singing mellifluously. The late May sun filtered through the leaves and dappled the clearing where Elisabeth stood looking at the apple. At last she took off the lid and gasped as her eyes widened; Julius had lined the box with dark green velvet, cut from an old scarf of Louisa's that she left behind in a trunk in the sewing room. From the little trinket box Elisabeth slowly pulled a silver necklace.

"That's incredible!" she almost whispered and turning to her mother she held it up to show her. There were murmurs of admiration from the others who had gathered around to see what it was, though Fabia recognised it at once. The necklace also once belonged to Louisa and had been her grandmother's. It was a quite large Victorian locket, oval shaped, engraved on the front with a rose-gold bird and a yellow-gold bee; it opened to hold a photograph each side. Elisabeth prised it open, "I've seen one of these before, I know what you do with them, you put pictures of people in them." She held it up, excited now to show everyone, her friends crowding round, taking turns to hold the apple, to pull the lid on and off, off and on.

Babette felt her eyes welling up, so surprised was she at Julius' gift. She crouched to talk to Elisabeth, her hand on her shoulder.

"I want to put Caspian that side and you this side," said

Elisabeth, pointing at the open locket and then turning to face her mother.

"This is a very special present Julius has given you," Babette told her, "this type of necklace is called a locket, and you're right, you can put photographs in it. You must promise to always look after it because it's very old and very, very special. It was so kind of Julius to give you this and to make such a beautiful box to put it in. You're a very lucky girl!"

"He made that apple?" Elisabeth asked, wide-eyed; Babette nodded.

"He's a really clever man then, isn't he? Not a tramp, see!" she said smartly to her friends. Elisabeth turned around; she wanted to thank Julius again, but he was almost out of sight, on his way back up through the woods to the hut.

8

Fabia's Prying

Fabia tiptoed into Julius' bedroom and quietly closed the door behind her. She realised that she had no need to creep about; no-one else was home. Elisabeth was at school, Babette and Caspian both at work and she'd heard her father leave the house at 6.30 that morning, presumably gone to the woods where he was spending more and more of his time lately. The sun rose at the front of the house, so the daylight had not yet filled Julius' room at the back, and it seemed gloomy, exacerbated by the low cloud that had been a dominant feature of the weather for the last few days. It all felt rather grey, and a perceptible doleful emptiness pervaded the room, which was quite monastic, a complete contrast to the clutter of Julius' sitting room, the disarray of his workshop and the untidy hut in the woods. He slept on a 1940's bedstead that was quite high off the floor, with a low dark wood footboard that was scratched and worn. The bed itself looked somehow flat, cold and spartan, not at all warm and inviting, as if seldom slept in. The green candlewick bedspread had been pulled up over the pillows and straightened down. Beside the bed was a small cupboard with nothing on it but a lamp, an alarm clock that was ten minutes fast, and white rings where hot cups had been placed and had stained the varnish. To one side of the room was a double wardrobe; both of the doors were closed, and the key in the lock. In the corner by the window stood a rush seated chair, on it lay a brown corduroy shirt, frayed around the collar, and an Arran wool jumper that had seen better days. The curtains were pulled back, though unevenly and Fabia noticed that on the one nearest the wardrobe the hem had come loose and was hanging down exposing crude stitching and the tendrils of old beige threads. On the other side of the room was an oak chest of drawers with nothing on it other than a chipped blue and white saucer with a few coins and an old watch in it.

It was to this chest of drawers that Fabia first went. She took a deep breath and very carefully pulled open the top drawer which was stuck a little so did not move freely. It contained only underwear; she pulled a face, put her hand in amongst it and felt around, flinching when the cold catch of a pair of braces touched against her hand. Deciding there was nothing of interest she arranged the underclothes more or less as she'd found them and closed the drawer, moving onto the next one. Socks; but again, she repeated the process of blindly feeling amongst them, finding nothing more.

'What am I looking for?' she asked herself. 'Anything, anything that proves that I'm right, that he drove my mother away.' Even now, when Louisa had been gone for years, Fabia still sought this evidence, but it was not all she wanted to find. Her dislike for her father had intensified since Elisabeth's party and she wanted to find something that justified this. She was vexed that he had given her grandmother's locket to Elisabeth, so she hoped to incriminate him. It had become an obsession.

The other three drawers were longer, running the entire length of the chest. Each had two handles and Fabia slowly pulled those of the topmost drawer, still trying very hard not to make a sound, even though she knew that she was alone in the house. Once open, the drawer revealed sweatshirts and jumpers, neatly folded. She slid her hands between and beneath each one, hoping to find something, a letter or a photograph, but her searching was in vain. The next drawer contained only jeans, tidily doubled over and she felt into the pockets of each pair finding nothing but a couple of small holes. She knelt down on the carpet and pulled out the bottom drawer which was almost empty except for a pair of beige shorts, still belted, and underneath them, something in a white carrier bag. Fabia took a deep breath and tentatively lifted it out.

Her heart was beating fast; she wondered if this was it, that in the bag she'd find photographs, of another woman, the sort of thing that Julius would have kept hidden. Fabia did not realise that this prying was futile, that she would find no proof that her father had instigated his wife's departure. Louisa had told her children that she left because she was unhappy in her marriage, that she and Julius led separate lives and she saw no point in them living together. She told them that whilst she would always be fond of their father, she no longer loved him and knew that she would be happier in France. This should have been enough for Fabia, but she believed there was more to it and she wanted to get to the core of it, to find out what Julius did to make her mother so unhappy. It could not be just his character, that he behaved as he did because that was the way he was. Quiet by nature, he kept his thoughts in his head where they were more likely to be compartmentalised than mulled over. His liking for solitude had always been there, but what no-one other than Louisa saw, and later understood, was that it increased when his brother, older than him by three years, had moved away and taken up his unconventional lifestyle living in squalid flats and rambling disorganised communes, and that it had been compounded even more after Nathan had lost his life in the accident. Fabia and Caspian, being only children had of course not known anything of this at the time nor through the ensuing years.

Had Fabia considered it more deeply she may have come to the conclusion that her father's apparent selfishness was in fact a manifestation of the depression that Julius suffered from, worsened by distressing life events. Not just his brother's death, but the gulf that grew between him and Louisa, and her eventual departure, his son moving away to university, Babette's failed relationship with Luke, and Fabia shutting herself away for hours on end. Had he sought help he may have recovered from this melancholy but that was not his way, and he fought against the proverbial black dog that had descended upon him by ignoring it until, in recent months, it had become a darkness lessened only by hours of solitude sitting in the quiet of the woods, and by alcohol.

Fabia took out of the bag a thin board and when she turned it over, she saw that it was an oil painting, signed in the bottom right hand corner by her mother. It was of a small red brick cottage, with a wooden porch that honeysuckle scrambled over; in the front garden pink and white geraniums tumbled onto the lawn from the flower beds around the edge. Fabia recognised it at once; it was the end house of the terrace in the village near Julius's woods, though it had changed considerably now, with a side extension and the front porch replaced by a larger, more modern one. The windows were now double glazed and much of the front lawn had been dug up and paved to allow for parking. She knew this was her parent's first home; her mother had pointed it out to her when they went for walks around the village in the summer holidays, long before Louisa started going to France for most of July and August. Fabia had lived in that house as a baby and now she spent a few moments looking at the picture of her first home. She touched the paint with her fingertips, feeling the different textures, the lines left by the brush when her mother painted the grass, and the daubing of the honeysuckle. Then she sighed, put the painting back in the bag and replaced it at the bottom of the drawer beneath the shorts, where she'd found it. Had she shaken out the bag or looked into it she would have found the tiny slip of paper that had fallen from the back of the board. In her mother's faded handwriting it said: 'Home at last! I love you so much. L x'

Fabia decided to look through the wardrobe next. As she passed the window she glanced out and saw Albert, their next door neighbour, in his garden wearing his usual tweed jacket and flat cap. He was crouched down pulling weeds from the vegetable bed at the top of his garden where he grew runner beans, broad beans, peas and potatoes. He loved his garden and he was a kind neighbour; being on good terms as they were, there was usually a time in late summer when he'd hand a bowl of beans over the hedge after there had been a glut. It was not unusual to arrive home to find a carrier bag full of vegetables hanging on the brass knocker of the side door. Babette always made good use of them; courgettes, green beans, new potatoes. Some were steamed to go with a pork chop or Shepherd's Pie for dinner, and one year she made chutney that they'd had at Christmas with cold ham, reminding them of the acrid vinegary smell that lingered in the house for weeks.

Fabia took a deep breath and slowly turned the key that was in the lock of the wardrobe door. It creaked as it opened and she was faced with a row of shirts and jackets on old wooden hangers; most were earthy colours, moss green, sage green, and varying shades of beige. Here were the clothes that Julius had worn for years; replenishing his wardrobe was not high on his list of priorities. There were checks and stripes, even a shirt with a diamond pattern that she hadn't seen before; some had stains on the collars, others were tattered around the cuffs or had buttons missing. She slipped her hand into the pocket of a jacket and grimaced when she pulled out a screwed up handkerchief, which she quickly put back. In the other pocket she found a small magnifying lens in a black leather slipcase, and a two pence piece. She turned her attention to the inside pockets, furtively delving into the dark of the wardrobe; but nothing. Then she straightened the fabric down and continued the same process, working through all the jackets in the wardrobe – corduroy, linen and wool, two of thick tweed, and a dress suit with a curious yellow stain on the lapel. Her fingers worked quickly, slipping in and out of pockets, finding nothing other than an accumulation of fluff, a spare button, a small brass safety pin, another two pence piece, a tattered invitation to John Ayres' 50th birthday celebrations at the Golf Club (whoever he was). Each time she found nothing, she hurriedly smoothed the garment down and went swiftly on to the next. But nothing, nothing; nothing at all.

Fabia was beginning to think this was futile. She wasn't entirely sure what she was looking for; what form it would take, that shred, that scrap of evidence that belied her father's true self and revealed what had been going on all these years, so bad that it made her mother leave. What was it exactly that she was expecting to find? Lipstick on a collar, a love note slipped into a pocket, an odd earring? She breathed deeply, looked again out of the window to the garden next door where Albert's wife was on her way up the garden path carrying a cup of tea for her husband. Her heavy bent frame testament to her old age, a noticeable limp the warning of wear and tear on her hip joint that needed medical attention. Fabia stood back, worried that if her neighbours glanced up, they would see her. They knew this was the room where Julius slept, they would wonder what she was doing there, and they might mention it to him: "We saw Fabia in your room the other day, I don't know what she doing in there, perhaps she was making your bed?" in the way of idle chatter that neighbours tend to exchange. She put this thought from her mind, at least this time having a notion of the irrational way people think when they know they are doing something intrinsically wrong; the misgivings of the guilty.

The open section at the top of the beside cupboard contained only a book: Leaves from a Moth-Hunter's Notebook by P. B. M. Allan. The corner of page 105 was folded over, the title at the top 'The Mazarine Blue'. Moths. Julius had been fascinated with moths for as long as Fabia could remember, spending balmy summer nights in the garden, picking among the flower beds, torch in hand, or brushing a dark sugary potion he'd made onto the bark of the trees. She remembered seeing a Tupperware container half full of it in the kitchen once, a thick and black liquid, smelling strongly of molasses and rum, next to it two over-ripe bananas, the skins brown and split, ready to be mashed and added to the mixture.

Fabia knelt down by the bed and pulled open the door of the cupboard, beneath the open section; inside it was divided into two compartments by a thin central shelf. On the top shelf was a bundle of papers, an untidy jumble not looking to be in any particular order. This looked promising to Fabia and she reached carefully for the topmost paper, a largish brown envelope, unsealed but folded roughly over along the top. Sitting back onto her heels she pulled it apart, slipped her hand inside and pulled out its contents. In her hand she now held several photographs, of varying sizes, some in cardboard frames, one in a small slightly tarnished silver frame. Most were colour, though some were black and white, and some were slightly out of focus. They were all of Elisabeth.

For a few moments Fabia was unable to move. Kneeling there on the floor in her father's bedroom, her legs began to feel heavy beneath her, her calves numb. Her heart was beating hard, her breathing shallow; she did not know what to think and was perplexed. This was something she had not expected to find. The photographs trembled in her hand; Elisabeth as a baby, Elisabeth as a toddler, her chubby hands holding an ice cream, pushing a toy pram in the garden, playing on the grass with her dolls and teddy bears, asleep on the sofa in Julius' sitting room. Elisabeth on a swing, dressed up as Snow White, as a fairytale princess, in her mother's clothes, strings of beads draped around her, a cerise pink handbag on her shoulder, red lipstick on her rosebud mouth. Elisabeth playing in the sandpit in her swimming costume, standing on the beach, a towel wrapped around her, at the table blowing out candles on a birthday cake...one, two, three candles, her third birthday. Elisabeth sat by the Christmas tree opening presents, holding a stocking, and several of her in the bath, bubbles on her chin and in her hair, playing with a long red and yellow ship, plastic ducks, multi-coloured sponge letters on the tiles along the bath spelling her name with the letters S and B missing. Thirty or more photographs of Elisabeth, straight dark hair, deep brown eyes; smiling, laughing, pouting, sulking.

Fabia took a deep breath, her hands dropped to her lap. Her thoughts ran amok. Why? Why did her father keep these photographs, these memories, hidden away in an envelope in his bedside cupboard, especially when there was not a single picture anywhere in this room or his sitting room of her or her brother? Why did he keep them? How often did he look at them? When did he look at them? This made no sense to Fabia; it even crossed her mind that he might be perverted, and she shuddered and began to cry. Julius did not outwardly show any affection towards Elisabeth, he did not make any effort to spend time with her, he never took her to school nor fetched her at the end of the day, he did not tuck her up in bed, read to her, play with her, talk with her. Did he ever do so? Fabia could not remember. But he had given Louisa's locket to her for her birthday!

A noise startled her; the front door slamming shut. Her heart raced; someone was home. Who could that be, at this time of day? Babette was at work, so was Caspian, Julius was probably in the woods and unlikely to come home until nightfall, if at all this time of year; he was more likely to spend the night up there in his hut. So they were all accounted for, but someone had come home; perhaps they'd forgotten something, or had come home feeling ill. She decided it was most likely to be Caspian or Babette as Julius always used the side door or, if he was taking something to the garage or to his workshop, he came in the back way. Fabia hastily put the photographs back in the envelope, taking care not to disturb the order she had found them in. She put them back in the cupboard and closed the door, then nimbly slipped out of the bedroom, taking care to close the door silently behind her. On her way down the stairs she heard Caspian whistling in the kitchen, filling the kettle and opening the cupboard door to get a mug, then lifting the lid from the biscuit tin.

"Hello. You're home early, or have you forgotten something?" she asked, appearing in the doorway.

"Neither," he replied. He put a teabag into a blue stoneware mug, "Want one?"

"No thanks," she folded her arms around her thin frame, pulling her cardigan around her, trying not to appear distracted.

"I had an appointment in town, the development at the stable block at West Grange. It's a mess down there, mud everywhere, and I didn't have the right sort of footwear, so I came home to change my shoes. I took my boots out of the car at the weekend and forgot to put them back."

Fabia smiled, "So you thought you'd have a cup of tea whilst you're here!"

"Yep, I'm parched. They never offer me a drink down there, bad-mannered lot. No-one's expecting me back till after lunch so there's no rush, I might even have an extended lunch break. The Stables are coming on well Fabia, you wouldn't recognise it. I think you'd like it though. I'm quite pleased with the way it's going."

"Remind me what they're doing down there," she sat down at the end of the table.

"Converting it to a house, probably a holiday let, if they

can get the planning permission for change of use. It would work well, it's a good site with the side garden behind it and it's actually got a lot more room than you'd think. They're hoping to put a big conservatory on it as well. That'll double the floorspace downstairs."

"It sounds lovely! Perhaps you could sneak me down to see it sometime," she paused and nibbled at her thumb nail. "Actually Caspian, I will have a cup of tea after all, if you don't mind. There's something I should to talk to you about."

"That sounds serious!" He stirred the tea and leaving the milk on the worktop by the sink, he pulled out a chair, sat down at the table and put a mug of tea in front of her. "Here you go. What's up then, little sister?"

'He's got such an air of authority,' thought Fabia. 'I can just imagine how good he must be at his job, no wonder he's done so well.' She tucked a stray strand of hair behind her ear and looked down into her tea, "Well... I'm a bit concerned about Dad actually. As you know I put the recycling out most weeks, not that I mind, but I've noticed a lot of bottles in it and it's not just the wine you and Babette have, and I'm not one for drinking, so it's obviously him. Unless there's something you're not telling me!" She smirked, then looked seriously at her brother, "I think he drinks quite a lot actually. I went for a walk in the woods the other day and when I went past his hut, I saw bottles lying around outside. Not just beer; all sorts – wine, whisky, brandy. I think he's got a drink problem."

Caspian leaned back on the chair, his hands behind his head, "Funny you should say this. Babette mentioned it the other day and I said that I'd look into it, but it slipped my mind because the recycling had already gone by the time she told me. I told her to tell me next time she thought there were a lot of bottles, but she hasn't said anything since." He paused, "Have you ever seen him drunk? He doesn't smell of booze, does he? I haven't noticed it."

"I don't get close enough to find out," Fabia replied answering his second question first. She took a sip of her tea, it was too hot to drink yet and caused a sharp pain in a back molar that she suspected needed a filling, though she had not seen a dentist about it. "I don't think I've seen him obviously drunk, no, but I saw him come out of his workshop once, late at night, and it looked like he was a bit wobbly. He gets that bad knee that makes him hobble though, so it might have been that. I mean, he drives home alright, doesn't he? He manages to park the car alright and it's quite tight in the drive."

She took another mouthful of tea and winced; she'd forgotten about the tooth and swore to herself at the sudden painful reminder. "I must see the dentist about this tooth," she mumbled.

Caspian pondered, his elbows on the table, chin resting on his hands; he was looking directly at Fabia, who felt a little awkward and went to the sink to add cold water to her tea. Even though Caspian did not know what she had been doing before he came in, she was aware that she was feeling guilty for prying in their father's room and she was sure that her brother would disapprove if he knew. He would think it odd, but then he probably had no idea how she felt about Julius, how she disliked him and how she wished that he had left instead of Louisa.

"I don't really know what to do. I suppose we keep an eye on it for now rather than confront him." Caspian was always very measured in his thoughts, and remarkably wise for his years. "Let's do that, shall we? We'll keep an eye on it and if it gets worse then I suppose I'll have to have a chat with him. He isn't easy to talk to though, you know that. He's the last person likely to admit he has a drink problem, especially to us. I don't think he seems depressed or anything, he seems the same as he always is, so I think we should monitor it. I'll talk to Babette about it tonight, I'm sure she'll agree."

"Okay. That sounds like a good plan for now," Fabia tucked her hair back behind her ear and inspected her nails, which she'd been biting. "Thanks Caspian. I just thought it worth mentioning."

9

Babette's Birthday

At the top of the street a barn owl lay dead on a garden wall. A small crowd had gathered to look at it, unsure if it had fallen there from the sky, or if someone had picked it up from the road and put it there.

"I've never even seen one in the country," one woman said.

"It must have been hit by a lorry," said another.

The bird was on its side, one wing bent tortuously beneath it and out to the side as if the body lay upon it. Ruffled feathers stuck up along its back, white as snow and speckled sandy brown. Its face was even more mask-like and composed in death than in life; eyes dark and blank, black speckles of dirt and dust between them where the beak began. A child began to cry.

"Someone should call a vet," the first woman said.

"But there is no point," remarked a tall man with spectacles and a large nose. "What can the vet do?"

"Dispose of it in the proper manner!" replied the woman. "We can't leave it here."

Such a scene at the top of the street would have caused Babette much consternation, but it was early in the morning and she was still sleeping soundly, so she missed it all.

When she opened her eyes, Elisabeth was standing by the bed. She threw her chubby little arms around her mother's neck and pressed her warm cheek against her face.

"Happy Birthday Mummy!" she said rather too loudly. "I've been waiting ages for you to wake up. Do you want to open your presents now or later? I want you to open them before I go to school."

Babette was surprised to see that Elisabeth was already dressed in her uniform; cardigan neatly buttoned up, and even her hair brushed, though she was wearing odd socks, one a slightly darker grey than the other.

"Open this first, I made it especially for you. And these are for you too, I picked them this morning when you were still asleep. I've been up for hours!"

She put a handmade card on the bed and, tied with thin lilac ribbon, a posy of flowers, which Babette recognised as being from the garden; Granny's Bonnets, Jacob's Ladder, Canterbury Bells, lambs' ears, pale pink geraniums and giant cat mint.

"They're like the ones you put on the kitchen table!" Elisabeth rocked to and fro against the side of the bed, her hands behind her back. She looked very pleased with herself.

"Do you like them?"

"I love them!" said Babette, slowly turning the posy round in her hands, admiring it. "They're beautiful, all my favourite flowers! These are the most beautiful flowers I've ever had! Thank you darling!" She pulled herself up straight, plumping her pillows high against the headboard, then leaned over and kissed Elisabeth on the cheek.

"I love you Mummy. Let's pull the curtain back now. I've got another surprise for you."

Elisabeth skipped round to the window and tugged at the curtains, clumsily pulling them wide open and bright sunlight rushed into the room, into every corner, dust motes floating all at once in the beams.

"Look Mummy, what a lovely day it is! The sun is shining for your birthday!"

"Yes, how lucky I am!" laughed Babette. "Is everyone else up yet?"

"Fabia is, she's making breakfast. She's not dressed yet though. She's still got her pyjamas on! She went outside in them, without her shoes on and her feet got wet on the grass, and when she came back in, she left footprints on the floor!" Elisabeth threw back her head and laughed and laughed.

"She should have put some shoes on, then her feet wouldn't have got wet! But at least they've had a wash!"

Babette laughed and stretched her arms out to her daughter, "Come here my darling, I think we've got time for a birthday cuddle before I get up!" She pulled back the duvet so that her daughter could squeeze into bed beside her and they held hands on the richly patterned quilt. "What a lovely start to the day! Something tells me it's going to be one of the best birthdays ever!"

"Oh, Mummy, I forgot!" Elisabeth jumped out of bed and ran over to the chair in the corner where she fumbled beneath the pile of her mother's clothes; skirts, blouses and dresses that she'd worn over the last week.

"Close your eyes!" Elisabeth ordered, hands fidgeting behind her back. Babette barely had time to close them before the little girl shouted: "Now open them!" And there on the quilt was a small string of glass beads, purple, pink, and bottle green, with others that were clear and flower-shaped, like little glass daisies. Elisabeth grinned from ear to ear.

"This is so beautiful! Did you make it yourself?"

"Mostly I did. Fabia helped me because I can't tie knots, and the string is so tiny, so she had to help me. We made it last night after my bath. We used some of her beads and some of mine. I chose them and she helped me thread them on the string, and then she tied the knot. You should see her beads, she's got hundreds! Some are old and they're nice, but they look dirty, so I didn't use them. Are you going to wear it now?"

"I certainly am!" Babette stretched the bracelet over her hand down onto her wrist and admired it. "Oh, my goodness me, Elisabeth! It's so beautiful! I'm going to wear it all day, it's the best bracelet I've ever had! I love it!" She grabbed Elisabeth, squeezed her tight and gave her another kiss, on a perfect rosy cheek.

* * *

Fabia nudged open the door with her elbow and in she came singing Happy Birthday and carrying a silver tray. There was tea in a china mug with dark pink roses on it; on a gold-rimmed plate hand painted with harebells and ivy, were two thick slices of toast, spread generously with butter and marmalade.

What a surprise for Babette! "Breakfast in bed as well!" she said. "I'm being spoilt! I could get used to this! I'm beginning to wish it was my birthday every day!" Elisabeth giggled and clapped her hands. "Happy birthday Mummy!" she shouted.

"I've left your present downstairs," said Fabia. "No room

on the tray and no free hands!" She moved aside a book and put the tray down on the bedside table.

"Oh Fabia, thank you! That's so lovely of you! Where's Caspian? Is he up yet? I haven't a clue what the time is, it must be quite early." She reached for her tea.

"He left ages ago, he's got a meeting in Salisbury and had to catch the early train. He's left you a note though, and a card. He said he should be back by six, and to tell you that he's cooking this evening, so that will be interesting! It's twenty to eight and as you can see, madam is already dressed and I'm taking her to school so you can stay in bed a bit longer, birthday girl. Plenty of time before you have to leave for the office."

How kind Fabia was on this morning, the morning of Babette's birthday. Babette would remember this and do the same for her on her birthday, though that was not until January.

Elisabeth had momentarily disappeared into her own world and was dancing a pirouette on the rug by the wardrobe, watching her reflection in the dressing table mirror. Babette felt a little disappointed that Caspian had already left the house; if only he had just popped his head round the door to say good morning. Now she would not see him until after work, but she consoled herself with the thought that it would be something to look forward to.

"Look at my beautiful bracelet!" Babette exclaimed suddenly, holding her arm out so that Fabia could see it. She brushed toast crumbs from the front of her nightdress onto her plate.

"Isn't it wonderful? I think the ladies in the office will be very jealous when they see it. In fact, I think everyone I meet on the way to work will be jealous, and they'll probably think I'm a princess or something because I'm wearing such a beautiful bracelet!" She sipped her tea and winked at Fabia. Elisabeth spun round, wrinkled her nose, sniffed, and blushed.

* * *

Caspian put his briefcase down in the hall, hung his jacket on the newel post and loosened his tie. He could hear what he thought was the television in the sitting room, the door being slightly ajar. He pushed it open and peered in.

"Happy birthday Babette! Have you had a good day? It's a bit dark in here, isn't it, why don't you put more lights on?" Despite the promising start to the day the weather had turned late in the afternoon. Darkish clouds had filled most of the sky and a few light showers had wet the pavements, a light wind picking up at the same time, whistling across the field at the back of the house.

What a wonderful sight met Caspian's eyes! It bordered on domestic bliss, and though something he was quite used to seeing, it still moved him. Babette was sitting in the red armchair, sewing what looked like Elisabeth's school pinafore, by lamplight. Elisabeth was kneeling on the floor at the low table silently pondering over a jigsaw puzzle, looking from the lid, which was propped up by the leg of the table, to the pieces she had laid out before her. The radio was on and Caspian thought how cosy it all was, the contented togetherness of mother and daughter.

"Shhh!" whispered Elisabeth, glaring at Caspian. "Mummy's listening to a play!"

Babette looked up from her sewing, surprised that she had not heard Caspian come in. "Five minutes," she mouthed, holding her hand up, fingers spread. The dim light concealed the smile that crossed her face; had he seen it Caspian would have immediately known how delighted Babette was to see him. Instead he raised his eyebrows and left the room, to return exactly five minutes later.

"All done?"

"Yes, sorry! It was Tess of the D'Urbervilles, you know how I love Thomas Hardy!" She stood up, placed the folded pinafore on the arm of the chair, smoothed down her dress, and went to him.

"Happy birthday!" He put his arms around her and kissed her lightly on the cheek, only narrowly missing her mouth, as if it was a last second diversion, something that he had thought better of. It took Babette slightly, though rather pleasantly, by surprise.

"Apologies for leaving without saying hello this morning. I forgot to tell you I had an early appointment in Salisbury, and I didn't want to wake you. Have you had a good day?"

"Don't worry, I got your note. I've had a lovely day, even though I had to work! Look at my bracelet. Isn't it beautiful?"

She held out her arm and he gasped; he held her arm with one hand and with the other, touched the beads. "Babette, it's not just beautiful, it's exquisite!" he exclaimed. "Is it a birthday present? Who gave it to you? I can see that it must have been someone very, very rich because this must have cost a fortune!"

Elisabeth was watching them, and she threw back her head, clutched her tummy and howled with laughter; all the while she wriggled her toes beneath the table. "No, it didn't, silly Caspian! I made it! Me and Fabia did it last night, it's not even from the jewellery shop! It's homemade!"

"No! I don't believe you Elisabeth! How could you and Fabia

possibly make anything as splendid as this?"

Elisabeth could barely speak for laughing and she wiped her eyes. "But we did! We secretly made it in Fabia's room. I chose the beads myself!"

"Well, how extraordinary! How very clever you are! And I'll tell you what; I think that if the queen sees that bracelet, she'll want one too and then you and Fabia will have to make one for her!"

"The Queen of England?" laughed Elisabeth.

"Yes, the Queen of England!" said Caspian, who had gone to her side, squatted down and ruffled her hair. "And then her friends the Queen of Spain and the Queen of Portugal will want one too!" Elisabeth roared and clutched her tummy again, then Babette and Caspian joined in and their laughter charged joyfully about the room, filling every corner, slipping behind the furniture, under the sofa, everywhere.

"Now come to the kitchen and see what I've got for us to eat. I'm cooking tonight and I've got things for us to munch on so we can all chat whilst I get started. I've poured you lemonade in your favourite glass."

Elisabeth was up and gone, heading pell-mell for the kitchen, where on the table were bowls of plump black and green olives speckled with dried herbs and garlic, fat juicy peppers stuffed with Greek cheese, spiced sesame sticks, and tiny savoury cheese biscuits. Beside them stood three flutes of sparkling wine, and in a glass that had lots of little blue stars on it, lemonade still fizzed as the bubbles broke away from the bottom and almost sang their way to the top.

* * *

Late that night Babette was still up, still wearing her bracelet, clearing away after having just made the next day's lunches for Elisabeth and Caspian; a sandwich for Elisabeth, four neat squares filled with grated cheese and lettuce, and for Caspian two granary rolls with ham and tomato. She'd wrapped two pieces of banana cake in tin foil and put them in a plastic tub to be put with the lunches in the morning. She did not need to think about herself; she only worked three days each week and tomorrow was a day off.

Babette worked in an accountants office in the town. Her job was largely secretarial and was not something she particularly enjoyed. She found the men quite dull in their grey suits, with their conventional ways, their routines and forced male camaraderie, but fortunately there were other women in the office, and it helped to ease the tedious and old-fashioned male-female divide.

There was Linda, who assisted the senior partner and founder of the business; though of a quiet disposition she had a sharp sense of humour and she and Babette concocted nicknames for some of the clients and made secretive, sometimes childish jokes about them. Linda was married with two teenage sons born when she was in her early twenties. She was quite plump and did not care greatly for fashion, wearing the same skirts and blouses she had worn for years, keeping the same straight bobbed hairstyle.

Geraldine was several years older than both of them and had been working at the office since she left school. Over the years she had taken considerable time off whenever the premises were redecorated, complaining that it caused bouts of debilitating asthma. She was clearly disgruntled to have a younger and more attractive female in the workplace after years of considering herself the office beauty; Linda did not matter; Linda was plump and plain and was no threat to her.

Such is the weakness of many men that Babette's good looks and curvaceous figure did not go unnoticed and she often received compliments from her colleagues and from clients. She brushed them off as she would a fly on her sleeve; they could flirt as much as they like, to her it meant nothing. Geraldine's reaction to this was like that of a very young child whose contemporary has more attention; she scowled and sank into tremendous sulks which caused a depressed and heavy atmosphere to hang about the office, thick and stale. Sometimes, it would go on like that for days at a time when Geraldine barely spoke to anyone and would not even look at Babette. No-one said anything; they all thought it piteous, but no-one said anything.

Geraldine had a habit of casting a very critical eye over Babette; her piggy little eyes, heavy with make-up, moved behind her thick glasses, up and down, up and down, taking in Babette's clothes, her shoes, her hair, her lipstick, every detail of her. There were furtive sideways glances that she thought went unseen though Babette was often aware of them. But it was water off a duck's back; Babette had no care for what other people thought of her. She genuinely felt a degree of pity for Geraldine and thought it a shame that her world was such a shallow one where physical appearance was of the first importance; that she judged people, especially other women, on appearance alone.

Babette believed that if Geraldine could only recognise her deeply rooted insecurities, she might somehow shake them off and then she would probably be nice, and easier to get along with. Instead, she constantly strove to be the most admired and the most attractive, in spite of the obvious advancement of her years. Although they were not the same, Babette thought that they might have found some common ground, as most women do. Perhaps they could have gone for a drink or lunch together, to the cinema, or browsing around the shops on their half days in the office, as she sometimes did with Linda.

Babette chose to ignore the animosity when it arose and she got on with the work she was there to do; after all, it was a job that paid her a decent enough income to buy the things Elisabeth needed, to contribute to the household, and to occasionally treat herself.

She was humming to herself and having just wrung the dishcloth out in the sink, was wiping away the crumbs from the surface of the worktop when Julius came in by the back door.

"Hello Babette." He took off his jacket and hung it on the peg by the door, "Was there any post today?"

"Hello Julius. Yes, there are a couple of letters for you on the table in the dining room. It doesn't look like anything important though."

He went into the anteroom and picked up his post. Quite unlike him, he noticed a vase of flowers on the table, not the usual garden sort, but the type of bouquet sold by florists.

"What lovely flowers! Where are they from?" Even more unusual was that he should comment on them.

Babette appeared in the doorway, yawning, "From work. For me. It's my birthday." The last three words she said so quietly they were almost inaudible.

"What was that?" Julius peered over the top of his glasses at her.

"They're from work. A present for me. It's my birthday

today," she repeated.

Julius glanced at the flowers, roses that were deep red, carnations in a similar shade, gypsophilia, and several stalks of greenery that he could not name. Red carnations, he thought, Louisa's favourite.

"Oh. I see! Happy birthday." He smiled but it seemed only a polite gesture.

"Thank you, Julius. Caspian cooked dinner, he made a vegetable lasagne. It was very good! There's some left if you want it."

"That's very kind Babette but I've already eaten. I'm sorry I forgot."

"What?"

"I'm sorry I forgot your birthday."

She smiled and shrugged. "Don't worry," she said. "You've never been one for birthdays, have you? Besides, they don't mean much as you get older."

"I suppose not. Certainly not when you get to my age."

Babette had gone back into the kitchen to straighten the chairs and hang the tea towels on the radiator where they would dry overnight. 'He never forgets Elisabeth's birthday,' she thought; he forgets his own son and daughter's birthdays, and mine, but never Elisabeth's. She thought of the wooden apple that he'd made for Elisabeth and her thoughts wandered back to the party in the woods, how the other children had thought that Julius was a tramp and how when they saw him come out of his hut they'd come running down through the woods terrified. Poor Julius!

She remembered that evening when they were all back at home, smelling of wood smoke, thoroughly worn out and a little giddy from the wine they'd drunk in the clearing; how

114

when Elisabeth was sound asleep in her bed, Caspian had come into the kitchen and put his arm around her. Then he pulled her to him and kissed her on the cheek, leaving his head against hers for a moment or two.

"Well done," he'd said quietly. "That was the most perfect day. Elisabeth loved every minute of it. You did a wonderful job, organising things, everyone really enjoyed it. I'm so.... I'm really proud of you."

Then he'd let her go, said goodnight and just like tonight, had gone quietly up the stairs, leaving her alone in the kitchen where she stood feeling rapturously happy, her cheek still warm where he had kissed it.

* * *

Two days later Caspian, hands in pockets, wandered through to the conservatory and stood by the door. It was still raining, as it had been, almost continuously since Babette's birthday, far more than had been forecast. It had kept him awake last night, the winds howling about the house, the rain lashing down, beating against his bedroom window at the back of the house where storms whipped down across the valley and the open field. He lay there thinking about the house, about the gutters, the slates on the roof, the wall in the bathroom that had a tendency to draw in moisture when it rained like this, and dark, damp splodges would appear, reminding him that it needed attention. His father either did not notice the repairs that needed to be done, or he overlooked them and so such things became Caspian's responsibility.

Not long after midnight he'd heard Elisabeth creep across the landing into Babette's room, and he thought of them snuggled together in the big bed with the velvet quilt pulled up to their chins, their arms around each other. He thought of Babette's clothes draped over the cast iron bedstead at their feet and on the chair in the corner by the door. He did not know why he thought of these things, but it warmed him.

The storm eased off during the day and the wind died down, but it continued to rain steadily. Caspian watched as it fell from a lead-grey sky that made it seem as dark as a day in late winter, even though it was still the afternoon and not long since Babette had come home from school with Elisabeth. Unabating big fat raindrops fell and splashed onto the patio and into the pond which was close to overflowing; there seemed to be no reprieve and Caspian found he was looking forward to supper and then to a few hours in the sitting room. He might even light the fire, he thought, such was the unseasonable temperature. Perhaps Babette would play cards with him after Elisabeth had gone to bed, or they could find a film to watch together.

He chuckled to himself; 'Like an old Derby and Joan', he thought. No wonder people often thought they were man and wife.

10

Caspian and Laura

At Tompkins and Parker Caspian was sitting at his desk, his shirt sleeves rolled up to his elbows, his tie folded neatly on the table behind him. He was eating his lunch and looking out of the window, daydreaming. Over the field he could see a line of washing hanging in the parched air in the garden of the cottage on the edge of the lane. The verdant midsummer landscape stretched out to the copse in the distance. Nothing stirred, all was still in the baking heat; the only sound was the whirring of the electric fan on his desk and the occasional burr of a telephone elsewhere in the building.

During the early hours of the morning he'd had an erotic dream about Babette. It had felt very real, as if when asleep he had gone off to some celestial plane or to a parallel universe that truly existed and was more than just the jumbled thoughts and happenings of the day that arose in his usual dreams. He had stirred, and lying there recalling his dream, he realised that he wanted it to be real. It had left him with an ache, a yearning in the pit of his stomach and in that instant, still drowsy with sleep, he realised that he was in love with Babette and that he desired her. His immediate reaction was one of shock and he instantly recoiled. Then he questioned whether such deep emotion was acceptable or appropriate. He and Babette had grown up together and lived more or less as brother and sister, or more accurately, as cousins, and though they had no blood ties they lived the easy and familiar existence of being part of the same family. True, theirs was not a typical family unit, Julius had his solitary ways and spent more of his time in his woods than at home, Fabia did as she pleased and though she was part of the very fabric of the house, she did not always join in their mealtimes or routines; depending upon her mood she flitted in and out of the household's patterns like a visitor and was usually either out or in her room. It was he and Babette who formed the nucleus of their 'family', who bought food and kept the house in order, arranging repairs and paying bills with Julius's cheque book. Caspian thought he could happily go on like this for years, for the rest of his life, and though he'd had girlfriends he had not felt that he loved them or that he could foresee any solid future with any of them. But Babette? They had been on the same family holidays, celebrated the same birthdays and Christmases, and shared the same meal table for as long as he could remember. She was a constant in his life and it was fair to say that they were very close.

This made him feel that his newly discovered feelings were wrong, but still he could not control them. He knew that he would marry Babette tomorrow if she would agree, and then he would always be happy. But he felt at the same time that it was no good to feel like this, that it was untenable, and ultimately, that it was improper, and yet for months, she had been in his mind constantly. He looked forward to going home after work and to finding her in the kitchen preparing supper, singing and chatting with Elisabeth. He enjoyed eating his packed lunches knowing she made them for him, he felt excitement when they were going out to see a band together or to meet with friends in the pub. He always felt proud to be with her and he relished her company above all others.

'What can I do?' he wondered. 'What am I to do?' He lay in his bed and pondered, eventually concluding that he would have to find a distraction, something that would put a metaphorical distance between them. Or perhaps the answer was for him to move away, to instigate a real distance and to leave behind all that was commonplace, then with several hundred miles between them, he would somehow move on.

* * *

Not long after Caspian's dream Babette had stopped making lunch for him to take to work each day. The impetus was jealousy. She was surprised at how disgruntled she felt because she knew that Caspian had started to see a girl he worked with. When she thought about it her stomach turned over and lurched as if it was full of some thick unwelcoming substance, and her heart began to pound the night he casually mentioned that he would not be having dinner at home, that he was going out to eat with Laura. Babette had hesitated for a moment, composed herself and quietly asked: "Where are you going?"

"To the new Italian restaurant on the corner of Broad Street and King William Street," he replied without looking at her.

"Who is Laura?"

"Oh, just someone I work with."

"A client?"

"Not exactly," Caspian mumbled. He was finding the situation difficult; he did not want to tell her that he was taking Laura on a date. It felt like a betrayal or even worse, as if he was doing something very bad, something that would change forever the happy and familiar world they all inhabited. He did not want to upset Babette, but he suspected that she might feel hurt and this troubled him. He had wondered over the last week or so how she would feel if he had a girlfriend, and how any resentment would manifest. He wasn't sure if it was merely that she would feel robbed of her companion, or if it was as he felt, something more profound than that. In any case, he knew that the alternative was for him, not a choice. He could not have a love affair with this woman he had shared his growing up years with, not when they had lived for so long in the same household, more or less as siblings.

He decided he must cut his losses and out with it; he must be honest with her.

"She's the new temp at work. She's there for a few months whilst we have this big project on. She started a few weeks ago and she's new to the area so she doesn't know anyone around here. I felt sorry for her, so I thought I'd take her out. It might help her settle in and make friends." He knew he was in part making excuses for his actions, trying to pass it off as nothing of importance, almost dismissing any possibility of the beginnings of a relationship.

"That's very kind of you." Babette looked away, stirring the ragout sauce she was cooking. She stared into the pot, blinking, "Well, have a nice time. I'm going to bed early, so I'll see you tomorrow sometime."

She'd tried to appear indifferent about it, although she felt that she could burst into tears at any moment. She felt as if her heart had now stopped beating in her chest, had been ripped out of her and all that was left was a huge black emptiness, like a hole. "Don't cry," she told herself, "Keep going. Deep breaths. Don't stop." And she took several deep breaths, one after another.

Upstairs, whilst he was getting changed, Caspian felt as if he had committed some dreadful crime. He felt as if he had brought a huge weight crashing down on him and Babette – and in turn Elisabeth; surely it would affect her too, and then it would resonate through the household causing an unsettled and awkward atmosphere. He was quite wrought-up and thought his actions utterly selfish. In his attempt to do what he thought was right, to distance himself from Babette, he knew that he had laid the foundations for a big and impenetrable wall to be built between them.

He thought about Laura. He knew he was not in love with her, nor anything like it, that she had not stirred his feelings nor aroused him in any way. He wasn't even sure if he particularly liked her because he did not yet know her very well. They had exchanged a few jokes and chitchat in the office but that was all, and he was wise to the fact that people are not always what they at first seem to be, or that they so often do not meet up to the expectations held of them. He thought her attractive yes, she was indisputably pretty, but she did not have the charm or the effervescence of Babette's character, that which had sprung to his attention as she settled back into the house after returning with the baby Elisabeth several years ago.

'What am I doing?' he questioned. 'Wouldn't it be better to talk to her and explain how I feel; to tell her that I am in love with her and that I can imagine no other life than with her?' He paced in front of the window, biting at the skin around his thumb nails.

'I'm going to do it,' he thought. 'I have to tell her,' and he imagined going back down to the kitchen, taking hold of her small wrists, turning her to face him and telling her: "Babette, I'm not going out to dinner, I've changed my mind. I don't want to go, I never wanted to in the first place. I'm having dinner here with you tonight, as I always do and like I want to do every night for the rest of my life. I'm in love with you, you are everything to me, and right or wrong, all I want is to be with you for always."

But he could not do it. He had no idea how she would react, and then he had to think of what Julius and Fabia and even his mother would think, what people who knew them would say, people at work, people at school. "But isn't she your sister?" his friends would ask, and to explain the true situation would take so long and so much deliberation to find the right words. He felt somehow perverse and ashamed to admit that he felt so deeply about someone he had grown up with and as he kept reminding himself, had lived with since they were children. He continued to pace about his bedroom and felt wretched and torn apart. How was it that something that intrinsically felt so right could at the same time feel so utterly, manifestly wrong?

Downstairs, Babette was crying. Her tears were initially of anger and then of a deep misery; she felt wounded and dejected. She loved the contented heartbeat of the house, of the rhythms and routines of the days and the quietness of the nights that would not exist if it were not for her and Caspian and the time they spent together. She loved the weekends when they put music on in the kitchen on Friday and Saturday nights and danced and drank wine together, when in the summer they sat in the garden and chatted until the early hours of the morning.

The times they went out made her so happy, the excitement of getting dressed up and strolling into town with him or driving somewhere for the day. She wanted it to go on like that. It had not occurred to her that anything would ever change, and she had not given it a moment's thought. What was Caspian doing? Why oh, why was he spoiling things? The truth was that they were both very content and hadn't until now questioned their bond or thought of the future. It was not just an acceptance of how things had become, it was more. They were happy doing things together and with Elisabeth, going everywhere together. It was a co-existence that they had created; its fathoms had not been foreseen.

She wiped her eyes and pulled out her hair corsage, tossing it onto the table, a sad and suddenly forlorn red flower, the brocade permeated with the smell of the cooking and of her hairspray.

'Fuck him then,' she said to herself. 'If that's what he wants to do then let him get on with it and I will have my own life too.'

She thought on an impulse of ringing the client who had invited her to lunch, or the man who lived next door to the pub and had given her his phone number when she was at the bar buying drinks one night. She thought of Jamie from her schooldays, who was now back in town and had been asking about her - was she still around, was she married? She was not short of offers but she turned them all down because she was simply not interested. She did not particularly feel the need for a man in her life, she had Elisabeth to consider and love affairs were not without their complications. She would not see her daughter hurt or confused. In essence Caspian was the only man in her life and though they were not lovers she felt that nothing could replace the profound devotion and loyalty that they shared.

"My God!" she said aloud, with a start, putting her hand to her throat, "I love him, that's the trouble. I've loved him for years!" She ruminated on how she had always known that she felt an immeasurable fondness for Caspian; at times she was aware that she was aroused by him, but this quickly subsided into the mere judgement that he was an attractive man. As if because they shared an existence akin to consanguinity, there was an unspoken rule which she abided by, not giving rise to any notion that their relationship could ever be carnal.

Babette had often thought that anyone who didn't know them would assume that Caspian was her husband, and Elisabeth their child. She supposed that most of the parents at Elisabeth's school thought so, being newcomers to the town. She wasn't sure about the friends she'd made there, what they thought, but it had never been necessary to explain the truth, which was complicated and somewhat painful. But Caspian and Babette had grown up in the town and there were people who knew them; those people sometimes conjectured that their closeness was perhaps a little odd.

"We must look like a little family. People at the school must think you're Elisabeth's father," she'd said to Caspian one afternoon when they were walking home, and Elisabeth had skipped ahead.

Caspian laughed, "I suppose they would if they don't know us very well. But that's up to them, let them think what they like. It's nothing to do with us."

"Actually, they probably think you're my latest boyfriend because Elisabeth doesn't call you Daddy," Babette continued.

"Well I'm the only father figure in Elisabeth's life, aren't

I? I mean, there's Dad I suppose, but he's not much cop." He shrugged, "I suppose one day she'll start asking questions but for now, she's happy and I don't really see any reason why we should complicate things. That my dear, would only discombobulate her!"

It was typical of Caspian to turn a serious conversation into something more jocular and dismissive. It was his way of ending a discussion, that to him, was by the by, or was something that he did not want to think about.

Babette turned the ragout off. She needed to think, and she could come back to the dinner later, when everyone would be ready to eat. She thought how she and Caspian had become responsible for the running of the house and how they jointly took all decisions on domestic matters. This had evolved because Julius was disinterested and lived more in his woods than in the house, and Fabia was still young and wrapped in her own world. Someone had to take responsibility and between them, without discussion of who would do this and who would do that, they had grabbed the rudder and steered the ship on. 'Other than the lack of a physical relationship, we are as good as married,' she surmised.

She recalled a time, many years ago, when they were both very young, when she was still at school and Caspian studying for A' Levels. One summer night on holiday at Dana's house in France they'd stayed in the garden talking after everyone else had gone to bed. They talked until the early hours of the morning, each lying on a separate sun bed with just a small gap between them, their young, slim brown arms hung loosely in the gap, touching now and then accidentally and after a while they had quite naturally held hands as they chatted. With the first light they crept into the summerhouse, not wanting to disturb the household, and they curled up together on the divan; nothing mattered, and no one cared, and they slept, arms entwined until sunrise.

It had not happened again, and they had not spoken of it. The days passed and they settled back into their usual habits, where small and intimate acts were commonplace, borne out of endearment, and they were not aware of them. Caspian would sometimes put his hand on her shoulder when he squeezed past her in the kitchen, at her elbow when they were out, getting in the car, or crossing the road, and she never reacted in any way because it was what he did and because she was so very comfortable with it and used to it. Not long after that he'd gone away to university and Babette moved out to live with friends in another town; he was not such a big part of her life then. Now, she realised that she longed to kiss him, she ached for him to hold her and that feeling went so deep it made her head heavy because she could not work out if it was wrong or right. Like Caspian, she could not make head nor tail of it all.

* * *

The next morning Caspian came down to an empty kitchen and missed the usual morning happiness; no Babette, no Elisabeth. They had left early to go for a swim at the public pool before school. Fabia was still asleep in her room, it being a Wednesday. She did not work at the gallery on Wednesdays as it was the one day in the week that they closed at lunchtime. Julius had presumably not returned home from another night in the woods where he would probably now stay for the whole day. Caspian was running late, he had slept only fitfully, turning this way and that. When he finally drifted off to sleep, he dreamed of Babette and awoke fighting the emotion that rose from deep within him, from the pit of his stomach, from his groin. He again experienced an overpowering feeling that he was doing something very wrong, as though he had committed some dreadful heinous act. During the night he got up and went to the bathroom; it was starting to get light and back in his bedroom he pulled the curtains apart very slightly and peered out into the early dawn. The garden was beginning to find its place in the day, the trees no longer dark shadows, and the birds were singing, a wondrous tribute to herald another day of fine weather. The tabby from next door was sitting stock still on the wall, and out over the garden Caspian could see into the field. The hedges were still dark there and the glow of outside lights left on overnight from the back of the houses in the estate across the field filtered through where the leaves allowed. A movement by the gate at the top of the garden caught his eye. 'Was someone there?' He stared out, narrowing his eyes, trying to focus. He was sure that he had seen someone, standing by the gate, looking into the garden, and he wondered why anyone would be about at that time of morning. A burglar perhaps, out on a reconnaissance, checking out each of the gardens that backed onto the field, seeing if there was anything worth coming back for another time, though the area was one of statistically low crime and break-ins were more or less unheard of. He made a mental note to check the garden each night before going to bed, to make sure that Julius' workshop and the garage were locked and secured. He pulled the curtain across and climbed back into bed.

Later on, just before he left for work, Caspian went to the fridge to get his lunch, as he always did. When he opened the door the eerie brightness of the light and the quiet whirring of the innards of the fridge spilled out into the dullness of the room. He looked on each shelf for his lunchbox, but it was not there, only hunks of cheese wrapped in cling film, a packet of sliced ham, a small green jug of salad dressing and bowls of leftover food; cold custard, potato salad, cooked pasta. He sighed and checked his wristwatch: 8.51. There was not enough time to make a sandwich so he would have to buy lunch from the café that had recently opened on the business park; coffee could wait until he was at his desk. He shuddered slightly. Work meant seeing Laura and reminded him of the irrepressible feeling of wrongness within him, not only of how Babette might be feeling but also that he was perhaps using Laura, being unsure of how he felt about her, knowing that she did not arouse him. Their dinner the night before was pleasant enough, he just did not particularly want to see her today but knew that it was unavoidable. A small voice in his head spoke to him: 'What are you doing Caspian? What the hell are you doing?'

He ignored it. He put on his jacket, took his car keys from the Moroccan bowl on the hall table and left for work by the side door.

11

Elisabeth's Picture

Babette took a deep breath, drew in her stomach and pulled a black lace pencil skirt up over her hips, zipping it up at the side. She smoothed her polka dot blouse down over the waistband and ruffled her hair, all the time keeping her eyes on her reflection in the full-length mirror in her bedroom. Then she poked jet drop earrings through the holes in her earlobes and carefully applied lipstick, the same vivid red as her blouse; she stood straight, half turned and smiled at the image in the mirror. 'That will do nicely,' she thought. She felt confident and knew she looked good, which today, was important to her. She picked up her bag from the bed and slipping into her wedge heeled sandals, went downstairs.

In the anteroom Elisabeth was sitting at the table, singing to herself and colouring a picture she'd drawn.

"What's that you're drawing, darling?" asked Babette, looking over her daughter's shoulder. "That's you Mummy, and that's Caspian. That's me in the car, look, waiting for you to hurry up. We're going out for the day, to the zoo, because

I want to see the monkeys, and our food is in the bag you're holding. We've got cheese sandwiches and cake and shiny red apples, but you can't see them because they're inside the bag."

"That's wonderful sweetie! What a lovely picture!" The drawing was typical of that of a young child; a man and a woman standing beside a car, stick-fingered hands touching, and inside the car a smaller person was waving, straight dark lines for hair, and a big U-shaped smile.

"I'd like to have a picnic at the zoo. That would be nice," said Elisabeth, her legs swinging to and fro under the table. "We do things like that in the school holidays, don't we? Can we go soon please? Later this week, when Caspian has a day off?"

"Well, that would be very nice, but I don't know if Caspian can take any time off this week, he's very busy at work at the moment."

"Oh, Mummy, please ask him! It would be a very special day, probably my favourite one of the holidays and I'll remember it to tell my class when I go back to school. I could write a story about it even."

"Okay, I'll ask him, but I can't promise anything. I'll see what he says. It won't be this week anyhow, because like I said, he's very busy. I'm sure we can do it another time though. We've got the whole of the summer holidays, so I expect we'll do lots of things and go to lots of places." Elisabeth chewed the end of her pencil, watching her mother.

"Did Fabia tell you she's going to take you out one day when I'm working? She said she'd take you to the beach!"

"No! She didn't tell me that! Brilliant! When is she taking me?"

Babette went through to the kitchen where she cleared away the dishes from their late breakfast. "You'll have to ask her!"

she called. "Now, we're going to Caspian's office in a minute, is that okay? I made him lunch, but he forgot to take it this morning, so we're going to go and give it to him. On the way back we'll stop in town and go to the café for ice-cream, would you like that?"

"Yes!" shrieked Elisabeth, jumping down from the chair. "Strawberry ice-cream! I'm ready! Shall we go now?"

"What about your shoes?" Babette laughed, "Are you going to wear shoes today or are you going in your bare feet?"

Elisabeth put her hands to her face, "Oops! I forgot! Which ones shall I wear? Can I wear my blue ones, or should I wear my lace-ups?"

"Put your blue ones on, they'll look nice with that dress. Be quick though! They're under the bench by the back door."

Elisabeth ran to find her shoes and sat down on the tiled floor to put them on, struggling with one of the buckles which dangled on loose elastic.

"You could bring your picture if you've finished it," said Babette. She'd had a thought and anyone who was watching her closely may have observed an unmistakeable glint in her eye. "We'll give it to Caspian with his lunch, he'll like that."

Babette felt a little ashamed at involving her daughter in this scheme of hers, but something had to be done and as she couldn't leave Elisabeth alone in the house, she had no choice but to take her along. Besides, they would go to the café on the way back as she'd promised. Elisabeth liked going to the café so that was a good reason for going out, not just to drop off Caspian's lunch. Two birds with one stone, it made perfect sense.

Caspian had been seeing more of Laura over the last few weeks. In that time, he'd become less communicative with

Babette and she'd started to feel that he was purposely avoiding her. He hadn't been about as much in the evenings and the marked change in their routine bothered her. She'd resolved to conceal her true feelings for him and made the decision that she should try to be happy for him, but she'd noticed that he didn't seem as happy as perhaps he should. He didn't seem to possess the lightness of heart or the euphoria that people usually have at the beginning of a relationship. Instead he seemed rather distracted and moody and he spent a lot of time in his room alone, going to bed much earlier than usual, and he didn't join in the dinner time chatter like he usually did. Things had changed and Babette didn't like it at all, she didn't like seeing him at sixes and sevens and she wanted the old Caspian back.

She hatched a plan to make him lunch and take it to him at the office, not just to surprise him but also to make Laura aware of her presence in Caspian's life. She had not met her rival yet and was very curious to meet this woman who had displaced her and unsettled her happy routine.

* * *

Babette parked Julius' old Citroen by the wasteland. As she expected, Caspian's car was not there. She knew that he had a meeting at a client's house that day and her plan was to deliver his lunch while he was out. She was a little anxious, not being entirely sure how he would react at her turning up unannounced, though this was only because she was aware of her true intentions. She knew him well enough to be convinced that he had not told his new girlfriend much about his unconventional homelife.

132

Laura looked up from the desk as Babette pushed the door open and with Elisabeth in tow, strolled nonchalantly in to the welcome cool of the air-conditioned reception office. She knew straightaway that this was Laura, because she'd met the other women who worked at Tompkins and Partners at the company's social gatherings she'd been to with Caspian. Laura was more or less what she had expected; averagely pretty, slim and well presented in her work clothes. Her light brown hair was styled in a tousled bob, her nose was rather long and thin, her eyes pale blue-grey with lashes lengthened by mascara.

Babette smiled at her, a big and confident smile, which belied the apprehension she felt and the lurching in her stomach, "Hello. Is Caspian not back yet? I noticed his car isn't here."

"No, he isn't," Laura replied. "We're not expecting him back until lunch time. Can I help with anything?" A professional countenance did not hide the fact that Laura was feeling unsettled.

"He forgot his lunch this morning," Babette explained, "So we thought we'd drop it in whilst we were out. We don't want him going hungry!" She chortled as she stood at the desk, the lunchbox in her hand.

"Of course not! Leave it with me and I'll make sure he gets it. I'll put it on his desk."

"You might want to put it in the fridge," Babette suggested with an air of authority as she handed over the lunchbox. "Oh, would you give him this as well? Elisabeth drew a picture for him this morning, she wanted to give it to him before he comes home."

"Of course." Laura took the picture and briefly looked at it. She was by and large lost for words; her heart was beating fast. She had been taken entirely by surprise. Caspian had not mentioned that he was married or had a partner and a daughter; she was suddenly wondering what kind of man he really was. She had not suspected he was the sort to cheat.

"I'll make sure he gets it," she said quietly and put the picture on the desk, placing the lunchbox on top of it.

"Thank you, that's very kind." Babette smiled at Elisabeth, "Come on then sweetie, we've got lots to do before he comes home this evening. We need to get the house nice and tidy for him, so we'd better be on our way. Thank you for your help," she said again to Laura. "Goodbye."

Babette virtually waltzed out of the office, feeling rather pleased with herself. It had gone just as she wanted it to. She was a little shaken, but she could see that Laura was put out, so she was pleased with herself. Her plan seemed to have gone well, though she could not help wondering just how much trouble she may have caused.

* * *

It was almost two o'clock by the time Caspian arrived back at the office. His meeting at Jane Darling Farm had gone on longer than he'd expected but the project was progressing well. The owners, Jonathan and Clare Sweeting had recently inherited the farm, along with over 700 acres of land and several outbuildings, from Jonathan's father. Although he had grown up on the farm, it was a life that Jonathan was not cut out for and after gaining an honours degree in economics he had progressed to a job as a stockbroker in the city, gradually working his way up to a position where he was in charge of a team of interns and earning a substantial salary. Now in his mid-thirties, he and Clare had decided that they should no longer delay having a family, but neither of them wanted to bring children up in the city. They had been toying with the idea of moving to a smaller town, perhaps within commuting distance so that Jonathan could retain his job, and they'd even been checking the property pages to see what was about within their price range. Jonathan had hankerings of giving up his job and working from home in a consultancy capacity so they sat down one evening at the kitchen table, papers and bank statements spread before them, and tried to determine if they could afford to up sticks and move further away, possibly back to the same area of the West Country where Jonathan lived as a boy. Around this time his father was taken ill so any fledgling plans they'd made were put on hold and they spent weekends travelling to and fro, helping to care for the elderly Mr. Sweeting. Fortunately, the farm had a very trustworthy and hard-working foreman who lived with his family in a tied cottage beyond the yard, so the day to day running of the farm could be safely left in his hands, whilst Jonathan took Power of Attorney and looked after the financial side of things. After nine months, his father passed away, leaving his whole estate to Jonathan, his only child.

"Well that settles that!" Jonathan said to Clare in the car on the way back from the meeting with the solicitors, "We'll go and live on the farm!"

"But we're not farmers!" Clare protested, "It's a very different way of life! It's a lot of hard work, and long hours, I know that! We wouldn't have a clue what we were doing!"

"I've already thought about that. We shouldn't uproot Keith, he's been there for years and he's very good at his job, so he can stay on in the cottage and take over the running of the farm. He'll be the farm manager. I'll pay him a good salary and keep my hand in with the paperwork, and we'll live in the farmhouse. We can eventually do it up."

"But we won't have any money coming in, other than from the farm. I doubt if that's enough to pay Keith and leave us enough to live on."

"We'll be okay for a while, don't worry. We'll soon come up with some way to generate an income." He gave his wife's hand a reassuring squeeze, "We could sell off some of the land for a start; with that and the money from the sale of our house we'll be alright for a year or so at least. We'll sort something out; we'll find new jobs or start up a new business. It'll all work out."

Clare didn't seem to share his optimism. "That house will need a lot of work!" she exclaimed. Her mind had already begun to wander, imagining how she would change things, opening rooms up, putting in a new kitchen, more bathrooms, and updating the central heating system.

Jonathan approached Tompkins and Partners to discuss the way forward for the farm. One of the partner's experience lay mostly in the development and modernisation of redundant farms and big country estates, finding ways to maximise profits. This was a fundamental part of their business and he saw this as a prime opportunity to let Caspian take the reins of what could turn out to be a fairly big project.

The outbuildings on the farm were mostly unused, other than for storage, and they were in relatively good condition. Standing around two quite separate yards across from the farmhouse, they offered a lot of scope for re-development. When at first the idea of turning the barns into workshops and offices was raised Clare felt uncomfortable. She thought that the comings and goings of people working there every day of the week, as well as their visitors, would be too disruptive, and it would also mean widening the narrow track that led around the farmhouse to the barns. The second and more obvious idea put forward by Caspian was to turn the barns into holiday cottages; farm holidays had become very popular and it would work perfectly with the two yards remaining detached and self-contained. Jonathan and Clare were quite excited at this prospect; it would give them a reasonable income and Clare could get involved with the design and furnishings, and help to run the venture until their family came along, by which time the business would be established well enough to employ a team of cleaners or to hand the properties to an agent. They shook hands with Caspian over the old pine table in the ramshackle kitchen and told him that they would like to push forward with this, and that they were excited to be working with him.

They were now halfway through the planning process and things were going smoothly. There had been no objections because the farm was relatively isolated, and the development would have no impact on nearby properties. The nearest neighbours were half a mile away so there would be no worries about disturbance from noise or traffic. Another bonus was that the overall character of the barns could be retained so there would be no detrimental effects on the countryside aesthetic nor on amenity value.

Laura was on the telephone when Caspian stepped into the reception; she glanced up and then averted her eyes, concentrating on the conversation she was having. Caspian gave a slight smile and waved and went up the stairs to his office. He hung his jacket on the peg on the back of the door and crossed the room to open the window wide. Then he sat at his desk to reflect upon his meeting and get the file updated.

He noticed the lunchbox on his desk, an unexpected but much appreciated surprise, as he hadn't had time to stop at the garage on the way back to pick up something to eat. He picked up the drawing, had a good look at it and smiled. 'Dear little Elisabeth,' he thought; she loved drawing and it delighted her to give her pictures to people as gifts. He put the drawing to one side and reached for his lunchbox, assuming that Babette had delivered it to the office on her way to some place or other with Elisabeth, and he was touched at her thoughtfulness. She hadn't made him lunch for a few weeks, and this had concerned him. His first thought was that it might have been some kind of punishment because he was seeing Laura, and this worried him, but one evening, in one of her crochety moments, Babette had told him that she was fed up with doing the lunches, that she felt like an unpaid skivvy and that he'd have to make his own or buy something from the café or the sandwich van that came to the business park each morning.

He took off the lid and found two small baguettes wrapped in greaseproof paper; cold beef, lettuce, tomato, and horseradish, and a generous slice of fruit cake, not homemade, he knew, but won at the Easter fete at Elisabeth's school, put into the freezer the same day and only taken out earlier this week when Babette was not working. One of her small pleasures was to sit down in a quiet spot, usually the small sofa in the conservatory, with a pot of tea and a piece of cake or two; just half an hour or so to herself that she savoured. 'Babette Time', she called it and she was temporarily happy to ignore any possible distractions, to let the telephone keep ringing, and to not get up to answer the doorbell. Caspian remembered Babette's delight at winning the cake and then Elisabeth dashing across the playground to tell them she had won first prize for her miniature garden. She'd made it in an old cat litter tray that Albert next door had given her, and Fabia said it was the prettiest miniature garden she'd ever seen when she and Elisabeth had put the finishing touches to it; a little mirror as a pond, a clothes line made with twigs and string, dresses and trousers hung on it, cut from scraps of fabric.

There was a soft knock at his door. "Tea?" asked Rachel. She had quite startled Caspian, who was lost in his thoughts and enjoying his lunch. Spread out on the desk before him were the plans of the farm; he brushed a few crumbs into his hand and put them in the bin.

"Yes, please Rachel, I'd love one. Were there any calls whilst I was out?"

"I don't think so. Laura didn't say so. Oh, she's gone home, she said she wasn't feeling well."

"Oh, what's the matter with her?"

"She said she had a headache. The weather I expect! I think we're in for a rattle up tonight."

"We certainly need it. It will freshen the air." Caspian was surprised; Laura was there when he came back from his meeting and she seemed perfectly alright then, but he supposed that headaches can come on rather quickly sometimes, particularly in thundery weather.

* * *

Babette was leaning over the table in the anteroom helping Elisabeth with her handwriting practice; Elisabeth's teachers had suggested she work on this during the summer holidays. Eager to help her daughter, Babette had gone into town and bought textbooks so that Elisabeth could write over dotted letters and then attempt them herself. Fabia was in the kitchen making a salad, peering closely at a dog-eared recipe book and checking the amount of lentils she'd weighed out.

"Hello," said Caspian, leaning over next to Babette to see what Elisabeth was doing. "Thank you for the picture Elisabeth, it was very good! I think you're going to be a very famous artist one day and we'll all be queuing up in galleries to see your work!" The little girl giggled and hid her face in her hands.

"And thank you for my delicious lunch!" he said, turning to Babette, with his dear old smile.

Babette could feel her eyes smarting with tears and she quickly turned away. She wasn't quite sure why she should feel so emotional, he was only thanking her for his lunch after all, but he had looked at her face in a way that was so familiar, and he'd smiled at her, and in that moment all was well.

"Was it okay? I felt bad as I haven't been making your lunch lately. I thought you were a bit grumpy about it, so I thought I'd surprise you with something you'd really like. I should have told you, then you would have known to look for it and wouldn't have left it behind."

She said this so sweetly, so demurely, no-one would ever have thought it was all part of a devious plan, that she had fully intended to throw a spanner into the works, to unsettle Laura and to remind Caspian that she was still here and very much a part of his life. He wouldn't know of course, that it had made her anxious and caused her to deliberate most of the afternoon because she wasn't sure how he would react. She eventually decided that as he had no idea of her intentions he would probably just see it as a kind gesture; simply that she'd made him lunch but that he hadn't realised and so she'd done what a lot of people with time on their hands would have done – delivered it to his office. She was right, of course; after all, she knew him well.

"It was really good, thank you, just what I needed, I was starving. I'm sorry I didn't look for it this morning, I didn't think to, I just assumed you hadn't made anything for me." He pulled his tie off and put it on the back of the chair at the end of the table.

"I should have left a note or something. I'm sorry, I didn't think, and I didn't hear you get up this morning. We had a lie in, didn't we?" Babette said, looking to Elisabeth; she was eager to change the subject, to stop talking about the lunch, to stop feebly apologising.

"Yes, we were lazy bones this morning!" Elisabeth replied, chewing the end of her pencil.

Babette's plan had, in effect, fired an arrow straight to Caspian's heart, greatly aided by Elisabeth's drawing of the three of them. He had no idea that it had upset Laura and had not really given it any thought. The intricate workings of the female mind were something he struggled to understand; he saw a clearer picture, one that was black and white and not subject to overthinking.

He had now seen Laura outside of work three or four times and although he rather enjoyed spending time with her, he was aware that something was lacking. He wondered if he would ever have any depth of feeling for her, but he held on to the thought that perhaps given time their relationship might blossom, and he would find what he so desperately sought: someone other than Babette. He wanted to feel for someone else more than he felt for Babette, but the truth was that Laura did not stir him. It was not her fault that he was not intoxicated

141

by her as he was by Babette, and he had lain awake at night wondering how long it would take, if ever, to find someone who could make him feel that way. His desire for Babette would not be subjugated and instead was growing stronger, only he had no intention of allowing it to surface.

12

Caspian Defends Babette

The next evening was a warm one, a balmy conclusion to a hot and heavy day. Caspian had travelled to London that morning for a conference, a two and a half hour train journey that gave him time to read and to sit wool gathering as he looked out of the window. He always thought when travelling by train, that it gave a different perspective of people's everyday lives. The train passed through countryside where tractors ploughed fields unseen from the roads, where men and women walked dogs along meandering rivers, away from the busier parts of the waterside. He saw allotments where runner beans scrambled up poles, nets hung from canes and draped softly over raspberry bushes; makeshift sheds hid all manner of tools, twine and flowerpots behind their paint-peeled doors, strawberries and courgettes grew in low polytunnels, along with peppers and tomatoes. The railway skirted around the edge of towns, the long thin strips of gardens at the back of terraced houses revealed the commonplace lives of families; swings stood on mown lawns, garden furniture on patios edged with flower beds, timber sheds with felted roofs held lawnmowers, bikes, rakes and shovels, deflated dinghies shoved away for another summer. On and on and on, through nameless conurbations, quiet country stations where the platform was no more than two carriages long, steep railway cuttings thick with nettles and rosebay willowherb, and along the side of a disused canal where red brick factories puffed out clouds of grey-white smoke into a cornflower blue sky.

Caspian always felt stale after a day in the city and as he walked up the hill from the station, he was looking forward to getting home and having a cool shower then a drink in the garden. He had not been home long before the telephone rang and reluctantly, he answered it, surprised to hear that it was Laura insistent upon meeting him for a drink.

"Can we make it another night?" he asked tetchily. "I'm exhausted, I've been in London all day. I thought you weren't well, anyway? Rachel said you went home early yesterday."

"I'm fine. I just had a headache, that's all, probably just the heat. I've been at work today."

"Anything exciting happen?"

"Nothing more than usual. Can we talk about work later? It would really mean a lot to me if we could meet for a drink tonight."

Although disinclined, Caspian agreed to a quick drink at the pub on the hill a few miles outside of town, stressing that he wanted to be back early for a good nights' sleep. They drove from opposite directions and wanting to make the most of the good weather, they sat outside in the little beer garden that overlooked the valley; it would be a spectacular sunset. The pub cat sauntered up the path, lay down and rolled over on the paving stones that were still warm from the heat of the day. Although twilight was yet a few hours away, several early moths hovered around the clematis that tumbled over the wooden fence and onto the roof of the old caravan on the other side.

An air of tension had descended over Laura and Caspian; they both sensed this, and it felt like an itchy blanket that neither of them wanted to wear. They sipped their drinks and it was a while before either of them spoke; at first they exchanged snippets about the weather and then about work.

When a moment came that felt appropriate to her, Laura cleared her throat and spoke directly to Caspian: "Why did you lie to me about your situation?" She rested her chin on her hand and looked at him intently.

"What do you mean, by 'my situation'?" He was perplexed but he could see that she was irked, her jaw fixed and firm, her teeth clenched.

"About your home life. You didn't tell me that you have a family, you didn't mention a wife and a daughter. Why not? Did it slip your mind?"

That was when the penny dropped, and Caspian realised at last how it must have all looked. Laura had been there when Babette brought the sandwiches to the office; it was Laura who had put his lunch and Elisabeth's picture on his desk. He was at first taken aback and did not know how to explain, then he ruffled his hair and laughed.

"Ah, you've met Babette!" he replied, "And little Elisabeth!"

"What's so funny about it? I don't see that it's anything to laugh at! A woman came to the office with your lunch, saying how you'd left it in the fridge that morning; with her was a little girl with eyes just like yours, and she'd drawn a picture, obviously of you and this woman who you say is

Babette, whoever she is, holding hands as you were all getting into a car. It looks a lot like happy families to me. Why didn't you tell me? You said you live with your father, your sister and your stepsister. No mention of a wife and daughter."

"She's not my daughter!" Caspian interrupted. "Babette is not my wife. Babette is my step-sister." He paused. "Actually, she isn't..." he trailed off. "Look, it's difficult to explain but I haven't lied to you at all. It was easier for the time being for me to say what I did. It's basically the truth, the real circumstances are complicated."

"What - having a wife and daughter is complicated?" snapped Laura. "So complicated that you have to lie about it and not even bother to mention them?"

"She is not my wife!" repeated Caspian, exasperated.

"Okay then, girlfriend, whatever she is. You live with her, she brought your lunch to work, and the little girl drew a picture of you and her holding hands, so that's obviously what she's used to seeing."

"It's not, it's just how she sees things, that's what she wants I expect, I don't know! She probably thinks I'm her father. She's never asked so none of us have bothered to explain it all to her. It's easier to let things be for now." He gathered his thoughts, aware that he was making a hash of explaining things.

"Look I know this sounds odd, but I'll grant you Laura, it's a strange set up, not a conventional situation by any means."

"For fuck's sake Caspian! This is getting worse! How can you expect me to believe a word you say? Just tell me what the hell is going on?" Laura buried her head in her hands; the conversation was maddening, infuriating to her.

"This is making my head hurt!" she fumed. "Look, try

seeing it from where I'm standing – some weird looking woman dressed up like a dog's dinner turns up at the office with your lunch and with her is a little girl who's drawn a picture of you holding hands and now you tell me she thinks you're her father! Honestly Caspian, I thought you were straightforward and level headed, perhaps a bit boring even, but it turns out you're involved with a woman who dresses like a tart and between you, you have this funny little child who thinks you're her father though you insist that you're not! What the hell am I supposed to think?"

Laura had waved the proverbial red rag right in front of Caspian's eyes. 'Tart! Funny little child!' He would not hear Babette and Elisabeth insulted like this, and so unnecessarily, so callously, not by anyone.

He slammed his fist down on the table, "Laura, you've gone too far! You've really overstepped the mark. You have no right to say that!" He knew that his voice was shaking, and that anger was rising up inside him.

"I've gone too far?!" she vociferated. "I'm the one who's gone too far? Oh, for fuck's sake!"

Caspian cut her off, "Yes, you bloody well have! Who the hell do you think you are insulting Babette and Elisabeth like that? You met them for a matter of minutes and here you are digging the knife in! You don't even know them! How can you insult an innocent child like that? I don't understand how anyone could do that! I don't care how angry you are, and I don't care what you think or what stupid conclusions you've jumped to; it's completely out of order!"

"Oh, you're very defensive, aren't you?" she shouted again. "What a surprise! That says it all!"

"I won't have them insulted when you have no reason to be so

147

rude. You've only met them briefly and you don't know the real situation, you've just jumped to your ridiculous conclusions and you're shouting and screaming at me when I haven't had a chance to explain properly! If you just shut up and calm down, I'll tell you how it all is – though only to stop you from blathering it around the office that I'm some sort of adulterer – or worse!"

"Well, what is there to explain? You have a wife, or a girlfriend, whatever she is, and a child that for your own convenience you chose not to tell me about. If you think you can fob me off with some pathetic story you can forget it. There's no point in trying to squirm out of it."

"Will you just shut up and listen! I said I'll tell you the truth and I will. Please stop being so angry. Just calm down and listen to me."

"I've every right to be angry, you're a fucking liar!" she yelled. "Does she know you've been seeing me? Well, does she?"

Caspian took a measured deep breath, "I am not a liar, and yes, Babette does know I've been seeing you. Look, my home life is not the usual set up, but I care very much for the people I live with." Laura attempted to speak again but Caspian continued, "No, don't interrupt, just listen. I live with my father and my sister Fabia. My mother left not long after I'd finished university; she moved to France, she still lives there. There are two other people who live with us – Babette and Elisabeth, who you met today. Babette came to live with us when she was eleven, after her stepfather died. Her stepfather was my uncle, my father's brother. He was killed in a road accident. Babette's mother and my uncle were married for a very short time, just a matter of months, when Babette was very young, when she was about five years old. Her mother was a very selfish person, she left them quite suddenly. She did a moonlight flit with some drummer from a band or something, ran off without a trace and left Babette with my uncle." He held his hand up warningly, "No, I said don't interrupt. Let me finish. This all had a very profound effect on Babette and like a lot of people who've been through things like that, she had a disastrous relationship when she was younger; she moved away with a guy she'd met and they were together for year or so before Elisabeth was born. Not long after that her boyfriend left her, and because she had nowhere else to go and she had a very young baby, she came back to live with us." Caspian paused and looked across at Laura, checking her response, "So you see, Elisabeth has never known her father, she wasn't even a year old when he left, and he's never been in touch. She knows that my father, Julius is not her father because he is old – not that that's a valid reason, but in this case it's right. So, Babette is in effect a cousin to me and my sister, that's how it's always been; I've always got on well with her and we're the only stability in Elisabeth's life. We take her out, we eat our meals with her, I sometimes take her to school or pick her up. It's what we do, so I suppose I'm the nearest thing to a father figure Elisabeth has, but she is not my daughter." He continued reflectively, "I don't know what will happen in the future; I think Babette is afraid of having another relationship and she places every importance on Elisabeth's wellbeing. We've lived in the same household since I was thirteen and she was eleven; we've grown up together, that's why I told you she was my stepsister, because it's an easy way to explain things. I would have explained it all properly when I felt the time was right, but now it's happened like this. When they came to the office you

149

made your assumptions, which are completely wrong, and now you've insulted not just Babette but also an innocent seven year old child just because you're angry and you think I've lied to you. You should think before you speak Laura, because you've shown a side of you that I really don't like."

He hesitated and shook his head, staring into what was left of his pint. He had never had to explain his home life at such great length and was now feeling quite emotional; mentally he was exhausted. Laura bit her lip, red faced, watching him. He sighed, "I can forgive you for jumping to the wrong conclusions, I can't quite understand why you did though, because I hadn't lied to you and you should have believed me, or at least handled this better. What I can't forgive you for is insulting two of the people I'm closest to and who mean the world to me. I've seen your true colours now and that's made me absolutely sure that I don't want to see you again."

He stood up and finished what was left of his drink. Laura began to protest, quietly this time, but he did not look at her and did not stay to listen. He walked to his car, got in and drove home where he knew he would find Babette sitting in the garden or in the conservatory on this warm summer evening. He would pour them both a drink and they would sit and talk about this and that until midnight and at least for that night, all would be good.

* * *

Julius ran into the hut, slamming the door behind him and pulling the bolts firmly across. His breathing was heavy and laboured as he gasped for air, his heart pounding, thumping loudly in his ears.

It had been there, just a few feet away from him; the shrouded figure. This time it was real, he had not imagined it and this time it could not be passed off as a trick of the light, or as a subconscious association with the entity he saw in his dreams. He couldn't remember which came first, whether the figure in the woods had moved into his dream world, or if the haunting incubus of his nightmares had so troubled him to the point of his imagining it elsewhere in his waking hours, which, he pondered, possibly suggested that he was going mad. But no, if he was going mad he would see the figure everywhere he went, not just in the woods; perhaps the woods are haunted, he concluded, though he had never heard any such stories.

He needed to cough to settle his breathing but dared not to in case the figure had followed him and was just the other side of the door. He leaned forwards, his hands on his knees, still gasping for breath. A noise startled him; 'What was that?' It sounded like scratching; his heart was beating wildly again as he imagined long claw-like nails scraping at the door; the domain of late night, low budget horror films, the sort he'd watched when a student. Then the scratching changed to an altogether different sound; a lighter tapping, and then a pitter-pat above him, one that he knew well. 'Squirrels!' he thought, with immeasurable relief. 'Squirrels scampering about on the roof! My god, I'm going mad!' His chuckle was that of a man who felt utter relief; his breathing settled and the memory of the frightening events higher up in the woods not ten minutes earlier began to ebb, to break up into tiny fragments that drifted around the hut and then unpredictably reassembled as Julius sank down onto the floor, his back against the still bolted door.

He tried to recall exactly what had happened, carefully

bringing to mind each moment, with as much detail as he could. He remembered thinking how eerily dark it was at the top of the woods, like those moments during an eclipse when the moon has just started to pass across the face of the sun and all goes quiet. The darkness came not just from the shade of the conifers but also from the exceptional cloud; the day was more grey and overcast than he had ever known for July. There was an overbearing, almost ominous threat of rain all morning and he had even needed the light on in the workshop after breakfast; it felt more like late autumn than summer.

He had walked up along the northern boundary of the woods and was heading along the topmost hedge line, re-tracing his steps from a few days earlier when he had been collecting kindling and lost his handsaw. He couldn't understand where it had gone, it must be there somewhere, where he had dropped it, most likely near one of the stacks of small branches and thick twigs he'd gathered over the last few weeks. He paced along slowly, poking about in the bracken with his foot, wishing that he'd remembered to bring a stick with him; it would certainly have been very useful. He'd crept along almost two thirds of the length of the hedge when he paused for a moment, rubbed his eyes and looked up, peering out into the lighter part of the wood. That was when he saw the figure, or thought he saw it, and off he went again, alternating thoughts chasing one another around in his head. 'Did he see it or not? Was it really there or wasn't it?' It frightened him, yes, but he had that strange feeling of being detached from reality, as though this was happening, but not here, not now; it was happening somewhere else to someone else. Yet he definitely saw it, it was real and it was there, just a little further down the slope, standing still as if surveying the woods, as if it was looking for him; a tall, slim figure in a dark grey hooded cloak that fell in shadowy folds to the ground.

Julius froze; the poor light only served to enhance that dreamlike quality. It created a fuzziness which added to the frightening possibility that this really was some sort of phantom, some spectre, doom laden, or with evil intent. 'What else could it be? It could not be human,' he quickly told himself. 'Humans don't walk round woods dressed in dark full-length capes, nor do they loom over you in your dreams, almost suffocating you. No, whatever it was could not be human.'

Slouched on the floor of the hut, his back to the door, he wanted to find an answer, something that made it not of an evil otherworldliness, but a figment of his imagination, a hallucination dredged up from his innermost self. That is how he saw the phantom that appeared in his dreams – a dark representation of the guilt he harboured, knowing he had let Louisa down, let his family down, and instead of facing these facts and offering some recompense for his foolish errors, he had shut down, compartmentalised his wrong-doings and expected everything to carry on regardless of any pain he had caused to his wife. He was unaware of the wounds that lay open, that would at times fester over the years. He thought his errors had been dealt with and put away, and he had attempted to tidy up their life together, though only by sweeping the fragments of broken vows beneath a threadbare rug.

He began then to convince himself that he must have imagined the figure in the woods that afternoon, and all the other times he'd caught glimpses of something or someone that looked similar. Likewise, the figure in his dreams; he reminded himself that it was only his subconscious taking over and shaping the figure as a manifestation of the turmoil within him.

This was not the rationalising of a sober man; Julius had, as usual, been drinking, and though he knew it was not enough to affect him greatly he further consoled himself with the suggestion that the alcohol must have clouded his judgement and made him see things that weren't there. Certainly, he felt that his eyesight was not as sharp, his vision blurred and lessened further by the darkness beneath the pine trees and by the disorientating light in the woods.

"I need another one," he thought, and he reached over, fumbling in a box to the left of the door for a bottle still half full of wine from this morning's musings by the fire. Julius had realised a long time ago that his dependency on alcohol was increasing and to the greater part, he did not care. He attributed the need to drink also to the sense of failure he felt in his familial situation; he knew he had driven his wife away, that no matter what she said, he felt that she would not have left if he had not betrayed her so terribly.

But his children were still there, the dearest people in his life were right there, pivotal to his very existence and he should have treasured them, but he did not know how to even begin to be close to them and he felt that in order to do so he would have to cross a wide abyss that gaped between where he now existed and where his family, and thus his happiness lay.

He could not do that, he could not find it within him to take that first courageous step, and he was not the sort of man to seek help or therapy, so instead he found solace in drinking. It gave him a façade, a wall to hide behind. It made him feel better because it made him not care.

13

Summer's Grip

Summer clung to the valley, an unshakeable oppressive heat that could not be escaped. Parched fields lay exhausted in its blazing grip, the sun beat down and an eerie silence invaded the copses. The stream that trickled down from the hill had dried, all life seemed numbed into a slow and sedated heaviness; insects droned wearily, even the effort of beating their wings seemed too much. Cows dozed in the shade at the edge of the field, the mud caked and cracked around the cattle trough, the stagnant water dotted with lazy midges.

Fabia had set out to walk to the woods but on reaching the open valley had turned back, unable to bear the sweltering heat. Her arms stung and itched from the heat of the early afternoon sun, perspiration had formed between the plastic frame of her sunglasses and the bridge of her nose. Her back was sticky with the patch of sweat that grew beneath her vest and through to the rucksack she carried strapped to her back. The cool of the woodland held much appeal, though getting there was proving to be tiresome; it was simply too hot. This was not a day for watching, Fabia decided; Julius wouldn't be doing much anyhow, he'd probably be lying in the shade of the beech trees, sleepy with alcohol, a verdant green canopy above him where the branches reached together, their emerald leaves merging, now and then sunlight glinting through, dappling the tree trunks and the dense dark leaf litter of the woodland floor.

Fabia walked on, her breathing more laboured, her pace regular but slowing. On she went, along the narrow strip of pavement that edged the road, left, right, left, right, left, right. A fly, aggressive in the heat, buzzed momentarily close to her ear; she brushed it away, wiped the perspiration from the top of her lip with the back of her hand, sighed heavily and returned to her stride, wondering if she was right to turn back.

'That woman might be there with him. They might be down by the stream on a day like this, having a romantic picnic together, though more likely they'll just be sat chatting on the bench at the top of the slope like they were last time.' She hesitated and thought of turning around and continuing to the woods after all, dithering over what to do.

'Who is that woman?' she repeatedly wondered. 'I've seen her before somewhere, I know I have. Who is she and why is Julius being so secretive about it? He has no ties, he's a free man, why hasn't he mentioned her or brought her home to meet us?'

She ruminated on her thoughts as she paced on, nearing the brow of the steep hill that rolled down into the town. A van sped past, rock music blaring from a tinny stereo, the driver in a blue vest craning his neck to look at her, then it was gone. On, on, on, she pushed in the scorching heat, her bare arms and legs reddening. 'It's so fucking hot,' she thought, wiping the back of her neck with her hand. She wished she'd saved some of the water that she'd stopped to drink by the cemetery gates at the bottom of the hill.

Her thoughts returned to Julius and the woman. She was now convinced that they would be there together in the woods and she was annoyed that the searing heat had thwarted her plans to observe them. Suddenly startled by the slowing of an engine behind her, she turned; a white van pulled alongside her, the same white van that had passed her in the opposite direction only a few minutes earlier. The window was wound right down.

"Excuse me love, do you know where the Crossbridge Inn is?" a man leaned towards her, near middle-aged, shaven headed, tattoos on his upper arm. Fabia felt uneasy of his sly smile as he looked her up and down, liking what he saw; her slim arms, her shorts, and her long slender legs. She noticed one of his front teeth was missing.

"It's back that way," Fabia pointed, in the direction the van had come from, not turning to look at him, not wanting to make eye contact. She carried on walking, her pace quickening, her heart pounding. The van rolled slowly along beside her.

"You're in a hurry aren't you love?" the man called, a slow disconcerting grin spreading across his face. "Do you want a lift? Why don't you come to the Crossbridge with me? Nice cold drink on a day like this, that's what you need. Come on, I'll buy you a drink love."

Panic surged through Fabia's body, and made her struggle for breath as she almost broke into a run. "No thank you," she replied, keeping her gaze straight ahead. A car was coming up the hill towards her, a blue light flashing. 'A police car,' thought Fabia and hoped that it was, then she would wave and flag it down. It must have pricked the van driver's conscience; he accelerated and sped off leaving behind the stifling stench of diesel fumes that hung in the hot air. Relief raced through Fabia's whole being as she ran the short distance to a gap in the hedge, climbed over the stile and briskly headed off on the footpath down across the field, her heart still beating frantically against her ribs. When she reached the footpath that ran alongside the bowling green on the edge of town, she stopped and put her hand to her chest in an effort to regain her breath and to compose herself. Even the bowling club was quiet today. Through the wire mesh fence the green lay flat and still, as if waiting for white haired men and women to come and stoop, as if in homage, rolling their offerings across the turf. On the veranda in front of the clubhouse half a dozen elderly people sat and alternated between long, strained pauses that sat suspended in the humid air, and short bursts of small talk that scattered out a few feet in front of them and then dissipated and fell to the grass, slipping down and away, into the earth.

In her last few years at school, Fabia often came along this footpath with her friends, using it as a short cut to the new housing estate where some of them lived. Polly had once remarked that the old people bending to play bowls reminded her of tortoises, stretching their necks out of their hunched shells, putting one foot forward, in long, arthritic slow motion, and the group had erupted into laughter.

Fabia straightened her rucksack, re-tied her hair away from her face and neck, and then set off for home. Twenty minutes later she pulled the latch that opened the gate from the field at the back of the garden, and still a little shaken, she went quickly down across the lawn. She was desperately thirsty and longed to be in the cool of the kitchen with a cold drink, her bare feet on the tiled floor, and the familiarity of the old house all around her.

On the patio at the back of the house Elisabeth was talking to herself and playing with an inflatable dolphin in a paddling pool. She was naked except for a wide brimmed yellow sunhat and a necklace of brightly coloured beads. On her lips was vivid scarlet lipstick, on her eyelids peacock blue eyeshadow, smudged and messy. The French doors were wide open and from the house swing music blared out.

Elisabeth looked up as Fabia's shadow fell across the paddling pool. "Fabia!" she smiled, narrowing her eyes against the sunlight, "Have you come back for tea? I'll tell Mummy, hang on." Then without moving she shouted, "Mum! Mummy! Fabia's back, better make sure there's enough for her as well!" She looked back at Fabia, "We're having... um.... Mum, what sort of tea are we having?"

"What?" Babette shouted from inside the house.

"What's that tea we're having? What sort of tea is it?" yelled Elizabeth, probably as loud as she could.

"It's just afternoon tea!" Babette stuck her head round the kitchen door, "Hi Fabia! I didn't know you were back. Are you joining us? We're having a refined afternoon tea on the lawn in our sunhats; cucumber sandwiches, little cakes and scones and everything. Go and put a flowery dress on, we're dressing up! Elisabeth, don't you think you should get out of the pool and get dressed now? You can't have afternoon tea stark naked!"

"I want Fabia to choose a dress for me."

"In a minute Elisabeth, I'm desperate for a glass of water, I'm parched! It's so hot today, it's unbearable! I'm all sticky and sweaty and I need a shower. Wait ten minutes for me and then we'll put our fancy clothes on for tea."

* * *

"Fabia?" Babette knocked lightly on Fabia's bedroom door, "Can I come in?"

"Yes," came Fabia's answer, and in went Babette to find Fabia in front of the mirror, pulling a wide toothed comb through her wet hair.

"Are you okay? You seemed a bit distracted when you got back. Is everything alright?"

"I'm fine now, thanks Babette. I had a bit of a fright, that's all, it was nothing really. I'm fine."

"What do you mean? What's happened? Tell me what's happened."

"Just something that made me feel uncomfortable. Maybe I should tell the police, thinking about it."

"About what? Fabia, tell me."

"I was walking on the top road and a van drove past. It slowed right down and the man driving had a good look at me. I didn't think much of it, you know how men look sometimes, but then a few minutes later he came back, the other way. He'd obviously turned around, and he stopped and asked if I knew where the Crossbridge was, so I told him and then he asked if I wanted a lift and he said he'd buy me a drink. The way he was looking at me frightened me, he was really eyeing me up, I felt really uncomfortable. It was horrid, I didn't know what to do, I was really panicking. I was worried that he might get out and try to force me into the van so I ignored him and kept walking really fast, but he just drove along beside me."

Fabia shuddered and began to wonder how seriously she

should have taken the incident. At the time, up on the hill she didn't really have time to think about it, she just acted out of fear which made her keep walking, as fast as she could.

"I was really scared actually, my heart was pounding. Luckily, a police car came up over the hill with its blue light flashing and the van sped off, so I ran back through the fields. I didn't stop till I got to the bowling club. I was so short of breath! I'm so glad that police car came along when it did, it was good timing."

Babette was horrified, "Oh my God, Fabia! You should tell the police! If they hadn't come up over the hill who knows what might have happened? Oh, you poor thing!"

She went to Fabia, put her arms tight around her and stroked her head, "Thank goodness you're alright!"

"It all happened so quickly, the whole thing was only a couple of minutes but it felt like much longer. I'm so glad that police car came along. It makes me so angry, men doing things like that! I felt so intimidated!"

"What a creepy bastard! I think you should tell the police anyway! You got away but his next victim might not."

They sat down on the bottom of the bed, Babette's arm still around Fabia's shoulders, as she drew out more details, what sort of van was it, did she get the registration number, what did the driver look like, did she recognise him? Fabia remembered the way he had looked at her, the way his eyes had run all over her, probably mentally undressing her, and although she was trying to convince herself and Babette that it was nothing, she knew that at the time it had felt like everything. She had been alone and vulnerable, over a mile from home with no one else around. She wanted to shake it off as if it was just a bad dream. She could hear Babette's voice, angry, indignantly opining,

161

"How dare they? Who do these bastards think they are, taking away our liberty? Women should be able to walk wherever they like! It's harassment, that's what it is. We should tell the police."

"I just want to forget it," Fabia said, having calmed down. "I'm home, I'm safe and I've learned a lesson. I shouldn't go walking on my own like that, especially not in these skimpy shorts."

"But that's exactly what makes me so angry!" Babette remonstrated. "Men like that destroying the freedom of women! We should be able to walk wherever we like on our own, wearing whatever we like. I hate it sometimes, the way men look at me in the pub. How dare they?"

The door was flung wide open and in came Elisabeth still wearing her sun hat and the brightly coloured beads, but with the addition of an old net curtain draped around her shoulders. Her rounded belly stuck out in front of her, her grubby hands clutched her mother's sunglasses, "Are we having tea now please Mummy? I'm so hungry I could eat an elephant."

Fabia snorted and laughed, Babette rolled her eyes, "Eat a horse, Elisabeth! We don't say eat an elephant, we say eat a horse!" She stood up and smoothed down her dress. Elisabeth fiddled with the sunglasses and looked petulant.

"If I'm really hungry why can't I say I want to eat an elephant? An elephant is bigger than a horse and I'm so hungry if I only ate a horse I'd still be hungry, but if I ate an elephant, I wouldn't be hungry anymore because it's enormous."

"Very good logic!" laughed Fabia. "Now, come on, I've decided which dress I'm wearing so let's go and find one for you and get you cleaned up a bit before we have tea."

* * *

Later that afternoon, Fabia mulled over Babette's words and made up her mind that she would not allow anyone to restrict her freedom, though she accepted that there were certain situations and certain parts of the world where it would be nothing short of madness for a woman to venture alone. Lately she'd begun to think that staying in this small town would hold her back and she knew she wanted to see more of the world, to experience different cultures. She thought a lot about the future, about what she might be doing a decade further on and about what she would have done during the time in between. She sometimes daydreamed of going to India, and to Africa and Hong Kong and hoped that by then she would have achieved that. Polly planned to go travelling when she'd finished university, to take a year out before looking for a job, and in a sudden flash, Fabia decided that she would go too. There was nothing to stop her and it gave her a whole year to save money and to make plans with Polly. Fabia didn't spend much from her earnings at the art gallery and she had plenty in her building society account. Louisa had made a generous gift to her and Caspian when she left, and a smaller amount to Babette. "It's not a lot," she said, "But it will be a help. Perhaps you could put it towards a deposit on a house or something. Just please don't fritter it away."

Caspian was speechless, "But Mum, that's a lot of money! Are you sure? It's really kind of you!"

"Don't worry, I can spare it! I've got enough to do what I want to do, and if I get stuck I can sell Granny's house in Brighton, so I want you three to have this. Babette, you might want to use some of it to start a savings account for

Elisabeth. Who knows, maybe you'll all use some of it to come and visit me in France! I hope so!" and she laughed at this, at the unlikelihood, as she realised that her children, as well as Babette had not particularly taken to Dana, and that they found her hubristic. She hoped that in time they would change their minds and that they would find out for themselves that Dana was a very intelligent and compassionate person who always put others before herself, and that she had a mischievous sense of humour.

* * *

Had Fabia continued to the woods that day she would have been shocked and saddened to see her father crying. From her usual position behind the bracken along the top hedge she would have had a good perspective of Julius sat beneath the huge beech tree, silently weeping.

'I've made a mess of my life,' he thought. 'I've driven my wife away and my children don't love or need me; they've grown up in a flash and I missed it all. I can't remember them being small. It's as if they aren't even a part of me, as if I existed on the periphery of their lives. I can no longer make the things I used to and I can't motivate myself to do so. I don't care about my house, my car, or my clothes. I don't seem to care about anything.'

He took a long swig from the bottle of scotch in his lap, wiping his brow with his unbuttoned shirt sleeve; the armpits were stained with wet sweat patches, as was the back. The bottle was almost empty and he knew there was more in the hut but he felt unable to stand and walk back there, and he wanted to go to sleep. He wondered how long he had been there beneath the tree and he looked at his watch, but his failing eyesight and the alcohol blurred his vision and he could not make out the hands on the face. 'My father's bloody watch! Hah! Why the hell do I wear it? He was nothing but a bully, he hated both of his sons and never forgave either of us for not wanting to join the forces, like he did. Stupid old fool, he just wanted to control us!' He took off the watch and raising his arm as high as he could in his inebriated state, he threw it into the brambles on the far side of the slope.

He reflected upon his relationship with his father, the constant belittling and the beatings, though these were not very frequent, and he remembered how unhappy a time it had been for him and Nathan, and how free they both felt when they left the suffocating atmosphere of home for university. When his father passed away Julius had felt an enormous sense of relief, a weight lifted from his shoulders. The proverbial millstone round his neck had been removed. He knew then that no more would he be criticised for almost everything he did, for how he looked, the way he drove, the music he liked, the company he kept. So intense was this feeling that it felt like a rebirth, as if at the age of thirty-six he was born again.

He then reflected upon his marriage. He wished that he had been a better husband and he was sure that if he had, if he had not made such grave mistakes, Louisa would not have left. She said that he went through life as if in a fug, unable to express himself other than through his wood turning, accepting the decisions that those around him made, as if he had no thoughts or opinions of his own. "For goodness sake Julius, you are a grown man, you don't have to live in the shadow of your father. No matter how much he held you back, you cannot live your life like this. You must break free of those old wounds, you must heal yourself." That is what Louisa often said, and she said it again the night that she told him she was leaving. He wished that he had been able to take her advice but habits formed over many years are not easy to undo.

'What has become of me?' he asked himself. He believed it was too late and impossible for him to change and so, on the hottest day of the year, he sat beneath the bosky canopy of the beech tree, his most-liked spot in the whole woods, and he wept.

* * *

And had Fabia not gone out at all, had she never had any notion of trying to find some evidence for her fallacious theories that her father was up to no good, she would have, had she walked into the kitchen at the right time, witnessed something that would have left her dumbfounded.

Elizabeth had gone out that morning with Anna. Anna's mother picked her up at ten o'clock and took the girls to the beach where they went to an aquarium and then on to a café along the sea front for lunch. Babette spent the morning working in the garden, mostly pulling out weeds; fat hen, enchanters' nightshade, dandelions and bindweed, and she carefully deadheaded the geraniums. She cut back the plants in the herb bed and took into the house a basket full of mint, lemon balm, flat leaved parsley, sage and rosemary. She cleared the table and spread newspaper out, laying the herbs in separate bundles and then tying them with garden string to hang from the open rafters to dry.

So had Fabia been there she would have witnessed this wonderful scene of opulent summer greenery, the tantalising scent of mint and lemon balm and parsley, but most of all, she would have been there when her brother came home unexpectedly after a business lunch in the wine bar. She would have seen how his face lit up when he walked into the kitchen; how he went to Babette, took the scissors and the string from her hands, held her face in his hands and kissed her fully and passionately on the lips.

14

The Bonfire

From her usual vantage point behind the ferns in the shadow of the top hedge, Fabia had a bird's eye view of Julius that day. He'd lit a fire in a different part of the woods, away from the front of the hut, and he was standing beside it, drinking a bottle of beer. 'It's quarter past eleven in the morning,' thought Fabia, 'Why is he drinking so early?'

He'd struck the first match not five minutes earlier so the flames hadn't yet caught and the wood was only smouldering, sending big fat clouds of smoke billowing around the brambles in the clearing and up into the trees, enveloping them in an ugly, dense grey-brown mist. Julius was staring down at the ground, swigging from the beer bottle, abstractedly kicking a rotting tree stump with his left foot.

When the smoke died down, he poured paraffin from a dented red metal can onto the fire and stepped back as it flared into action. The dry twigs and branches crackled and spat in the sudden blaze as Julius bent to his side, untied a sack and began to throw things onto the bonfire, handfuls at a time, one after another, not pausing to look at any of it.

Fabia watched with curiosity, her eyes narrowed in concentration. 'What's that he's burning?' she wondered. 'Old papers - bills, letters, magazines?'

She watched as he carried on, stooping and feeding the flames, time after time, his face furrowed, intent on what he was doing, as if it were some essential cathartic exercise. The flames were now roaring and reaching a considerable height, the fire fuelled further when Julius began to pile tinder dry bracken on to it, using the garden fork that Caspian was looking for in the garage a few days earlier. Julius took a final swig from the bottle, slung it into the undergrowth and hands in pockets, turned and stumbled off, down the path in the direction of the hut.

Fabia remained rooted to the spot behind the ferns, pulling her hood down over her face slightly. She always feared she might be caught off guard and spotted by someone walking in the woods, more so now she knew about the blonde woman with the little terrier.

She was puzzled as to why her father had walked away leaving the fire at its height. The woods were sheltered but out in the open of the fields there was a discernible breeze and if a sudden gust blew down into the woods from the field gate at the top corner, it would blow the flames into the brambles and quickly spread the fire further. Surely Julius would not risk burning his beloved woods down? The woods were his refuge, his sanctuary; he spent so much time up there, Babette joked that he might as well live up there, foraging for nuts, berries, and fungi; eating squirrels and hedgehogs for a treat! And the way he threw the bottle aside, that wasn't the sort of thing Julius did – he hated litter! When Fabia was a little girl, they'd all been picking blackberries at the edge of the woods one afternoon, long before Julius owned them; she was eating crisps and when she'd finished she absent-mindedly dropped the empty packet onto the ground. How Julius had scolded her! He'd made quite a scene, shouting at her to pick it up and take it home to put in the bin. And yet here he was now, tossing a bottle into the bushes as if he had no care for the woods! So unlike him, so out of character! Was he drunk already, before noon?

Fabia shifted position, from crouching to kneeling. Her legs were beginning to ache, and she badly needed to stand and stretch. Julius reappeared from the lower path, carrying two more sacks over his shoulder, and in his hand, two more bottles of beer. He put the sacks down by the fire and opened one of the bottles, taking a long slug. Picking up a stout stick, he poked at the fire, which made it pick up again. He splashed on more paraffin and then bent over and delved into one of the sacks, again pulling out bundles of paper, throwing them onto the fire, armful after armful, as if he could not get rid of it all fast enough. When the first sack was empty he sat down on the ground and finished his beer, then he opened the other bottle, drank half of it and slowly stood up. Grabbing the last sack, he upended it, tipping the entire contents, sack and all, onto the fire. It raged and spat like some ferocious orange beast unleashed from a pit, Julius taunting it, goading with his stick as it roared angrily.

Again, he walked away from the fire, returning minutes later carrying a large cardboard box. He staggered slightly on the path up to the fire, and on reaching it he dropped the box to the floor. He then pulled out of it another bottle; not beer this time, but a bigger bottle with a red top – perhaps whisky or brandy. He took a long gulp, put it to one side and turned his attention to the fire. It was burning well, and though it was not necessary, Julius forked another mound of bracken on to it. He began to take things out of the box and sling them onto the fire, without stopping to have one last look at whatever it was. Fabia squinted and focused intently on what her father was doing, desperately trying to see what he was burning. She determined rectangular and square shapes, then round objects of different sizes. Onto the fire they went. It suddenly dawned on her what it was; Julius was burning the breadboards and bowls he had made, the ones he had exhibited that did not sell, that had been in a trunk in the corner of the garage loft for years, covered in dust and cobwebs.

'That is not like him,' Fabia thought. 'Why on earth is he doing that?' He usually took the things that were no longer wanted to one of the charity shops in town; anything broken beyond repair would go to the tip. Julius was a strong advocate of recycling, of re-using; one man's junk was another man's treasure, he maintained. Even his hut was made from bits and pieces of timber from the stack behind the garage, oddments that he'd salvaged from various projects over the years. Burning things like this was quite out of character for him.

The drinking on the other hand seemed to be altogether part of his routine these days. Fabia had sometimes found him late at night, asleep in his sitting room, in an alcohol induced slumber, evidenced by the empty tumbler and the bottle of whiskey on the low table in front of him, and having watched him for months she knew that he frequently drank when he was in the woods. She rarely ventured down as far as the hut so it was impossible for her to know exactly how bad his habit had become, but today it looked as though he'd had a lot and he was showing no signs of stopping. 'Has he become an alcoholic?' she asked herself, believing that her father now had a serious problem. She thought she should mention it again to Caspian, but if she told him or Babette she would have to explain how she knew and then they would know that she had been spying on him in the woods.

Fabia often questioned why she pried on her father like this. She was aware that it would be thought of as odd behaviour, or might be suggestive of some psychological disorder, especially as she always wore the cloak, which made it more sinister and more unnatural.

She also questioned why she had a very distant relationship with her father. She accepted that she had never felt close to him, or loved by him; in fact, she had felt that he did not particularly like her. He was not supportive of her, had never expressed any interest in her schoolwork or her hobbies, and he didn't show encouragement in any way. He got on better with Caspian, but was that merely because Caspian was a boy, or because he was his first born? Fabia knew that she had been a particularly fractious baby and infant, keeping her parents awake most of the night for several years, and her birth had been long and troublesome, so that her mother became quite ill and had to stay in hospital for two weeks. She wondered if because of this, Julius subconsciously blamed her for the breakdown in his relationship with his wife – oh, the irony! Whether or not it was the case, it would surely have been repairable had he been able to make some effort or to show feeling. In any case, what remained was that as always, Fabia blamed her father entirely for Louisa's leaving them. She often reminded herself that he must have done something to drive her mother away and she felt impelled to satisfy herself that it was him at fault. 'No wonder my mother could not stay with him! I knew it! I knew he was up to something!' That is what she wanted to say, so to her, this gave her a reason to follow him to the woods and observe him unseen.

At length, Julius turned his back on the bonfire and lurched away, back towards the hut. When he had not returned after almost fifteen minutes, Fabia decided to venture out from behind the ferns. There was no sign of him and she wouldn't have been at all surprised if, considering the state he was in, he had fallen into some drunken stupor. He might have slipped and rolled into the ditch at the bottom edge of the wood, she thought, or perhaps he had fallen headlong into the hut, crashing onto the dirty floor where he was now snoring deeply.

She waited ten more minutes and then deftly darted through the trees stopping almost in line with the hut. Hiding behind the thick trunk of an aspen she could see that the door of the hut was wide open, her father's legs half in-half out. She snorted an almost derisory snort. She was right; he had obviously staggered as far as the threshold of the hut, tripped over the step and crashed onto the floor, falling into a sleep that only the drunk could sleep. Confident that he was out for the count, she pulled her hood down, shook her hair free and walked back to the bonfire. The flames had by now abated and only the centre of the fire still burned; the rest smouldered cruelly, a blackened mess of twisted, crooked shapes, a pile of black-dark-grey flakes of ash. She walked around the edge of the fire, looking at the debris, surprised and saddened at what she picked out amongst it; photograph albums and the remnants of clothes among the ashes. A navy and green striped tie, a sleeve of a jumper that she was sure her mother had knitted, a thin waterproof jacket she remembered from a holiday in France. She plucked a piece of paper from beneath it and immediately recognised her mother's sloping handwriting: *must tell her one day.*

Fabia froze for a moment. Was this just an innocent part of a note or a letter, or was it something important, the sort of thing she hoped to find? Was it a clue? Tell who what one day – what did it mean?

She picked up a thin branch from the ground and prodded the jacket, lifting it up and away from the papers smouldering beneath it. She used the end of the branch to sweep out a pile and then crouched down to pick them up, smoothing them out as best she could. Mostly indecipherable now, she read more of her mother's handwriting: *secrets that are harder to live with each day.*

Fabia realised she was trembling. She felt this was something crucial, but she could not fathom what it meant. What secrets was her mother referring to? This must be something to do with why she left – because of something so secretive that her father felt it necessary to destroy all evidence. She turned the paper over in her hands, very slowly, as the bottom corner disintegrated: *has a right to know* her mother had written. No date could be discerned on the paper, and having been in the fire briefly, it was impossible to tell whether it had been written in recent times or years ago.

Fabia was perturbed. She turned these words over and over in her mind, trying to work out what this could be about, but she realised it could be anything and though she desperately wanted to know, whatever it was, her mother had not chosen to discuss it with her. She committed the words to her memory and threw the letter back onto the fire. She poked among the smouldering remnants, pulling out what she could to study more closely, sifting through the papers, old bank statements, household bills, instructions for a fridge that had been replaced several years ago, invoices for car repairs, the name of the garage still legible. The sort of stuff that everyone burns from time to time, but why all the other things, the breadboards and the bowls, and now, she saw, her mother's artwork, and photographs of two women playing tennis, dancing in a field, reclining on a rug on a lawn in summer, cloche hats on, strings of beads. Two happy women smiling together; her mother and Dana in their younger days.

Fabia plucked a photograph from the fire and tucked it beneath her cloak into the pocket of her jeans. She stood to her feet and pulling the hood right up over her head, she tiptoed through the trees again, running soundlessly through the woods until she could see the hut where her father still lay slumped in the doorway, fast asleep. She wiped a drop of mucus from her nose and realised her cheek was wet beneath her eye, both from tears and from the acrid smoke of the bonfire. She felt weary and shaken, as if she had seen too much, delved too deeply into things that didn't concern her, and she was suddenly conscience-stricken that her prying had gone too far, that she really must stop this. She must absolve Julius of any blame, rid herself of this obsession, and move on with her life.

She realised that she did not know her father at all, that her conspiratorial treatment of him was in reality, unfair. It was a persecution, and she knew that beneath his sullen and emotionless exterior there was a human being who had secrets, or if not secrets as such, then things that for some reason, right or wrong, he chose to keep to himself. "Is that not something we are all entitled to?" she thought aloud.

She looked again at the doorway of the hut. The man slumped drunk and asleep in the doorway was her father; she began to cry as she understood that no matter what had happened, her father was a broken man and he needed help. Whether or not he wanted or would accept help was another matter. More than likely he would shun any offers of support, but in any case, she had no idea how to help him and she knew that before she could do so she would need to resolve the ill feeling she had towards him. Slowly and solemnly, wiping her nose with her sleeve, Fabia turned quietly to the top of the wood where she slipped off her cloak, tucked it into the rucksack she had left under the hedge, and began the long walk home.

By the time she reached the house, large raindrops had started to fall, darkening the pavement as they landed. The wooden gate at the side of the house squeaked on its hinges as she pushed it open. Rounding the corner of the house she was greeted by the welcome sound of laughter. Caspian and Babette were in the garden, rushing to bring washing in as the rain came quicker. "Help me with this sheet!" called Babette as Caspian lowered the line and reached for the pegs.

"Hi Fabia!" she smiled, picking up the basket and placing it on her hip, swinging it down the steps to the back door. "Cup of tea? We've got the kettle on, I'm making a pot."

"I'll have one later, thanks, I'm going for a bath now. Perhaps when I come back down." Fabia had realised on the walk home that the smell of the bonfire had got into her hair and permeated her clothes and she needed to rid herself of it. She certainly didn't want anyone to notice it.

"I'll bring one up for you before you get in, shall I?" said Babette, putting the basket of washing down.

"That will be great, thanks," Fabia replied and turning her head as she went through to the dining room she was surprised to see her brother slip a hand round Babette's waist as she leaned over the washing. She raised her eyebrows and felt a prickle of discomfort. A day for revelations! The burning of long kept secrets, and now Caspian flirting with Babette! She felt a change coming and did not know if it was entirely welcome.

The bathroom quickly filled with steam as Fabia undressed, dropping her jeans and checked shirt to the floor. The scent of the bath oil was arresting, attar of roses that her mother had sent her from France, and all at once a memory of them both at the top of the garden one hot summer morning came to her. They were cutting flowers for the house the soft fragrance of the Gertrude Jekyll roses that grew in front of the hedge filling the air; the long bed of pink blooms vivid against the silken dark green of the laurel. A thorn had caught Louisa's finger and she hurriedly put the rose into the trug and her finger to her lips as a drop of blood rose to the surface.

'I am of my mother's blood,' Fabia thought, and she remem-bered the photograph in the pocket of her jeans. She took it out and studied it; her mother and Dana from their later school days in Paris, arms around each other, smiling, satchels on their shoulders. Dana, the woman Louisa now lived with, but back then how carefree, how happy they looked. 'How wonderfully happy,' thought Fabia.

* * *

The previous evening Caspian and Babette had taken a bottle of wine out to the garden and sat beneath the arbour in the top corner, hidden from view by the tall shrubs that grew around it. Ceanothus, holly and viburnum provided a sense of solitude and a dense habitat for garden birds. Sparrows chirruped from its depths and this year, a blackbird had built a nest there and raised three broods.

The preceding days had been warm and this was the last of relatively high temperatures before the weather turned again. "Might as well make the most of it," Babette said putting a bottle of French Sauvignon and two glasses on the mosaic top of the table in front of the arbour. They talked about the changes to be made in the garden in the coming autumn, particularly to Julius' vegetable plot next to the workshop. It was no longer tended and was overrun with weeds. Babette liked the idea of continuing to grow things, to provide sustenance, and she cultivated lettuces and rocket there which they ate in salads and sandwiches, but the demands of her job and being a mother took priority and she found that she did not have the time to nurture the things she grew. Caspian felt that he did not have the time nor the motivation to do so either and he suggested that the best solution was to return it to lawn.

As dusk fell they opened a second bottle and brought blankets out to put over their shoulders. The sky was still clear and they were determined to sit out enjoying the good weather as long as they could. The wine loosened their tongues and their talk became more intimate. They sat closer together and Babette rested her hand on Caspian's knee.

"Why did you kiss me the other day, when I was doing the herbs?" she suddenly asked.

Caspian hesitated. Here was the chance to tell her, to let go of the turmoil he had been struggling with over the past few months, to end the inner battles that had kept him at odds.

"Why do you think?" he put to her seriously.

"I'm not really sure. I want you to tell me."

Again, he vacillated. "Because I love you," he said. "Not just the way that I've always loved you, it's more than that now, it's different. I suppose I kissed you because I'm in love with you."

Babette's eyes filled with tears, not of sadness but of joy. "I think that's how I feel too," she said earnestly, "I mean, I've felt like it for a while, but I didn't know what to do about it. I don't suppose it's right, is it?"

"I've thought about that such a lot. I have to keep telling myself that we're not related by blood, that we're not really related at all. Nathan wasn't your biological father, was he? If he was we'd be first cousins, but he wasn't, so we're not."

"The Queen and Prince Philip are cousins!" Babette interjected.

"They're not first cousins though, and they didn't grow up in the same house like we've done. That's what makes this so awkward. I don't know what Dad or Fabia would think, I don't think they'll be very happy about it." He pushed a strand of hair back from her face, "I realised I was in love with you a few months ago. I tried to suppress it, but I can't. It doesn't matter how hard I try, I can't do anything about it, and I don't really want to fight it anymore anyway."

He took her hand, and awkwardly paused again, "We must be careful, we mustn't rush into anything. For now, it's enough that we know how we both feel, but we really must go slowly and find a way that makes it alright. A way that we can be together without it seeming like it's wrong."

Babette slowly nodded, "Yes, I agree. I hope we can find a way, I really do. I love you so much Caspian."

High above them the almost full moon shone brightly, and from somewhere over the far edge of the field a tawny owl called, a lonely but hauntingly beautiful sound that carried on the late summer night.

15

Fabia's Violin

"Listen! Fabia's making screechy noises! Can you hear it? Oh, my ears, it's hurting my ears Mummy!"

Babette laughed at her daughter jumping about in the kitchen, her hands over her ears, pretending they were hurting. There was indeed a 'screechy noise' coming from Fabia's room, a screechy noise they didn't often hear but when they did it became a household joke as it always had.

"Let's go and see!" Elisabeth grabbed her mother by the wrist and led her to the kitchen door. On the first landing Babette stopped and plucked at Elisabeth's sleeve, "You've got a hole in your cardigan. How did that happen?"

Elisabeth looked down at the floor, stuck out her bottom lip, then looked up again, "I'm not sure, I think Marsha did it." Her face reddened a little, "You're not going to tell me off, are you? It wasn't my fault, Marsha did it by accident."

"How did it happen?" Babette asked again.

"I told you Mummy, Marsha did it. She didn't mean to, she was going like this," and she demonstrated, a scissor action with her fingers on her mother's arm.

"Snip, snip, that's what. She did it like that and it accidentally cut my sleeve. She said sorry three times. No, four! No, three! She said three sorries. I was worried about it; I was afraid you'd tell me off. Are you cross with Marsha?"

"Well, I don't suppose I'm that cross because it's an old cardigan, but you must tell Marsha to be more careful. It's a good job you weren't wearing your best clothes!"

"I'm sorry Mummy. She's silly sometimes, that Marsha. I'll tell her not to do it again, I'll make sure she doesn't. I won't sit so close to her next time. If she does it again, I'll make her go in the teapot and she won't be allowed out for a week."

"How do you make her go in the teapot?"

"Well, I sort of put her in there. Sometimes I just tell her to go in there and she does."

Babette chuckled to herself, "Well luckily that cardigan is an old one, it's a bit tatty round the cuffs anyway, so it doesn't really matter too much. Perhaps we should get you a new red cardigan, you look so pretty in red! What were you and Marsha doing with the scissors?"

"Making paper flowers to stick on a picture. We haven't finished it yet. Can you help me finish it later?"

"We can do it this evening before dinner if you like. We don't want Marsha helping though, do we? She's not very good with scissors!"

"No, she's in the teapot, she's not coming out today, she's sulking because she's been naughty."

"What were we doing?" asked Babette nodding towards the stairs where the ragged high-pitched din scurried about, like a trapped wasp frantically whirring at the window, desperate to get out and find its way home.

"We were going to see what that noise was! Come on!" Elisabeth bounded up the steeper second flight of stairs and along the short landing to Fabia's attic room.

"Knock, knock!" Elisabeth shouted, rapping on the door. "Knock, knock! Can we come in please Fabia?" She pushed the door open and went into the room, her mother close behind her.

Fabia was standing almost in the middle of the room trying to play her old violin. On the chest of drawers was a piece of sheet music, held to the cover of a heavy book with a clothes peg. She stopped and turned to face her visitors, still holding her violin under her chin.

"Hello you two. What are you up to?"

"We heard a screechy-scratchy noise and we wondered what it was! It was hurting my ears!"

Babette chortled and joined in with her daughter's teasing, "We thought there was a cat stuck up here somewhere, didn't we Elisabeth?"

Elisabeth fell onto the bed chuckling. Fabia could not help but join in; "Very funny," she said gently poking Elisabeth with her bow, which only made Elisabeth snicker even more, and then she was off, she couldn't stop, laughing and laughing.

"Have we got the giggles?" asked Fabia smiling, and Babette, Babette laughed so much that tears ran down her face!

The three of them composed themselves with sighs and sniffs. "I went to the bookshop on the way home from work," Fabia told them, "the second hand one at the end of West Street. There's some good stuff in there, lots of children's books, Elisabeth, you'll like it. They had two boxes full of sheet music, I spent ages going through it all and I found a few pieces I used to play. I bought this but I can't play it! I seem to have

183

lost the knack!" She held up the piece of music she had been studying; Minuet in G by Beethoven, "I used to play this at school, I even played it at concerts but I'm so out of practice now."

"I thought I recognised it," said Babette.

"Well, that's good! I wouldn't have thought anyone would recognise it! I'm so rusty, I haven't played my violin for years!" She put the music sheet down on the book, "It's really weird, I've been thinking lately about playing it again, and then they had all that music in the shop, so I thought: 'Right, that's it, I'm going to give it a go.' I'd forgotten how much I enjoyed it! I kind of thought I'd be able to pick up where I left off but it's not that easy."

"You used to be very good! You even played in the school orchestra! Do you remember that funny little man who you had lessons with when you first started?"

"Mr. Greylake. Yes, remember his house? Stuff everywhere and loads of cats, it stank of cat pee! He's dead now."

"Who's dead?" Elisabeth's interest in the conversation suddenly returned.

"The man who taught Fabia to play the violin."

"Why is he dead?"

"Well, he just is. He got very old and died."

"What's an orchestra?" Elisabeth slid her feet to and fro on the thick rug beside Fabia's bed, wriggling her toes in the tight pile.

"A group of people who play music together," answered Fabia.

"Like a band? Like The Who and The Buzzcocks?"

Fabia and Babette laughed. "Well, no, not really," explained Fabia, "an orchestra has lots of people, loads more than The

Who or the Buzzcocks, and they all play different instruments like flutes and clarinets, and violins and cellos. They play classical music."

"I know what classical music is, it's when it hasn't got any words," Elisabeth interrupted.

"How do you know about The Who and The Buzzcocks?" Babette asked.

"Caspian showed me his records. Do you know how many he's got? About a hundred!"

"Anyway, I've got something to tell you," announced Fabia, suddenly changing the subject. "I'm going to France next week! I'm going to see Mum! I'm going for three whole weeks!"

"Really? How come?" Babette's eyes widened.

"I booked a ferry crossing at the travel agents today. You know the gallery is shut for a month while the conservatory is being finished? Ali and Will are going away for three weeks and there won't be anything for me to do. They reminded me I haven't had any time off since Christmas, so I thought I'd have a holiday too."

"Lucky you! I wish I could go on holiday for three weeks!"

"And I met a very handsome man today. He asked if I'd like to have lunch with him tomorrow!" Fabia blushed a little.

"Ooh! Who is he? Are you going?"

"Yes, I am! I'm quite nervous about it actually, I can't believe he asked me!"

"Are you going to marry him?" Elisabeth interrupted. She was standing in front of the dressing table, fiddling with Fabia's necklaces, as she often did. "Then you'll have to change your name to Mrs...Mrs.... What's his name?"

"No, I'm not going to marry him Elisabeth, I've only just

met him!"

"Who is he?" Babette asked again. She was very interested and wondered if this was why Fabia was in such high spirits, much brighter than her usual dreamy self.

"He's called Ben. He's Ali's son, from her previous marriage. She's talked about him a lot but he hasn't been down when I've been there, so I haven't met him before. He's been working in Switzerland for the last two years, running a big art gallery but he's come back to the UK now and is living in London. He's SO handsome, and such a gentleman!"

Babette smiled and rubbed Fabia's arm, "He sounds nice! Who knows, maybe he's come into your life for a reason! Is he much older than the twins?"

"Only a few years. I think he's about your age."

"Am I good looking?" Elisabeth had adorned herself with several different necklaces, a long many stranded shimmer of multi-coloured beads, fake pearls and glistening stones.

"Oh yes Elisabeth, of course! You're absolutely beautiful, especially with all my necklaces on!" Fabia went and stood behind Elisabeth who was admiring herself in the mirror. "Shall we go to the park and feed the ducks?" she asked, stroking the little girl's hair.

"Only if I can wear these."

"That's a bit fancy for the park, but you can put them on when we get back. We'll dress up for dinner tonight, that will be fun!"

"Yes!" Elisabeth shrieked with delight and skipped out of the bedroom. Then she jumped down the stairs, two at a time.

* * *

Earlier that afternoon when Fabia was alone in her room, inspired by the music she'd bought, she got out her violin, wiped the dust off with her sleeve, and attempted to play. It had been a few years since she'd last played and she was surprised at how she initially found it so difficult. She wondered if it would soon come back to her and hoped that it would. It was true that she'd forgotten how much she used to enjoy it; she had always felt that her soul, or some other very big part of her went into the music that she played, and she always felt very moved by it.

At school the music teacher had been impressed when she first heard her play the piano; "Look at those long slim fingers, see how they move!" she said to the headmistress, and they agreed that Fabia had a natural musical flair. She often performed in assemblies, and in school concerts, to an audience that was visibly stirred by the talent of such a young girl. The praise was something she took in her stride, though in truth she felt embarrassed by it, such was her self-effacing character. She was familiar with music from a very early age, from when her mother practised the piano in the conservatory. Louisa would lift Fabia onto her lap and show her how the keys made notes and then tunes. She taught her easy pieces, first Chopsticks and soon, she progressed to Moonlight Sonata and Für Elise. Fabia had lessons from the age of five with Mr. Greylake in his tall thin house opposite the doctor's surgery and he told her she must pursue it, that she was naturally gifted. She played very well by ear, but he taught her to read music, and one day after her lesson he played the violin to her and gently persuaded her to have a go. She could not explain what it was that roused her, but she found it beautiful; it was her Eldorado. She loved the warm sound of the bow

187

midway between the bridge and the fingerboard, the pellucid brightness of the higher notes, to her as clear as the air of a cloudless May morning. "Practise whenever you can Fabia, don't ever let that talent slip away. Nothing has the power to move like beautifully played music," Mr. Greylake told her, and so the sound of Fabia's violin became commonplace in the house; blithe and chirpy, tripping down the stairs, in and out of the rooms, exciting and seductive, spinning in the air, and sometimes a pervading melancholy came with it that seemed to make the entire house sigh.

She played in the town hall, and in auditoriums in regional cities, both with an orchestra and solo. It was after one of these performances that she found her mother wet eyed in the foyer of the cathedral where she'd played Ave Maria. She initially wondered why she should be upset, her concern etched on her eager face as she went to her mother, but Louisa bent over and put her arm around Fabia's shoulders. Wiping her eyes, she said: "I'm so proud of you my darling. I had to come out here because otherwise I'd cry, and I didn't want everyone to see me crying. I'm not sad, these are happy tears! You've made me very, very happy. I'm so proud of you."

Fabia was looking forward to going to France, to seeing her mother; she decided she would take her violin and practice it there.

* * *

Julius, as usual, was alone in the woods that afternoon, fast asleep beneath the enormous beech. By nature a solitary character, he had whilst at university been more affable, though not in the same hail-fellow-well-met manner of his contemporaries. Louisa was of a quiet disposition and they had suited one another during their student days and in the early years of their marriage, which had been happy. They never felt the need for a large circle of friends and found all the pleasure they needed in their life at the cottage.

Julius often thought of those times and he regretted how he had altered the very fabric of that existence with his wrong doings, things which Louisa for a long time was unaware of. He tried to forget it all, to lock it away in a compartment that could be pushed to the back of his head, but the truth was it could not. It would not lie and he became distant, spending more and more time on his own, leaving his wife with their young son in the evenings whilst he passed the time in the woods. There he sometimes allowed his regrets to surface, briefly wept over them, and in an attempt to brush them aside, absorbed himself with watching the wild animals that fed and made their homes in the wood. One year he spent almost every spring evening observing badger cubs creep out of their den at dusk. Sitting very still upwind of them he saw them tumble about together at play, furtively snuffling about for grubs and fungi; their mother was never far from them, alert for any danger. He took great delight in this, and during the day when he was working in the timber yard amidst the noise of the saws and the clattering and banging of the stacking, he looked forward to the time after supper when he could go to the quiet of the woods to watch his badger family.

Another time he saw a vixen and her cubs emerge from the top bank of the woods and ferret along the hedge; little balls of orange-brown fur rolling down the slope. In late spring he enjoyed seeing deer come into the glade to feed among the bluebells, leaping off into the dark of the conifers when they sensed him nearby, the flash of their white tails arcing into the gloom. The wood became his sanctuary and though he enjoyed telling Louisa about the animals he saw; he was reluctant to invite her to be part of this silent world he could escape to and be alone. She didn't seem to mind, she was quite happy to spend her evenings reading to Caspian, bathing him and tucking him up in bed. Then she would sit in the armchair beneath the glow of a standard lamp, marking papers and planning lessons, or at the table with her sewing machine, busy making curtains and tablecloths, pinning paper patterns on to fabric to make dresses for herself.

Their life together continued in this way and despite Julius' misdemeanours and consequent woes, no notable cracks had appeared in their marriage. After his father passed away, he and Louisa decided to move into the town and they were lucky to be able to just about afford the big house with his inheritance and a small mortgage, slowly making it their family home over the years.

It was about this time that Julius first became interested in wood turning, so he made the barn at the end of the garden into a workshop where he spent much of this time turning spoons, lamps and bowls. He progressed to candlesticks and chairs after he joined the local Guild of Craftsmen where he quickly learned new skills and even took part in their exhibitions. By the time Caspian was ten, Julius was exhibiting solo. He travelled to shows, sometimes taking his son with him, paying the boy pocket money to help set up the stall and to wrap pieces in tissue paper for customers. Later, his work became sought after and it commanded a high price tag, being in demand at renowned galleries. On the surface, it was a good life, they were all happy, though Julius still suffered much inner torment.

When Nathan was killed that torment intensified, not only because of the shock and the grief at losing his only brother but because he felt he was to blame for the accident. There was also the huge question of what would happen to Babette.

"She must come and live with us," Julius said. "That is the obvious solution."

He and Louisa were drinking tea and eating biscuits in the sitting room of Nathan's neighbour, whose daughter was best friends with Babette. Babette had been with them when the police had called next door after the accident and she'd stayed there whilst Julius and Louisa made the two hundred mile trip to be with her. On the journey they discussed Babette's future, sometimes at odds; Julius was resolute in his decision that they would take the girl in, he would have it no other way.

"Don't you think we should try to find her mother?" suggested Louisa. "She should know what's happened, Babette is her daughter after all. As far as we know she has no other family."

"Absolutely not! I don't see any point in that! That woman buggered off and left Babette with Nathan when she was only six years old, she doesn't care for her. She can't call herself a mother! What kind of mother does that? Babette can't even remember her! Why should anyone go to the trouble of trying to find her? Besides, where would you start? She was trouble right from the start, Nathan should never have got involved with her. Babette is better off without her. We don't want her in our lives."

"So you really think we should take her in?"

Julius was concentrating on the road, "Yes, of course we should! There's no alternative. For God's sake Louisa! What else do you suggest?"

"I suppose the only other option is for her to go into care."

"That's ridiculous. I won't hear of it. That wouldn't be right at all. She has to come and live with us."

"It's difficult for me Julius. I know Babette is more or less a cousin to our children, and yes, I suppose I do love her, but, well... I'm not sure how to say it? She can be quite wild and if I must be honest, I wonder how that will affect Fabia as she grows up."

"Wild? What an earth are you talking about? She can be very single minded at times and she's a bit highly strung, but she's not wild Louisa! Think what the poor girl has been through! It would be good for both the girls; Babette might bring Fabia out of her shell and if Babette does have a 'wild' streak as you seem to think, then I'm sure Fabia will temper it."

Julius was resolute. His mind had been made up as soon as he heard that Nathan had died, and Louisa knew that in spite of her misgivings it would be wrong if they did not take Babette home to live with them.

There was much that Julius and Louisa were to discover. Not long after his marriage Nathan had taken the necessary steps to legally adopt Babette. When her mother disappeared he made a will appointing Julius as his step-daughter's legal guardian and he left every penny he had for her care. He never discussed this with Julius, whether this was because he was sure that his brother would take care of Babette, or because he was afraid that he would not be in agreement with it, but it did not matter. His wishes would be granted and for Julius and Louisa, the matter was resolved.

So Babette came to live with them in the big house on the edge of the town. Though she was at first inconsolable, in time she settled in well and did not prove to be difficult, as

Louisa had suspected. She got on well with both Caspian and Fabia, already quite used to spending weekends and school holidays with them. The wheels of the family unit trundled along perfectly well, the bereaved cousin was now part of their family and was loved and made to feel an intrinsic part of their lives. There was a headstrong streak in Babette; she sometimes did just as she wanted though only to the extent of staying out late and playing music too loud, and she showed independence of spirit, always the one who climbed higher in the trees, the one who was first to launch out across the river on a tyre swing. She was not especially tolerant of people and quickly became incensed at what she considered to be stupidity in others; some would say she did not suffer fools gladly.

The years raced by and day after day Julius returned to the house from his job at the timber yard where in time he rose up through the ranks to become general manger and then a director. In the evening when Louisa was at her easel in the sewing room, he retired to his sitting room to read or to watch television with a nightcap of single malt whiskey on ice. He did not spend quite so much time woodturning but on lighter nights and at weekends he still went to the woods, which in time he owned, and he spent the daylight hours observing the wildlife, clearing brambles and bracken, and stacking fallen branches for firewood. He looked forward most of all, to the time when dusk began to fall, when he would light a campfire, pull up a fold-out chair and enjoy a solitary tipple, just enough to send him into a deep and dreamless sleep.

16

Fabia in France

The sunlight filtering through the trees dappled the lane to the chateau that was Louisa's home. The journey had been long and arduous, the roads busy with holiday makers not used to driving on the right-hand side of the road. Fabia was looking forward to getting to the chateau, to some food and a bath. She hadn't been there since she came over with Caspian four years ago this summer. and whilst she had happy memories of that time, she felt that she had not really got to know Dana, and that she found her somewhat intimidating.

Louisa and Dana had been at school together since they were very young and had been very close as teenagers, taking their separate courses in their twenties but sporadically keeping in touch. About fifteen years ago they had re-established their roles as confidantes to one another and since then Louisa spent a lot of time in France visiting Dana, sometimes taking the children with her. Her eventual departure to live there permanently came unexpectedly when Fabia was fifteen and Caspian in his final year at university.

Dana was a tall and very attractive woman who could certainly be described as bohemian. She had spent years in Paris hanging out in the streets of Montmartre, renting rooms that looked onto courtyards strung with washing, where footsteps echoed on the cobbled pavements at night and the laughter of people leaving the bars and cafes made the night hours shorter.

"But darling, your children are so nervous! Why do they not run free here, there is so much for them to explore!" Fabia remembered overhearing Dana and her mother talking one evening, years ago. They were preparing supper in the kitchen on the ground floor of the house, with its huge limestone flags and an enormous stone inglenook where an old range rumbled and belted out heat that somehow never seemed to pervade the cool of the room, even on the hottest of days.

Fabia felt sure that Dana did not particularly like her. "I doubt it," Caspian said when she mentioned it to him. "I don't think Dana dislikes anyone. You must remember that she has an artist's temperament and you are sometimes over sensitive!"

Caspian was probably right and, as he also pointed out, Dana had no experience as a mother. She had no children of her own and had never married though she had a circle of erudite male friends, as well as women, who came and went, leaving clothes strewn upon bedroom floors, puddles of water in the bathrooms, empty wine glasses and cigarette ends in ashtrays on the tables and the terrace. It was impossible to tell which of them, if any, were lovers, though they could certainly all be categorized as admirers.

Dana inherited the chateau when her parents passed away. It had been inhabited by her family for five generations, and long before that, served as a fortress in the Hundred Years

War. It was much in need of repair; crumbling walls revealed crevices flimsily sealed by gossamer spiders' webs, some of the window shutters would not close and banged incessantly in the slightest breeze so had to be tied to huge nails in the frame. Paint and plaster flaked from the walls inside, leaving strange map-like shapes, continents not yet discovered.

The whole house was quite powdery with dust and superficially lacklustre, yet it retained an air of nameless beauty. On warm days sunlight poured in through the tall windows and rested in long beams heavy with dust motes. It had a certain grace, as though in some far off corner of the house someone was always playing the piano, very gently, very finely, and the lightness of the notes danced through every part of the house, slipping up the stairs, filtering through cracks under doors, and up through floorboards.

It never seemed to rain there; the huge kitchen door was always left open onto the terrace where a saltwater pool remained covered, and out of use. "I hope that soon I will have enough money to make it good," Dana had said one day, strolling around its perimeter. Her long red dress trailed on the ground, "The bank will release some more money or perhaps I will sell a painting and become rich, who knows!" Meanwhile she wafted from room to room in her diaphanous robes, her long dark hair wrapped in a richly coloured turban, arms full of papers and heirlooms she had unearthed from a cupboard or from a colossal chest in the cellar. "See what I have found!" she announced in her heavily accented English, "The inventory of my grandfather's library! Who knows what we have here? Books that are three hundred, maybe four hundred years old! Maybe priceless works by Le Sage, Marivaux or perhaps Voltaire. My darling, we have our work cut out!" she exclaimed to Louisa, stubbing her Gitane in a saucer on the Japanese lacquer work side table.

Wisteria tumbled over the railings on the bridge over the dry moat to the front door, long dried up; Dana said not even her grandmother could remember when it last had water in it. Frothy lilac flowers cascaded from the walls where bines scrambled to the windows on the top floor; frogs croaked in the lavoir where the lawn met the path, butterflies busied themselves among the herbs that spilled out from the beds in myriad shades of green. It seemed to always be summer there, endlessly summer.

The conversation in the car had mostly been Louisa telling Fabia about their plans to renovate the chateau and how eventually, they hoped to hold residential art courses there. The difficulty was, Louisa explained, that Dana desperately wanted to remain living there but did not have the income to maintain the place, so they had come up with the idea of getting it up to scratch enough to open the art school. It had all been discussed with an adviser at the bank who thought it a worthwhile project and had suggested they might diversify into writing workshops and yoga retreats.

"We have a few people staying at the moment," Louisa told her daughter, "and work has already started, so there are men busy plastering and wallpapering, things like that, but I'm sure you remember, it's a big house, so there's plenty of room for everyone." She indicated to turn right, off the main road, "Oh, and Dana's cousin, Yanis is staying, and his son Samuel. Yanis is a sculptor, he's very good, his work is incredible actually. He has a big exhibition coming up in September so he's getting everything ready for that. Samuel is about your age; he's just finished university and he's here helping in the gardens."

The heat was quite suffocating and had reached temperatures that Fabia was not used to. Being so fair of complexion she found the strong sunlight too much and preferred to spend hot summer days beneath the shade of a tree or in the cool of the house.

"The beauty of these thick stone walls is that they keep the hot sun out but the warmth from our fires in. That is how we like it, it's perfect!" Dana explained as she greeted her. "Did your mother tell you, we have made a bed for you in the Spring Room at the back of the house! You will be able to use the little bathroom in the tower now that the plumber has installed new pipes – even a bath! Such luxury! It is all painted as well, a beautiful pale yellow, like those flowers you have in the hedgerows in England, I forget what you call them, but it was your mother's idea – the Spring Room should be the colour of an English spring."

"Primroses," said Fabia as she took her bag off her shoulder and put it down on the huge tin trunk in the hall, "they're the only pale yellow ones I can think of. Mum loves them."

As hot as it was, she was looking forward to exploring the grounds again, to strolling beneath the willow trees along the canal, or in the shadow of the poplar grove at the back of the house. It was all just as she remembered it. On that first afternoon she found a seat by the hedge in the orchard where she took her notebook to sketch and write poetry. Bumblebees and butterflies were busy among the flowers that grew untamed in the beds, dog roses twisted their way up the thick hedges, crickets chirruped in the long grass. When it grew cooler in the evening Fabia wandered on the lawns at the front of the house, into the woods behind the coach house; she paused on the little stone bridge over the lavoir, watching fish lazily jumping, a cloud of midges that moved as a busy almost shimmering mass above the water.

The next morning, she was sitting with her back against the huge red trunk of a sequoia, deep in thought, when she noticed a young man walking up the lawn towards her. She'd seen him earlier from her bathroom window, working amongst the fruit bushes in the walled gardens at the back of the house. She noticed how his white shirt stuck to his back in the sweltering heat as he bent to pick plump redcurrants. Now and then he stood up, put his bowl and secateurs on the ground, and removed his straw hat to wipe his brow.

"Hello, you must be Fabia," he greeted her, "I'm sorry, I missed you last night, I've been to the coast with friends for a long weekend. I got back very late and everyone had gone to bed - except Dana. She never seems to sleep!" He sat down on the grass beside her.

"I'm Samuel," he held out his hand. "You've probably met my father, Yanis?"

Fabia shook his suntanned hand, "Yes, I met him at breakfast this morning. He showed me some of his work, it's amazing!" She paused, searching for something else to say: "Your English is very good," is what she nervously came out with.

"Thank you," he blushed a little, which made him look younger, more boylike. Fabia immediately thought him handsome; short mid-brown hair ruffled back from his forehead, brown eyes fringed with dark lashes. He had a strong, quite angular face, was what you call 'chiselled' she thought. Her friends would say, "Oh, he's very chiselled, he could be a model," or, "He has a fine chiselled face, a very good looking man."

"I've had a lot of practice," Samuel explained, "I went to

university in England, I finished in June this year. I think I'd like to study more one day to perfect it. There are still so many words I don't know, but for now I have a job. I start work later this year."

"What did you study?" asked Fabia. "Which university did you go to?"

"Canterbury," he replied, stretching out his long legs, rubbing his left calf. "My degree is in Plant Science, or Botany, I suppose you could call it."

"That's a very interesting subject." Fabia was quickly beginning to feel more relaxed and she turned her body to face him more. The grip on her sketchbook slackened a little, her pencil slipped onto the grass beside her. "Tell me about your job?" she blushed; "I'm sorry, all these questions! I don't mean to be nosey!"

"It's okay," he smiled, happy to be chatting so easily with her. "I'll be working in England, though I don't start my job until December. Officially, I'll be an assistant gardener, but I will also be doing some work as a research entomologist, studying the effect of pests and disease on the plants. I'm really looking forward to it, I was delighted when I was offered it. I couldn't believe I would be so lucky."

"Where is it?" she asked.

"In Wiltshire, in the gardens of a country house. It's part of a big estate, all very English, very picturesque. I have to find somewhere to live though, which worries me a little. There are cottages on the estate, but they all have tenants, so I'll have to look in a village nearby, or in the town, which is about 6 miles away." He looked across the lawn and smiled, then looked back at Fabia, "What about you? Are you an artist like your mother? I thought I saw you sketching before I interrupted you!"

"Oh, I'm not very good," she shrugged, "I did art at A' Level and I'm very interested in it, but it doesn't come naturally to me like it does with Mum."

"Can I see?" Samuel held out his hand to reach her sketch-book. She handed it to him; her sketch of a view of the hills, perfectly framed between two very tall and straight trees. She bit her lip as he studied it.

"I might paint it, with watercolours," she explained.

"It's very good! Why do you say you're not very good? You do have a talent! Keep sketching, the more you do something the better you become at it."

"Practice makes perfect!"

"Yes, that's right," he handed the book back to her, as she blushed again, pleased that he had complimented her on her work.

"Where in England do you live? My Aunt told me it's in the South West, but I can't remember exactly where she said it was, I'm sorry! I like the South West, it's a lovely part of the country, I spent one of my summer holidays in Devon. I worked so hard that year! I was gardening in the grounds of a castle, I picked raspberries on a fruit farm, and worked in a pub in the evening!"

"We live in Somerset, the next county to Devon. The town where we live is small and not much happens but it's alright; I grew up there, I've never lived anywhere else. I work in an art gallery, only three days a week, more when it's busy, if there's a big exhibition or something."

"Sounds nice! Do you like it? Do you enjoy your work? I think it's important to take pleasure in what you do, if you can."

"Yes, I do. I like it because, well, it's a nice thing to do, but

I can learn from it, and the people who own the gallery are lovely, like friends." She thought of Ben and how well they had been getting along. They'd been for walks together and for dinner a few times, and she was surprised to feel a pang of guilt that she was here now, quite enamoured with this handsome man in such a very short space of time.

"That's why I'm really looking forward to starting my job," he replied. "It's good to be able to earn a living from something that you are really interested in, in my case quite passionate about, that's what I would say."

Fabia was enjoying Samuel's company more and more. Even though they'd only been chatting for a few minutes, it already felt like she'd known him much longer. The conversation felt easy and relaxed.

"Mum says you're working here for the summer?" I saw you this morning in the garden at the back, it looked like you were working hard."

"I was," he sighed. "So much to do but it's so hot. I start work very early in the morning because it's cooler then; by midday I've had enough. Tomorrow the grass must be cut so I'll start early before everyone is up. I'm sorry if the lawnmower wakes you." He stopped and looked about him, then glanced at his watch. "It's lunchtime," he said, "Shall we go and find something to eat?"

"Good idea! I didn't have much at breakfast, so I'm famished," said Fabia, standing up, straightening her sundress.

They walked back to the house together and went into the shade of the kitchen through the door on the ground floor, by the corner of the moat. Voices on the terrace told them that the rest of the household had decided to eat outside. Dana was busying herself, going to and fro from the kitchen to the terrace with bowls of salad, plates of cold meat and cheese. By the pool, Yanis and Louisa were laying the table, putting plates, cutlery and napkins in their rightful places.

"Ah, there you are!" exclaimed Louisa. "I was just coming to find you to say that lunch is ready. Yanis is going to put the sunshade up so that we can eat out here, we have to protect our pale English skin!"

Yanis was comically struggling with the sunshade, an old one that he had dragged from the store at the back of the house, thinking it would be more suitable than the smaller one they had been using that was not quite big enough to shield them all from the strong rays of the early afternoon sun.

"Have a seat Fabia," said Dana, bustling past with a wooden board laden with cheeses and thick slices of bread. "I see you've met my nephew. I hope he's being a gentleman."

"I am always a gentleman!" tutted Samuel. "It's how I was raised, isn't it, Dad?" He took a pair of dark sunglasses from his shirt pocket and put them on. 'How distinguished he looks,' thought Fabia and she momentarily imagined her friend's reactions if they were here. Jenna, she thought, would be flirting with him, looking up at him with her wide doe eyes, leaning towards him.

"It's so hot! Far too hot to do anything this afternoon!" said Louisa as she passed the bread around. "You don't mind if we don't go out, do you Fabia? I thought we'd go to Poitiers tomorrow and I'll show you all the sights. There's a wonderful medieval quarter, with lots of original timber framed buildings, and I want to show you the cathedral."

"It's not exactly a cathedral," interrupted Dana, "it's a church, but" she said turning to Fabia "It's very beautiful, quite magnificent. I think you'll enjoy it. There are incredible carved statues on the façade, which makes it look very Gothic, like a Spanish cathedral."

"It sounds very interesting," said Fabia, a fork full of salad leaves poised to go into her mouth. "I like that sort of thing! I'm looking forward to it Mum. Is there a market? I love the French markets, so much better than the ones we have in England, I love the atmosphere."

"There is," replied Louisa, "we'll go in the morning, so we don't miss it. We'll have a good browse and I'll take you to one of our favourite cafes for lunch." She leaned forward and cut a slither of goat's cheese, "Later this afternoon, when it's cooled down a bit, I might tackle the cupboard in the tower. It's quite a dusty job but we're finding some very interesting things."

"Old and interesting!" remarked Dana, "Like Yanis!" She winked at him as she raised her glass and took a sip of wine. He smiled back at her, laughing, and he blew her a kiss as if to say: "You too my darling, you too."

That night in bed, Fabia smiled and settled down with her book by lamplight. The next three weeks stretched out before her, in her mind already full of places to see, idling in the grounds, more lunches on the terrace. Her thoughts of home were far way and she gave no thought to what her father might be doing in the woods or to the minutiae of Babette and Caspian's daily lives. She would write to them whilst she was here, and send Elisabeth postcards, but for now, she was looking forward to spending time with her mother, and to getting to know Samuel better.

Was it the magic of the chateau and the beauty of the grounds, in parts a tumbling wilderness, in others a reflection of the height of summer on the water, that weaved its charm and drew

Fabia in so that she slipped calmly into the days and nights of the life there? People came and went, came and went; the boy from the baker's shop in the village who cycled up the lane each morning with fresh bread, the woman from the farm who came with her two small children to pick fruit. In return for their labours Dana gave them a bowlful to take home, with a small payment, and she urged them to stay for lunch. There were the students who arrived one day in a battered Citroen, prodigies of Yanis', whom he'd invited for a brief sculpture course; the couple in their thirties, who were the nearest neighbours, he dark and olive skinned, she short and plump with a belly round and expectant with their first child.

Each morning the sun blazed in through the windows of the kitchen as breakfast was prepared; thick crepes, eggs scrambled with generous slabs of butter, fruit, fresh and firm, picked at sunrise. In the evenings they gathered by candlelight in the dining room and talked over a simple supper late into the night, Fabia often retiring to her room a little giddy after too much wine. One night, not long after midnight, there was a light tap-tapping at her door and when she opened it there was Samuel, as she had hoped. He came in with two glasses of brandy and cigarettes; handsome as ever, always so handsome. Fabia did not turn him away.

She did not turn him away for the rest of the holiday; with him she was so delightfully, almost deliriously happy. She wrote home to Polly and Jenna: 'I've met the most gorgeous man,' she told them, 'I'm in love and I don't want to come home!'

But all holidays must end, as did Fabia's and though sad at being parted from Samuel she was excited about his coming over to England to visit her as soon as he could. She would ask Julius if he could stay with them for a week; she knew he wouldn't mind at all, because he never seemed to mind about anything, and she couldn't wait to introduce her new friend to Caspian and Babette, and to little Elisabeth.

She could not wait to tell them of her plans; that when Samuel came to England to start his new job, she would be moving to Wiltshire with him.

17

Fabia Attacks Julius

That afternoon in the woods there was no sign of Julius. Fabia had moved tentatively along the top hedge and pulling the hood of her cloak down over her face, she ventured down to the edge of the clearing where ash still lay thick on the floor from Julius' bonfire. She crept among the trees to the point where she could get a clear view of the hut; the door was wide open, but her father was nowhere to be seen. Fabia speculated about where he might be; he couldn't be far away because his car was parked on the track when she came up to the woods earlier and she hadn't heard the engine start, so she knew he hadn't driven off. He must be somewhere close, possibly walking in the fields, or he might even have gone down to the pub in the village.

She went back closer to the hedgeline where she felt safe but could still keep an eye out for her father. It had begun to rain; a very light drizzle, and she was starting to feel cold. Pulling her cloak tighter around her she glanced in the direction of the beech trees where she thought she saw something move. She heard rustling, very close, from somewhere behind her, then a twig snapping underfoot, too heavy for the kind of animals that lived in the woods and she was instantly petrified. Julius, or someone, was very near, possibly stalking her. She froze, not daring to turn around; she must not under any circumstances be discovered. In a panic, she turned and started to walk hurriedly towards the hedge where she could push through the trees and quickly climb over, then run down the track. She was afraid that her cloak would hamper her, but there was not time to take it off and put it in her rucksack, and in any case she could not risk being recognised so she would have no choice but to gather it up as she ran. By now her heart was thumping against her chest and her legs were trembling.

In the space of two minutes, more happened than she could ever have imagined. Her foot suddenly became caught in thick tendrils of ivy that crept across the ground by the ditch, and struggling, she realised she could not free herself. Glancing down she saw that her shoelace was tangled in rusty wire that was exposed through the leaves, part of the old fence that had previously ran along the hedge and had collapsed long before Julius bought the woods.

Without warning, close behind her, Julius bellowed, an indecipherable but violent shout and in a flash, he grabbed at her cloak. The blood was thumping in her ears; she could not, would not be exposed, not at any costs. She pushed her foot back and forth forcibly, and then from side to side in an attempt to free herself; she bent down to tug at the tangled lace and in that instant she felt Julius' hand upon her as he gripped her upper arm, clutching wildly at her cloak. Without thinking she picked up a thick branch that lay in the ditch and swung it blindly over her shoulder. Again, and again she swung it, with more strength than she knew she had. She felt it land on what she presumed was her father's head, what felt like blow after frenzied blow in the impending struggle, and he cried out in shock or in pain. The third blow must have knocked him unconscious; his heavy body fell to the ground with a dull thud.

Fabia did not stop to look. With one almighty wrench she pulled her foot free and wiping her nose on her sleeve, clambered over the hedge. On quaking legs, she ran into the dense conifers the other side of the track and sped down among them, not stopping until she reached the bottom of the plantation where she at last shook off her cloak and leaned forward to catch her breath. She knew that she had not been followed and that this meant Julius was probably still lying unconscious.

Fabia now felt an overwhelming sense of horror, of some terrible devastation that could not be undone. Should she go back and see if her father was alright? It occurred to her that she may have killed him, and she did not know what to do. She slumped down on the floor that was carpeted with pine needles and she began to cry, huge sobs between which she could not catch her breath. Her nose was running, mucous trickled down over her top lip into her mouth. She coughed violently and spat, fighting a strong urge to vomit, then she leaned over, retched and bought up a viscid white fluid.

'What on earth was she doing? Why was she still doing this? She was happy now, surely? She had a future with Sam to look forward to, why could she not leave her father to his hapless and miserable ways?' She resolved to stop this snooping once and for all, and began to pray to for forgiveness, for salvation.

After a while Fabia composed herself as well as she could and stood up. Her legs were still shaking but she wanted more than anything to be home. She began to cry again when it dawned on her that if Julius was still alive he might already have driven home, and he may be waiting for her, having realised it was she who had attacked him. Fabia could not face that possibility but neither could she bear the thought that he may be dead or seriously injured. She considered going back up to the woods to see if he was there or not, but she was worried that if he had regained consciousness, he might see her. Then she would have to somehow make it seem that by coincidence she was innocently there, as if she was just taking a walk. It occurred to her how terrible she must look and how much she was shaking, and she knew that she would not be able to feign a casual discourse nor act surprised if she found her father hurt. Yet she needed to know that he had recovered and that he was not maimed or worse. She remembered reading in a novel that a murderer always returns to the scene of the crime and again she started to shake and to sob. She wrung her hands and silently begged, 'Please, please dear God, please let him be okay, please, please, please let my father be alright.'

She sank down against a tree and her sobbing intensified and became loud. It had started to rain and as the dusk fell darkness had crept into the gloom of the forest, skulking between the dark trunks of the conifers like some hungry black beast that would eat her up if she did not leave. 'Let it come,' she thought, 'Let it come and kill me, after all I may have murdered my own father. Don't I deserve to be eaten alive?' Those thoughts raced wildly in her mind and her sobbing continued; she thought of Sam, and of Elisabeth, Babette and Caspian, of her friends and her job at the art gallery, of home, and though it seemed like a different world that she was now detached from, she knew that she desperately wanted to be there, for all to be normal.

She stood to her feet again and on trembling legs began to walk slowly and carefully to the edge of the plantation.

Out on the lane Fabia worked up a brisk pace, somewhere between running and walking, on the footpath through the fields in the half-light, until she reached the outskirts of the town. She took the quickest track, along the side of the bowling club, already lit with the orange glow of the streetlamps. In her preoccupation and her hurry to get away she had left her cloak thrust deep into a large clump of brambles and she now worried that whatever had happened to Julius, it was this that would give her away. She was sure that she would be arrested. She cursed and swore because she hadn't stuffed the cloak into her rucksack as she usually did; she had acted hastily out of fear, she had panicked and now her cloak would be found, forensically analysed and traced to her. She worried that Julius might have come round after a few minutes, recovered quickly and driven into town to tell the police that he had been assaulted. By now they would be in the woods, searching for shreds of evidence. They would extend their search into the undergrowth at the bottom of the plantation and there they would find her cloak; if they had sniffer dogs this would take no time at all. By the end of the night she would be arrested and locked up in a police cell. Her entire world, her future that had been so full of hope would lie in ruins.

She dwelt again upon what state her father might be in and was consumed by remorse and anguish. She felt that she was drowning, engulfed by wave after wave of compunction. She desperately wished this was not happening and she had a feeling of unreality, as if this was a dreadful nightmare from which she would soon awake. Over and over Fabia worried about whether Julius had recognised her or not; then in a more rational moment she consoled herself that it was unlikely because he had probably been drunk and would not have had his wits about him. That strange bloodcurdling yell, utterly indecipherable; yes, he must have been very drunk.

Reaching the drive at the side of the house, Fabia noticed in the light of the streetlamp that her shoes were very dirty. The right one that had been stuck in the hedge was much worse than the left; the loam of the woods clung to the sole and covered the upper. Clumps of pine needles, bits of leaves and small twigs stuck to it and had worked their way into the eyelets. She went quietly through the gate, meticulously lifting and closing the latch so it barely made a sound, then crept up onto the lawn by the hedge where there was just enough light from next door's bathroom window for her to see. She turned her foot to the side and pushed it back and forth through the long grass. She fumbled in her pocket, pulled out the remains of a used tissue and bent over to wipe the mud off the upper and the lace. Then Fabia went silently into the garage, removed both shoes and pushed them down behind the tent that was leant against the back wall. She stood shaking in the dark of the shed for almost ten minutes, taking deep breaths to try to calm herself. She wondered who would be in the house, whether she could creep in without being seen. She did not know what the time was but guessed that it was about half past eight which meant that Babette would be clearing away the dinner things and that Elisabeth would be in bed. Caspian, she knew was away on business in Devon, something to do with the plans for a harbourside development he was about to start work on. Fabia peered out of the garage window and saw that the kitchen light was on, so she decided to go in through the side door where she could quickly go straight up to her room without being noticed.

* * *

In her room, Fabia quickly stripped off her clothes and stuffed them into the laundry box in the corner. She felt the need for a shower or a bath, to wash her hair, as if the mere action of water running over her would have a cathartic effect, ridding her of the jumble of emotions that had taken hold of her; as if it would bring back a sense of reality or would magically make everything return to normal. She had a violent headache now and was shivering almost constantly, still fighting an irrepressible urge to vomit. She paced around her room and wrung her hands, recalling the horrific moments when the branch had struck Julius, the crack of the final hit and the dull thump as he fell to the floor. She cried again, not wanting any of it to be real, unable to believe what had happened. She felt as if she would die. Her anxiety was compounded when she thought again that Julius might be dead, that she had killed him, and of the insufferable consequences. She did not want to go to prison; her stomach turned over at the thought. She felt crippling pains across her abdomen, that her legs had turned to a jelly like substance and could not support her, so she threw herself down upon the bed and sobbed, distraught, into her pillow. "Please let him be alright, please, please, please dear Lord, please let him be alright, please forgive me," she whispered in her anguish.

That thought came back to her again: 'A murderer always returns to the scene of the crime.' But she would have to go back to retrieve her cloak and destroy it. She decided that she should go as soon as possible and proposed to do so after her

213

bath; she knew that she would find the darkness terrifying but she must do it and so she would take a torch and be brave. But what if the police were already there, what if they had already found her cloak?

An hour and ten minutes passed; Fabia was still sitting in the bath, clasping her knees to her chest, staring into nothingness. The water had gone cold and she had not noticed the rain lashing against the window, nor the wind whistling down the chimney of the bathroom fireplace. She got out of the bath and dried herself roughly, catching her reflection in the mirror; she looked dreadful, her eyes were swollen, beneath them dark shadows, and her nose was red. Her head ached and she felt a heaviness in her whole body; she felt terrible and was desperate enough to creep downstairs to find painkillers.

At the bottom of the stairs Fabia heard voices in the kitchen; Julius and Babette talking. "I don't know Babette, I'm not entirely sure. I shouldn't go wandering around in the dark," she heard her father say; "I must have walked into a branch or something. My eyesight's not what it was you know. I've done it before, I knocked my head on the doorway of my hut the other night and knocked myself clean out."

Fabia went falteringly into the kitchen. Although she was shaking, she was so relieved to hear Julius' voice, and especially to hear him say that he thought he had walked into a branch! That was all! That was what he thought! Of course! So, he had been drunk, so drunk he thought he walked into a branch! Oh, the release, the relief! And he was alright, he was here, at home in the kitchen, talking to Babette!

Julius was at the sink washing his hands. Babette had slipped on her shoes and gone out to the dustbin with the scraps.

Fabia cleared her throat and spoke, "Hi Dad, how are you? I

feel dreadful! I think I'm coming down with a cold, I've been in bed all afternoon." She pulled her dressing gown around her, felt in the pocket for a handkerchief and blew her nose.

"Oh dear, Fabia, you poor little thing," Julius half turned in the direction of the doorway where she stood. He did not look any worse for wear other than a small gash and a bruise above his left temple. Fabia's relief was magnified, to actually see him, to know that he was alright! Never in her life had she been so pleased to see someone standing at the kitchen sink washing their hands!

"Silly fool walked into a branch in the woods," said Babette coming back in with the washing up bowl now emptied of vegetable peelings. "Look at that cut on his head! Serves him right, messing about in the woods in the dark. It's not as if we need more logs, the shed is full of them. Really Julius, you should be more careful."

Fabia feigned sympathy, "Yes, you should Dad. You're too old to be messing about in the woods in the dark."

"Good grief Fabia, you look terrible!" exclaimed Babette, wiping her hands on her apron.

"I know! I feel terrible too! I was just telling Dad how I don't feel well. I think I've picked up a cold, I've had a thumping headache all afternoon. There's a lot of it about."

"An early night will do you good. I'm going to hit the sack early tonight; I've had far too many late nights lately and it's catching up with me. I've got dark circles under my eyes."

"Take some aspirin, that will make you feel better," Julius lightly touched Fabia's arm as he passed her in the doorway and went through the hall to his sitting room. She did not turn to look at the gash on the side of his head because if she did, he would have seen that she was about to cry.

* * *

Although the branch had rendered Julius unconscious he had not been knocked out for long. When he came round, he was surprised to find that he was lying on his back at the top of the woods, beneath a low cover of blackthorn. He wondered how he got there and as his senses returned, he had a vague, almost dream-like impression of the figure that he saw in the woods, of the phantom, and of him pursuing it into the thicket. He sat up and brushed the leaves and dirt from his coat, trying to piece together what had happened but his recollection was flimsy. As he stood up, he realised his head was throbbing above his left eye and putting his fingers up to it, felt a sticky wetness. The blood on his fingertips confirmed what he thought: he had hit, or rather something, had hit his head. He was perplexed and tried desperately to remember what had happened, but still nothing came. Looking around, he noticed a low hanging branch that had snapped, and on the floor near to it was the part that had broken off. This offered a rational explanation for the state he found himself in, so he pushed the cloaked figure to the back of his mind; another dream or a figment of his drunken imagination. He concluded that he must have walked into the branch and knocked himself out; it was the only plausible explanation. He acknowledged that he had been inebriate and could not be sure if the headache that he felt was due to the injury to his head or to the amount of alcohol he had consumed in the hut that afternoon, possibly both. He couldn't think what he had been doing up in this part of the woods but dismissed it as drunken wanderings, like the time he had woken up by the wire fence at the bottom of the slope, with his head almost in the stream.

* * *

"Caspian, I've just brought Friday's meeting forward to this afternoon, three o'clock. The Americans are on their way back from the coast, they're very excited about the development and rang to ask if we could see them earlier. I said we were all okay with that so if you have anything in your diary could you please ask Rachel to re-arrange it? And tell her to block out the rest of this week – we're going to be very busy. When you've finished your lunch can you come to the meeting room? We need to check the plans and get everything straight before they get here."

Ed Tomkins looked a little flustered standing in the doorway of Caspian's office, shirt sleeves rolled up, his tie loose below his unbuttoned collar.

"No problem Ed. I have an appointment at Jane Darling Farm at four, but I'll get that rescheduled. Give me fifteen minutes and I'll see you in the meeting room."

Caspian finished the ham and salad baguette that Babette had made for him that morning, then he stood up, stretched, and walked over to the window. Autumn hung over the landscape like a blanket draped over summer fruit canes. The trees were now turning colour, myriad shades of red, brown and gold, and leaves were starting to fall in the woods at the edge of the field. The weather had turned noticeably chilly in the last week or so and at home they had already set the central heating to come on and warm the house in the evenings.

A sudden movement caught Caspian's eye; last week a camper van had turned up on the track that led to the forest behind the field. A dingy, faded yellow-green, noticeably rusting even from a distance, it had been parked just under the trees and those who had noticed it did not know if it had been abandoned or if someone had taken up temporary residence there, though no occupants had been sighted; until now. The side door slid open and a man stepped out, dressed in jeans and a green jacket; his dark hair was quite long, down to his shoulders. Other than that, he was too far away for Caspian to be able to work out any discernible features, or even to tell how old he was, though if the vehicle and his attire were anything to go on, he was quite young. Caspian watched as he shook out a red and yellow patterned blanket, momentarily disappeared back in the van with it, and then climbed out again, pulling the door to. Zipping up his jacket, he strode off along the track towards the business park, a determined and slightly arrogant swagger.

Caspian checked his watch; nineteen minutes past one. He called Rachel and asked her to ring the Sweetings and reschedule his appointment with them, then he picked up a thick blue file from his desk and hurried off to the meeting room. An hour and a half to prepare for the conference with the Americans, very important clients. Caspian knew that working on a project as big as the harbourside development could make a huge difference to a small firm like Tompkins and Parker.

18

Luke

The fairground was ablaze with colour, light and sound, a phantasmagoria in the chilly early October night. The shrieks and screams melted into laughter, the constant chugging of motors and generators in the background. Aromas of hot dogs, chips and candy floss tantalised nostrils as the merry throng wandered past dodgems, roundabouts, the ghost train, waltzers and the Ferris wheel. Music blared out from every side stall, from every ride; a group of young girls in skin-tight jeans and leather jackets sang along, clapping their hands and swaying to the beat of a rockabilly hit, hips swinging. Children jumped excitedly up and down, tugging at parents' sleeves, pleading with mothers and fathers for candy canes, toffee apples, a go on this, a go on that.

The field had been wholly transformed; it was usually only that – a field, vast and green, behind a small estate of local authority housing, where people came to walk their dogs, to push sleepy toddlers in buggies and babies in prams, along the tarmacked paths. Children played there after school and in the holidays, rode bikes around before going home for tea or before the dusk descended and youths hung about, chewing gum, smoking cigarettes, chiding one another, canoodling.

"Babette! Caspian!" Emma called in her high-pitched voice, and came rushing towards them, with Daniel behind her, just about keeping up. She was wearing a very big and furry ushanka hat with ear flaps that hung down to her shoulders and made her look like an exiled Russian princess. In her usual effusive manner, she kissed both Babette and Caspian on each cheek in turn, "I'm looking for Will, he's here with the twins, have you seen them? We were supposed to be here half an hour ago, but someone forgot to put the rabbit away!" She looked down at her son accusingly, eyebrows raised.

"Oh Daniel, did you forget about Big Ears because you were excited about coming to the fair? It's easy to forget about things when you're in a hurry to go out but it's a good job you remembered. He'll be snug and warm in his little house now," Babette said looking down at Daniel, diffusing his embarrassment.

"We've only just got here," she explained, turning her attention to Emma. "We haven't seen anyone we know yet, only you two."

"Hello Elisabeth! How are you? I like your hat! It really suits you!" Emma gushed. "Are you coming to the party on Saturday? I hope so! Daniel's Granny is making a birthday cake, chocolate of course because it's his favourite, and we have a magician coming, so we're going to have a lot of fun! Maybe he'll produce Big Ears out of a big top hat – imagine that! You are coming, aren't you?" She bent down and said quietly to Elisabeth, "Make sure you bring Mummy and Daddy, won't you because the grown-ups are invited too."

Elisabeth smiled and nodded shyly. Babette looked sideways at Caspian and raised her eyebrows. 'Mummy and Daddy,' she thought, 'No-one seems to know any different!'

"Ah, there they are! Come on Daniel, we'd better go and join them. See you all Saturday!" and Emma merged into the crowd, heading towards her husband and sons who were queueing to buy toffee apples.

"Please can I hook a duck?" Elisabeth asked her mother.

"That's a good idea! Let's see if we can catch a duck! We can all have a go, and then maybe we'll get three ducks and extra candy floss! Come on!" Babette slipped her arm through Caspian's and off they went, into the hustle and bustle to the hook-a-duck stall, bright lights glaring, music bellowing.

Caspian stooped behind Elisabeth at the front of the stall, holding her little wrists and guiding her aim as she concentrated. Her narrowed eyes focused on the tiny hook suspended above the plastic ducks as they bobbed up and down in the water on the carousel, a multitude of yellow ducks with bright orange beaks, dancing along, up-and-down, slowly turning round and round. Caspian's aim was perfectly judged. Beyond the stall the colours were a blur, the sounds a cacophony; the food smells hung like smoke in the air.

"We've got one!" squealed Elisabeth, "We've got one!" Babette cheered enthusiastically; it was as if they'd won a million pounds. Caspian stood up straight; "Now let's choose your prize!" he said, and he lifted Elisabeth up so that she could see the array of toys displayed around the stall, hanging from the awning and from the central pillar. Disinterest registered on the young woman's face behind the stall as she waited and chewed gum, a money belt strapped around her thin hips, fishing rods gripped in her hand. She managed a thin smile as she gave Elisabeth the prize she'd chosen; a garish bright pink rabbit wearing a blue and white polka dot dress with a small lace collar, a slightly crochety expression on its face from brown plastic eyes that had been stuck on too close together. Elisabeth grabbed it and squealed, hugging it to her.

Neither of them had noticed that on the other side of the stall a man had been watching them and he now followed them as they turned away into the crowd. He was unkempt, with a short beard, his longish hair tied back, a ring through his eyebrow, more in his ears, dark shadows beneath his eyes. He walked with a swagger that was cocksure and almost aggressive, hands in the pockets of his denim jacket, frayed at the collar, a dark stain on the shoulder. Although he kept a measured distance, he trailed them with purpose, pushing past the people who hindered his progress, never taking his eyes off his prey, his gaze fixed most intently, determinedly on Babette.

By the dodgems they met Fabia and Polly, where they stood with a small group of friends. "Hiya Elisabeth!" Fabia shouted over the music; they were standing beneath one of the speakers where it was almost impossible to hear. "I like your rabbit! Where did you get it? Did you win it hooking a duck?" Elisabeth nodded, holding up the rabbit for Fabia to see.

"Lovely, isn't it!" Babette winked.

"Want a go on the bumper cars?" Fabia asked Elisabeth. "Is that alright?" she checked with Babette, already counting the coins in her hand. "Of course!" Babette nodded and Fabia took Elisabeth by the hand and led her towards the cars as people clambered out. "Green or blue?" Fabia pondered aloud, and Elisabeth skipped towards a blue dodgem, silver and red stripes glittering along each side and over the bonnet like ribbons.

Babette stood close to Caspian while she watched her daughter. She smiled at her happy round face, looking up at Fabia as she steered the car around, this way, that way, the two of them chatting all the while. Despite her coat and scarf Babette felt the cold creeping into her bones and she shivered, stamping her feet to keep them warm. She glanced over her shoulder, "I'm just going to get candy floss for Elisabeth, I'll be back in a minute." She looked up at Caspian and he nodded in return.

The sweet stall was right opposite the dodgems; a board hung from the red and white awning, displaying the prices of candy floss, toffee apples, bags of multi-coloured sweets and sticks of rock. Standing in the short queue she felt a hand on her shoulder.

"Babette! Fancy seeing you here darling!" The voice was gruff and sneering; Babette recognised it at once and she froze in surprise. Alarm spread over her face as she half turned, unable to speak.

"I thought it was you. Well, well, well, you've changed, haven't you? Look at you all done up with your fancy coat on. I saw you snuggling up to your brother or your cousin, whatever he is, with my daughter. Playing happy families, are we?"

Neither of them had noticed Luke watching them as Elisabeth tried to hook a duck, they had not seen nor even sensed him following them through the stream of people going in all directions about the fair.

"Cat got your tongue, darling? Where have you been these last few years then? I've been looking for you. I guessed you'd come running back to this dump, can't quite make it on your own, can you? Don't worry, I don't want you back, nothing like that, but the thing is you owe me money, and well, let's just say I'm a bit down on my luck at the moment and I could

223

do with it."

"I don't owe you anything you liar! Leave me alone, just fuck off! I don't want to talk to you or see you," Babette was trembling. She was angry but also felt intimidated at this very unwelcome intrusion, like some huge monster had reared up to confront her from a past that she had shut away and moved on from, a past that she did not want to remember.

"What's the matter babe? We need to have a little chat, you and me," Luke moved closer to her, blocking her path. "Get out of my way! Leave me alone," Babette hissed. She tried to move around him, to the side, but she was not quick enough, and he grabbed at her arm as she stepped away.

"Let go of me, let go! Fuck off Luke, leave me alone!" shouted Babette at the very moment that Caspian turned round. Without hesitation he jumped down from the platform around the dodgems and rushed to Babette's aid, "What's going on? Who the hell are you?" He glared angrily at Luke and in that moment he recognised him; this was the man who was camping out at the edge of the field in the green camper van, there was no mistaking him.

Luke snapped aggressively at Caspian, "Keep out of it mate, me and Babette have got some talking to do, she owes me money, but she's going to sort that out. Leave it, it's got nothing to do with you."

Luke still had a firm hold on Babette's arm and try as she might she could not shake him off. "Get off!" she yelled again.

"Well she doesn't want to talk to you, does she? So you'd better let her go," Caspian put out his arm to push Luke away.

"Oh yeah? Or what? What are you gonna do about it four-eyes?"

Caspian was not expecting the blow that Luke then threw

at him, a strong swipe that caught him on the side of his face, knocking his glasses askew; but Luke had let go of Babette and she rushed to Caspian's side as he returned a well-aimed punch to Luke's ear.

"Caspian! Stop it! Don't lower yourself, come away!"

The commotion had quickly drawn attention from onlookers. Two well-built middle-aged men stepped in and swiftly pulled Luke away to the side of the stall. Caspian was shaken, he rubbed his face as Babette steered him away, and then she suddenly stopped, put her arms around him and buried her head against the collar of his coat, quaking with a mixture of emotions; shock, fear, embarrassment, and amongst it all, with pride.

She held on to his arm as they walked back to the dodgems where Fabia and Elisabeth were just climbing out of the car. Elisabeth ran to them, "Mummy, that was brilliant! Fabia's such a good driver!" Then she slipped and went crashing to the floor; Caspian dashed forward and picked her up. She put her little head against his shoulder and bawled.

"It's alright darling, you haven't broken anything, let me kiss you better," Babette looked distraught as Caspian, still holding Elisabeth, put his arm around her shoulder.

"Come on," he said gently, "I think we've all had enough for tonight. It's time we went home."

* * *

The incident at the fairground had made Babette angry and was exactly the type of situation that she would later dwell upon. Predictably the questions, the irrational thoughts spilled out, at times an endless stream of what-if-that and what-if-this and why is he here? What does he want? Then it would subside, and she would become pensive and distracted, only for it to pour forth again, a babble of illogical and absurd conjecturing.

Caspian told Babette how Luke had taken up residence in the van at the edge of the plantation a couple of weeks ago. She immediately became suspicious and fearful, saying that he had been watching her and that she must not let Elisabeth out of her sight for a moment, that he had come here to find her for some reason and though he said she owed him money that could not be it, because she owed him nothing. One night her thoughts span out of control and she became obsessed with the thought that he had come here to take Elisabeth from her. At other times she said that he wasn't even remotely interested in his daughter and that for some reason, it was herself he was after.

"I think we should tell the police," she said a few nights later, "at least then they'll have it on record and if he tries anything else, they can arrest him. Surely that's the right thing to do?"

"But he hasn't been to the house or anything. He hasn't called or followed you to work or anything, and he hasn't been hanging around the school," Caspian was quick to point this out, hoping it would reassure her.

"Imagine that! Imagine him turning up at school! That would be so embarrassing! I don't want anyone to know that he's Elisabeth's father. They all think you're her father, I don't want anyone to know that her real father is a waster!"

"I think he'll clear off now, I really do," surmised Caspian. "He was probably trying it on about the money. I think he just came here out of curiosity; it's possible he did want to see Elisabeth, but he wanted to see you too. He's probably on his own and he might even have thought there was a chance of a reconciliation, although he should know that would be ridiculous. From the things he said to you he must have seen straightaway that you're not like him anymore, that you've grown up and moved on, and so he'll go away now, and you probably won't hear from him again."

"He'd better do. I've always dreaded him coming back into my life. I really hope he'll go away and stay away for good. But he says I owe him money and I know what he's like about money, he'll keep on until he's got what he wants. I don't owe him a penny though, honestly, I don't. How could I? He never had any money, he had nothing."

"Well look darling, if that's what he really wants I'll give him money. I'll give him money to bugger off and leave you alone. I'll pay him whatever he wants to get out of your life, I mean it."

"No, you won't Caspian! I won't allow it, never! But thank you for offering, I know you mean it and you would do it, but I won't let you. If he does show his ugly head again, if we hear another word from him, then we'll tell the police, is that agreed?"

"Okay. I think that's fair. If he bothers you again, or if he goes to the school causing trouble, anything like that, then yes, we will tell the police. It would be the right thing to do then. That would be harassment."

Babette wrapped her arms tight around him and with an audible sigh she laid her head on his chest, "You are so lovely Caspian, I don't know what I'd do without you sometimes. I love you so much."

"And I love you too, you know that."

* * *

Eight days later, all was well again. There had been no word or sight of Luke and as Caspian predicted, the old green camper van at the edge of the field had gone, leaving no trace other than a few bags of rubbish which the foxes scavenged and the farmer cleared away after a couple of days. Babette's anxiety had dissipated, and she was again her usual effervescent self.

Caspian was sitting at his desk one afternoon, working on the amended planning application for Jane Darling Farm. The telephone rang and he leaned across to pick it up. "Private call for you," whispered Rachel, "I think it's one of the Americans."

"Okay, put him through, thanks Rachel."

"Good afternoon, Caspian! It's Jared Cole, how are you today?"

"Very well, thank you Mr Cole. This is a surprise! I hope it's nothing serious. What can I do for you?"

"Well, actually, I guess it is serious Caspian, or at least we think so. I'll cut to the chase, shall I? I have a proposition for you, but I'd appreciate it if you didn't mention it to the partners, keep it to ourselves if you don't mind."

"Right...What is it?"

"Well, we were having a chat yesterday, me and John, and we'd like to put something to you. Let's not make any bones about it, we'd like you in charge of the harbourside plans. We were very impressed with what you've put together and we want you to be chief architect for the entire development, to oversee things for us as we're not going to be over there much for the first phase. I appreciate it's a little underhand to speak to you direct like this; we certainly wouldn't want to cause any bad feeling between you and the partners, but like I said, we were very impressed and we think you're too good to slip

228

through our hands. We recognise talent when we see it."

"Wow! Well! I don't know what to say. I'm very flattered of course – thank you. Yes, thank you. I think it might be best if you discussed this with the others though. Would a written proposal be a good idea, something we could all talk about?"

"I don't think it would work like that Caspian. I think Ed Tompkins wants to take control of this, he wants to be in charge, but you're the one who came up with the plans, and you're the one we want working on it. We love your ideas, you're younger than the others, more forward thinking and we need that. We want to set a model with this development because we've got similar projects in the bag and we need someone like you to take it forward, someone young and dynamic. If you're in agreement with this then our next step is to tell the partners we want you in charge; they don't need to know we've already spoken about it. You see, if I went to them first not knowing if you were interested or not it could damage relations, but I'm confident that if you're happy to take charge we can find the right way to put it to them."

This had all come as a shock to Caspian and he was to some extent lost for words, "I see. Thank you, Mr Cole, like I said, I'm incredibly flattered. I'd love to take the reins of course, but I need to think about it, I'm not really sure how comfortable I'd be with this. I have to think of the partners as they're my bosses, and there's a lot for me to consider. I'd hate to put Ed's nose out of joint."

"Of course, of course, I understand. We don't need an answer for a couple of weeks so why don't you chew it over? You can call me anytime if there's anything you're not sure about, we can talk further. There's something else I'd like to ask you whilst I'm on the phone. We were wondering Caspian, if when the harbourside is finished, if you'd like to come and join us. I can offer you a job as senior architect, you'll have six juniors, a full-time secretary, and I can promise you a very good remuneration. Plus, we have some beautiful apartments not too far from our office."

"To join you? You mean..?"

"Yes, I mean join us, come and work here. To up sticks and move to the states, come over the other side of the pond. I don't know how that sits with you, you probably have a wife or partner to consider, maybe children as well, but I can assure you it's a very serious offer."

"I don't know what to say! I do have people to consider and I'll need to talk to them, but I'm not dismissing it. It's a fantastic offer and such a huge compliment, thank you. I'm delighted that you like the plans and well... this is all a bit of a shock to me, a very nice one, but a shock all the same. Excuse me if I'm not making much sense, it's just that I really don't know what to say!"

"I understand Caspian. Like I said, have a good think about it, talk to whoever you need to. But the two aren't dependent on one another in any way, we'd be mighty pleased if you can take the harbourside project and we'd be over the moon if you want to come and join us but it's not a question of all or nothing, I want you to understand that."

"Absolutely, thank you Mr Cole. There's a lot for me to think about but I'd certainly like to give it all some serious thought. I don't mean to sound rude in any way, but can you bear with me for a few weeks?"

"Of course, Caspian. We're not back in the UK until early December so let's meet up and have a private chat then. I'm happy to leave it till then, something this important can wait,

I appreciate that."

"Thank you, Mr Cole, I appreciate it too, thank you. We'll speak again in December."

"It's my pleasure Caspian, I'll look forward to hearing from you, but don't forget, you can call me anytime if there's anything you want to know. Oh, and one other thing."

"What's that?"

"It's Jared. Please call me Jared."

"Thank you, Jared. Goodbye."

19

Caspian and Babette

Fabia was travelling back from Cornwall, coming home from a weekend spent with Polly in her student digs. It was a dull afternoon in early November, the light fading fast as the train sped along the estuary. Now and then she caught sight of her reflection in the window as she strained her eyes to see outside; a young boy walking along a raised causeway, lifting his hand to a gull as it flew low over his head; the ebb tide exposing the mud flats, rocks usually unseen projecting above the surface, a twisted piece of metal, driftwood, the carcass of an old boat. Towering cliffs of red sandstone stood as if on sentry, woodland rose protectively behind them, and then the railway cutting. It was a strange coastal landscape that seemed almost alien as it was left behind by the rolling hills and wooded valleys that stretched out to meet the endless grey sky. Fabia turned momentarily into the fuggy warmth and security of the carriage, the quiet voices of passengers chatting, people on their own absorbed in a book, a newspaper, or in their thoughts.

Autumn was absolutely everywhere, spread out over the valley like a quilt of brown and gold, yellow and red. It crept softly through the trees that lined the side of the main road back down to the town; it hung limply from the branches and scattered at the foot of the hedgerows and across the lanes. A mist hung like a dense hoary curtain on the hills, slowly unfurling down across the fields to where the hedge, thick with drizzle, muffled the sounds of traffic and farm dogs barking, cattle lowing, and sheep bleating at the edge of the woods.

It had been a good weekend. Fabia had enjoyed telling Polly all about Sam and their plans. She hadn't felt so excited about anything since she was a child and she was happy to declare that she was floating on the proverbial cloud nine.

"What happened with Ben?" Polly asked.

"Nothing really. He asked me out for dinner when I got back from France, but I made an excuse and said I couldn't make it and it was left at that. When he went back, he said I was welcome to stay with him if I fancied a weekend in London, but I didn't say much. I didn't have the heart to tell him I'd met someone else."

"But you liked him. You must have felt a bit torn between the two of them, surely?"

"Not at all! I forgot all about Ben the minute I met Sam. Did I tell you about the first time I saw him? He was working in the fruit garden at the back of the house and I couldn't even see his face, but he fascinated me even then. It's like I was captivated right from that moment. I kept wandering around the garden hoping I'd bump into him that morning, I couldn't wait 'til lunch time to meet him. There's something incredibly special about him Polly, he's completely blown my mind. I don't mind admitting I'm well and truly hooked!"

"What does your Dad think?"

"I haven't mentioned it to him. What's the point? He's not interested in anything I do! He's only interested in himself." She paused and took a sip of coffee, "I've told the others though and they're really pleased for me, they're looking forward to meeting him. Oh my God, do you know about those two? I haven't told you, have I?"

"Who?" Polly's eyes widened.

"Caspian and Babette! They're an item!"

"No! That's weird, isn't it? Is that legal? Aren't they related?"

"No, they're not, not really; she's not our real cousin, my uncle wasn't her biological father, he was her stepfather."

"But it's like she's your sister - and Caspian's sister. She's lived with you for so long, I've always thought of her as your big sister. Or maybe as a cousin, I don't know. Now that I think about it, I'm not sure what I thought, or what I think, but you know, she's just always been there, part of your family."

"I know what you mean, but she isn't really related to us at all. There are no blood ties, so I guess it's alright for them to get together."

"I can't help thinking it's weird. You must admit, it does seem a little incestuous, I'm sure that's how everyone else would see it."

"That's what I thought at first, I must admit. It was quite a shock, but the more I thought about it the more I thought they aren't really doing anything wrong. In a way, it was inevitable; they've always been close and they're like a little family, them and Elisabeth, they have been for ages. They all go out together and they both take her to school and that. I don't think they care what anyone else thinks, but everyone assumes they're a couple anyway, and now they definitely are."

"Do they share a bedroom now then? That would be really odd! I wonder what your Dad thinks."

"I doubt if he's even noticed, he's usually too drunk these days, for a start. They still have their own rooms, I don't suppose they can share yet because Elisabeth often goes in with Babette if she wakes up during the night. They probably don't want to confuse her." Fabia thought to herself for a moment and then said, "It would definitely seem odd if they suddenly started sharing a room!"

"Surely Elisabeth's a bit confused anyway? If everyone thinks he's her father, she must think that too? You know, kind of assume it, and she must realise that her friends' parents share a room when she goes to their houses."

"I don't know. As far as I'm aware she's never said anything or asked any questions about that sort of thing. She's always called us all by our Christian names, except Babette - she calls her Mummy, of course. The main thing is she's very loved. Let's face it Polly, we're not the average family, are we? I bet most people think we're a strange lot!"

"Well, you're certainly not conventional but I like the way you lot are, it's so relaxed. I used to wish my family were more like yours, until your Mum left. It all changed then, and I felt really sorry for you."

"Well, we get on much better these days and I'll be seeing a lot more of her now that Sam and I are together. I expect we'll spend most of our holidays in France." Fabia glanced at her watch, "Hey, come on, we'd better get ready, we'll be late for the party if we don't get a move on. I've got to do my hair and put make-up on."

* * *

"To me this doesn't feel wrong in any way," Caspian stated quietly and calmly. He was propped up on one elbow, on his side, next to Babette who was lying on her back on his bed. He was in that moment completely besotted by her and he thought her the most beautiful woman on earth; how gorgeous her thick dark hair falling about the pillow, how defined her bone structure, and how strikingly green her eyes!

"It isn't really, is it?" she replied. "We keep reminding ourselves that we're not actually related by blood, and that's completely true. It's a fact. We've grown up together, yes, but that doesn't make us brother and sister. We're not even cousins. I just keep thinking how can it be wrong when it feels so right. That's the thing Casp, it really does feel right, but I don't know what we're going to do, what we're going to say, or how we're going to face everyone as a proper couple."

Caspian sighed, "I can't help thinking that we spend too much time worrying about what other people will think. All we really need to worry about is what the people closest to us will think. Fabia knows, so it's just Dad, Elisabeth and Mum to think about. Other than that, most people assume we're an item anyway, so what are we fretting about? In any case, I'm not throwing this away just because it might seem wrong in anyone else's eyes. I don't care what they think."

"Me neither!" Babette ruffled her hair and sat up, pulling her knees to her chest and clasping her hands around them. "It's quite right what you say, about most people already seeing us as a couple, and anyway, it's no-one else's business. So you're right, it's our family we're worrying about. I'm dreading telling Julius though. How do you think he'll take it? I have a feeling he won't be very happy about it, I'm sure he'll say we're perverted or something. I know we're going round and round in circles, but it's not incestuous, is it Casp? It can't be, not at all, we aren't related by blood, so it isn't. We're not doing anything wrong. There you are, you see, the same old ground, we talk and talk, and it always comes back to the same thing."

She stopped talking, sank her face in her hands and sighed, "We have to tell Julius, we have to tell him soon before he notices. I know we shouldn't really be afraid of his reaction because like we keep saying, we're not doing anything wrong, but it's still difficult."

"Yes," Caspian agreed, "we should tell him. Why don't we do it tonight when he comes home? He won't stay in the woods tonight, it's too cold now. He'll be home later so we can tell him together, after dinner."

Caspian's thoughts, however, were suddenly crashing about in his head. Despite what he said, like Babette, he couldn't help fretting about how his father would react. Fabia wouldn't be a problem; she had obviously noticed that he and Babette had grown closer in recent months and the flyaway comment she made when they dropped her off at the station proved that. "Have a good weekend, love birds," she'd said, and she smiled as she got on the train, turning to blow them a kiss. She was younger and more liberal minded, and it was like an acceptance, the way she said that, like she was giving her seal of approval. Or maybe she was so wrapped up in her new boyfriend that she just wanted everyone to be as ecstatically happy as she was, typical Fabia with her airy-fairy ways.

Since that night under the arbour at the top of the garden their relationship had taken a new tact and it was not easy to hide the truth. Their actions that spoke far more than words; those small gestures – a sympathetic, grateful, or even mocking pat on the shoulder, a certain intensity when they spoke, a gaze held for longer than an instant, that's what was becoming hard to conceal. One morning as Caspian was leaving for work Babette had run on her bare feet to the hall with the lunchbox he'd almost forgotten, and as she handed it to him, she stood on tiptoe and kissed him lightly on the lips, just as Fabia had come down the stairs. She couldn't have missed it, and though they worried about it what they didn't know was that to Fabia it merely confirmed what she'd suspected for a while; that her brother and Babette had become lovers.

And what about Elisabeth? Would it make much difference to her? Probably not, and besides, there wasn't really anything to explain to her, although she might notice displays of affection and inevitably, there would come a time when they would share a bedroom. She might ask questions then, but that was a bridge that would be crossed when it came to it. Caspian was sure that Elisabeth saw him as her father; for his part, he loved her beyond measure and he naturally acted in a fatherly way to her. He gave her a great deal of attention, he played with her and took her out sometimes, just the two of them, holding her hand as she skipped along beside him, chattering to him about her school day, what she'd seen on the television, or what Marsha was doing. He and Babette often took her out together, to the wildlife park, the beach, the cinema; the three of them went to the supermarket together to buy groceries. That's how it had been since he came back from university, without deliberation or discussion it was a step they quite naturally fell into, and it worked; they were all three of them content.

Could he put a name to his relationship with Elisabeth? What was she to him really – a much younger sister? A niece? Or did he not give it a name and just take it for granted, a given closeness that would not alter much when he became her stepfather? He did not foresee any huge change in himself nor within the dynamics of their relationship. He had always felt very protective over Elisabeth and he knew that he would always care for her, that he would guide her and continue to protect her as she grew up. He would cherish her as his daughter, and if anything should happen to Babette, he would without hesitation take full responsibility for Elisabeth.

* * *

That night it was as if the thoughts had been taken out of their heads and swapped around. Caspian was now calm and sure of his feelings. He was concentrating on re-arranging the contents of the oak cupboard behind the sofa. Babette had lost the confidence she had found that afternoon and had been thinking of nothing else for the past hour. The same thoughts churned round and round in her head, the same questions over and over, and still she could not come to any final conclusion.

She was sitting in the leather chair in the sitting room, absentmindedly picking at the skin around her thumb nails, a habit she had when she was worried or tired. She was brooding and suddenly questioned out loud, "What will people think Caspian? Honestly, what will people think?"

Caspian stood up, looked at her and sighed, "Babette, we talked about this earlier. I thought you had it all straightened out? You seemed so sure about things this afternoon. It doesn't matter what anyone thinks. You know that I love you deeply and that I have no intention of being without you. I really don't care what anyone else thinks and that is final. As far as I'm concerned, this is it, this is my life. My future is with you and Elisabeth. You have to accept once and for all that what others think can't be our concern."

He went to the window and looked out, hands in pockets, "I'll tell you what we'll do. We'll move away, where no one knows us. It'll be better that way, we'll find somewhere to live, and another school for Elisabeth. We can both get jobs easy enough. Trust me darling, it will all work out. I think it could be the answer."

His reassurance only made Babette tearful. She wanted to believe him, to believe it could all be that simple, but still she agonised.

Caspian turned to face her, "Look, I've been meaning to tell you something. I just needed to find the right time because it's such a big thing."

Babette faltered and sat up straight, "What is it?"

"I've kind of been offered another job. Well, not kind of, I have. But there are two parts to it. You know this big project I'm involved in at work, with the Americans?" Babette nodded, wondering where this was leading.

"They've offered me two things. One is that they want me to oversee the work, the whole project, and the other is that when it's finished they'd like me to work for them permanently. To go and join their company."

"But that's in America!"

"Exactly. It's a lot to think about, I know. But think about it, Babette; it could be just what we need. The money would be really good, it would be a new start for us, and there's even an apartment we could live in near the office."

"What did you say? Did you accept? The job, I mean. It's

great that they want you to be in charge of the project, but did you say you'd take the job when it's finished?"

"No, I told them I wanted to think about it, that I needed to talk it over with you. They're okay with that, they weren't expecting an immediate answer anyway, they appreciate it's a huge decision. They're coming over again early next month and they want to talk about it then. I think we should seriously consider it, Babette, I really do. We should have a proper talk about it. Not now though, we've talked enough today, we should talk about it when our heads are clear. It could be the perfect solution for us."

"I don't know what to say! You've sprung that one on me, good and proper! Moving away yes, it's a great idea – but to America?"

"I know, it's a lot to think about. That's why we'll talk about it another time, when we're both in the right frame of mind."

Babette was quiet for a few moments, "We said we'd tell Julius tonight, that's what's bothering me. I'm so worried about how he'll take it. How do you think he'll react?"

Caspian laughed out loud, "I was thinking about that when you were cooking dinner and the conclusion I came to was that he'll be completely indifferent. Think about it, Babette, since when did Julius ever react to anything? You could take the shirt off his back in the middle of the High Street on a Saturday morning and he'd just shrug and walk home half naked. He never reacts to anything, does he? You know that! When can you ever remember him getting excited or angry about anything?"

"But this is different Caspian. I'm effectively your cousin, we've spent the last fifteen years living like brother and sister. He won't be happy about it at all, he'll say it's wrong, I'm sure he will."

Caspian went to the chair and knelt down next to Babette. He took both her hands in his and thought for a moment before he spoke again, "Babette, we seem to be going over the same ground again. We're not cousins, for God's sake! We have no blood ties; we're not related at all. Yes, we've both lived in this house for years, we've grown up together here, but it makes no difference. I said the other night that even before I went to university the way I felt about you was different to how I saw Fabia. Fabia IS my sister; it didn't feel anything like that with you. I've been in love with you for years Babette, I just didn't realise it until recently. And don't forget you weren't here a lot of the time - you moved out when you were sixteen, I went away to university, we barely saw one another for a few years. It changed the way we'd lived before. That gap, that was when we grew up and that distance made my feelings for you stronger, I've told you that before." He looked at her intensely and then kissed her hand, "I knew that what I felt for you was very deep, more than the sort of fondness I'd feel for a cousin. I didn't want to admit it then because like you I thought it wasn't right and I was worried about how everyone would react if I told them, but I don't care now. When you came back it didn't even matter that you had a baby. Do you remember I wasn't here the night you came back but when I came home I knew the minute I walked in and saw you sat in the kitchen that I loved you more than anything, it was like it jumped up and hit me in the face. I was so happy that you'd come back, but I thought it best not to show those feelings, and I certainly didn't think you'd ever feel the same. How I've kept my feelings hidden these last few years I really don't know."

"Caspian, you're making me cry!" Babette put her arms

around his neck and kissed his face, "You're right, I know you are, it's always been there, hasn't it? It took me a long time to work out how I felt about you, but I kept thinking about you and then I thought that I was in love with you and had been for a while, but I felt I had to fight it. When I was in the cottage on the farm with Luke I used to get so frustrated with his ways, I used to watch him, and I used to wonder how you would behave in that situation. I used to wish he was you sometimes. I thought about you so much, I dreamed about you, I even wrote a letter to you, asking you to come and stay, but I didn't post it. I was trying to make things right with Luke and it wasn't working. He wasn't what I wanted, and I just longed to come back here to you, to lovely reliable old you. Even though I knew you couldn't be my boyfriend, I just wanted to be here with you. I love you so much Caspian, no way in the world is this wrong!"

"It isn't wrong, of course it's not. How many times do I have to tell you? We've said it enough, but I'll say it again: we are not blood related. It isn't illegal. We are not doing anything wrong," he held her face in his hands and wiped a few tears that had fallen from her eyes as he studied her intently; those eyes, how he loved them! "Don't cry. I don't like seeing you upset. We should be happy that this has finally all come out. Please don't worry what others will think."

Babette took a deep breath, "Okay. You know what they say - true love conquers all."

* * *

Julius did not come home until very late that night. He had cooked himself a supper of edible boletus and penny bun in the frying pan over the campfire and had then drank several bottles of beer and half a small bottle of whiskey, before falling asleep in the hut. When he awoke it was pitch dark in the woods and tawny owls were calling, staking out their territories. A light breeze sifted through the nearly bare branches, drying leaves rustled as mice scuttled about among them and foxes moved through the bracken looking for food. Julius packed up by torchlight and stumbled down along the path to his car, then drove slowly home under a night sky lit only by a waning moon.

Babette and Caspian had waited up for him and had just begun to think he would not be returning until the morning when they heard his car pull up into the drive. They had spent the last hour discussing exactly what they were going to say to him, and how they would say it. Although they were both nervous of his reaction, they had agreed that it could not make any difference; they would still be together regardless.

They waited in Caspian's bedroom a while, whispering as they listened to him moving about downstairs, opening cupboards in the kitchen, clattering plates. A chair scraped on the kitchen floor, silence followed and then the door of his sitting room banged shut.

By the time they had composed themselves and gone down-stairs Julius was drifting off to sleep in the armchair with only the soft light of the table lamp casting shadows across the walls and floor. Caspian coughed.

"Dad?" his voice was soft and low, "Dad, are you awake?"

Julius sighed and drowsily opened his eyes, turning his head towards them.

"Dad, sorry for disturbing you. We have something impor-tant we want to tell you."

Julius rubbed his eyes, "Is Elisabeth alright?" His speech

was slow and slurred by both alcohol and weariness.

"She's fine, it's not her, don't worry. We want to talk to you about us, us two, me and Babette." he faltered and drew a deep breath, then put his arm around Babette's shoulders. "Well... the thing is, we're... we're an item. That's about the best way I can say it because well, that's how it is. I appreciate you might not approve but nothing will change things. We've spent hours talking it over these last few days, and what we want to do is move away so that we can live as a family without anyone gossiping about us. We'll go somewhere where no-one knows us, where we can feel free and be happy. It would be good if you could be pleased for us, but we understand if you're not, and I know this might have come as a shock to you. We're both very sorry if it has, but, well, this is how it is, and we thought it was the right thing to tell you."

A thick silence filled the room as Julius stared ahead of him. He said nothing, made no sound for a few minutes and then suddenly he let out a loud and woeful sigh, covered his face with his hands and began to sob.

Caspian and Babette did not know what to do. They had not anticipated such a reaction and they looked at one another in dismay.

Julius began to make a high-pitched groaning noise so distressing that Caspian and Babette wondered if it really came from him. "Leave me!" he wailed and turning on his side he curled up tight and hid his head in his arms. Caspian and Babette were so shocked that all they could do was stand there, mouths agape, and watch.

"Go!" Julius muttered, "Leave me!"

20

A New Place To Live

Fabia had driven Caspian's car to meet Samuel at the airport, almost two hours' drive away. They were ecstatic to be reunited and they held hands almost constantly on the journey back, stealing a brief kiss at road junctions and traffic lights. They chattered non-stop, of how each had passed the time since they had last seen one another, repeating things they had already told one another on the phone, and talking feverishly of their plans for the near future. It seemed that the grey of November had broken just for them and the sun shone, unseasonably strong, as if the earth had temporarily forgotten it was autumn and had returned to late summer. Such a fine English day that stretched languidly across the fields, lolloped lazily over hedges, then tumbled softly down the hillsides, winding its way out over fields thick with the brown stubble of summer wheat.

They went in through the door at the side of the house, Fabia's key turning with a customary clunk as she pushed the door open and Sam squeezed in behind her with his suitcase and bulging rucksack. The hallway seemed to be full of sunshine and smelt of furniture polish. Babette had cleaned and tidied the house and was now busy in the kitchen; water sloshed in the sink and gurgled down the plughole, the inviting aroma of a cake baking wafted enticingly through the downstairs rooms, and cheerful ragtime music greeted them.

"Well, this is home!" smiled Fabia, turning to Sam. A grin stretched from ear to ear across his handsome face, golden-brown from his outdoor work in France; that sparkle in his eyes, the exultation, the honour he felt at stepping into this very private life of hers. He could not put it into words.

* * *

"It was where they hung the meat," explained the agent. "Not terribly romantic, but it's a lovely flat." She pushed open the door to Flat 2 in the East Wing and they stepped into a long, narrow hallway, brightly lit by daylight pouring in through the windows that ran along one side. On the opposite side two doors led off to the bedrooms and straight ahead, a door was open to the sitting room. The ceilings were high, the windows tall, with shutters that were pulled back. There was a pronounced air of faded grandeur even here, in what was the basement of the 18th century stately home.

"Let's start down the end," said the agent and she led the way through to the sitting room. It was quite a large room, with two windows in both the east and south walls, almost full height with low sills. A refined light pervaded the room, a trapped tortoiseshell butterfly fluttered in a corner behind a seal brown velvet curtain. The walls were papered white, the carpet the same mid-green as in the hallway, and in a small fireplace was a black enamelled wood-burning stove, swept clean. The windows looked out on to the gravelled car park to the side and at the end, over low box hedges on the narrow strip of lawn in front of the flat, was a vista along a woodland walk where a metal gate stood open.

"I like it very much," smiled Sam. "This room is a good size and it has a nice feel, very calm and peaceful." Fabia nodded in enthusiastic agreement.

The kitchen was of adequate size, ochre yellow walls that were bumpy and uneven, fitted units around the edge of the room, space in the middle for a small table. As its former use dictated, meat hooks hung from the ceiling; above the ceramic butler sink and wooden draining board a high window gave a glimpse of the back garden. To the right was a door through to a lobby which connected to the bathroom, and a door that led to the small utility space and to the back door. It was very agreeable, a formerly more practical, beneath-the-stairs area of the main house, and still in essence a part of it; a cosy and welcoming apartment. Even the slight smell of mustiness did not matter.

"We've kept the vital character of the house as much as we could. Obviously certain updating was essential, but these flats retain the ambience you would expect, being part of a stately home," the agent explained. "The sash windows are original, all the fireplaces and door mouldings and the cornicing too," she smiled, "though not the wood-burner of course, that's a modern addition! And beneath the carpets are the original flagstones. Seems a shame to cover them up but keeping the warmth in is important with these high ceilings."

The back door opened to a small area of lawn, hedged with tall laurel. To the right-hand side was a long double storey building, the bottom part open and used as a car port. "Your parking," the agent told them. "Of course, you can also park in the courtyard at the front, but with all the staff, it can get busy during the day, and it's where the tenants' visitors park as well. You just continue around the side of the house to park here, or you can access it from the track that runs past the obelisk in the field at the back of the house."

"It's lovely, really lovely," smiled Fabia. "What do you think Sam?"

"I love it!" he answered, looking around.

"Of course, you have access to the gardens anytime," the agent informed them, "All tenants have access to the gardens, which is a huge benefit as it's unbelievably peaceful when the visitors have gone home, and when the gardens are closed to the public in the winter. It's quite a spectacle when it snows, really beautiful. And you have your own part of the walled garden further down the drive. You can do more or less what you want with it, within reason, as long as it's kept tidy. Most of the tenants grow vegetables in their plots and there's a communal greenhouse, one of the original glasshouses that was rescued. Someone even managed to grow a pineapple in it last year! It's all very private and that bit isn't open to the public."

"Will you be living here too?" she turned to Fabia.

Sam answered for her, his hand on Fabia's shoulder, "Yes, she will. She hopes to find work nearby."

"What sort of work do you do at the moment?" the agent asked her directly.

"I work in an art gallery. Only part time, but I enjoy it and I'm hoping to find the same sort of work around here."

"I should think you'll find something. There are quite a few galleries in the towns around here, and in some of the villages. This area seems to attract art lovers. You know there's a big art collection in the house? It's of national importance. Well, international really. We have plans to make it a permanent exhibition in its own right. It's fine art, mostly landscapes, portraits, and some 18th century miniatures. Several major pieces have recently been returned from a house in Italy, so we feel that as a collection it should be available for the public to see."

Fabia's eyes widened, "That sounds interesting, I'd love to see it when it's open."

"We haven't decided exactly how we're going to do it, or where we're going to house the exhibition, it's in the very preliminary stages. One idea was to renovate part of the stable block, where the café and shop are. Actually, it might work out well for you because it will inevitably generate a couple of part time posts. I can't promise anything, but we'll definitely need some help with it and you never know. Come to my office when we've finished looking around and I'll take your details."

The two bedrooms also looked out onto the back garden. One was slightly larger than the other, and though both were quite dark as they faced north, they were pleasant rooms, brightened by white painted walls and light carpet. The bigger room had an ornate cast iron fireplace and a small walk in closet for hanging clothes; it had even been fitted out with rails and shelves, and lower down, a built-in shoe rack.

It was a foregone conclusion; of course Sam would take the flat, he needed no encouragement nor persuasion. He and Fabia were both very excited at the prospect of living there in less than a month's time and they practically jumped with glee as soon as the agent was out of sight. They decided to have a walk around the grounds, and to wander down the front drive and find the tenants' walled garden.

"We can grow our own vegetables!" Fabia enthused. "Won't it be wonderful? Home grown veg for dinner every night, lovely fresh salads in the summer! You should see the gardens in the autumn with all the colours reflected in the lakes, it's so beautiful then, people come from miles around to see it."

"I can imagine it very well! I've seen pictures, though there is probably no comparison to the real thing. I cannot wait Fabia, I am so much looking forward to starting this job and living here – and now I have you, my little Fabia! The cherry on top of the cake!"

Sam may have noticed that Fabia blushed a little when he said this. She had not told him that she had been walking on air ever since that first day beneath the tree in Dana's garden.

They held hands tightly as they strolled along the paths that wound their way around the lakes, a larger one closest to the house and at its end a waterfall that flowed into the second smaller lake. Now and then were glimpses of follies; a neo-classical pantheon, a rotunda that stood above a boathouse, and high up on the hill above the gardens a temple to Apollo, the sun god, reached by a dark tunnel cut into the rock of the hillside. Overlooking the lake was a cool and shaded grotto, inlaid with shells, and fed by a natural spring; in its corners several types of fern grew. This vast formal garden was built on one man's romantic recollections and sketches of a youthful grand tour on the continent and was now enjoyed by thousands.

Sam turned suddenly to Fabia, not loosening his grip on her hand, "Can you believe it?" he exclaimed, "just a few weeks and we will be living here! Life is good, Fabia, life is so good!"

* * *

The police car pulled up on the road outside the house and two officers took their time getting out, a man and a woman. They spoke quietly together for a few moments and then walked to the door, the man lifting his hand to the heavy brass knocker which he rapped loudly.

Babette was in the conservatory watering plants. She put down the watering can, not noticing the droplets that fell on the tiled floor, and quickly went through the hall to answer the door. She was surprised to see police officers on the doorstep. All kinds of thoughts flashed through her mind; Elisabeth, Caspian, Fabia, even Luke; perhaps he'd been up to no good and they wanted to ask her a few questions. Julius, it must be Julius – had he been caught driving whilst under the influence of alcohol?

"Miss Mortimer? I'm PC Bastable, this is WPC Dunn. May we come in?" They held out their identification cards.

"Yes, of course. What's happened? Is it my daughter? Is she alright?" Babette was trembling, her heart beating fast.

"It's not your daughter we've come about. Is there somewhere we can sit down?"

"Yes, we'll go in here," she led them into the sitting room where she sat in the brown leather chair and the two officers sat side by side on the sofa.

"We're here regarding Julius Mortimer," PC Dunn began. "Are you Fabia, his daughter?"

"No, I'm Babette, his niece. Well, sort of. His brother was my stepfather. I live here, I've lived here since I was a child. Oh my God, what's happened? What has he done?"

The officers questioned Babette further, noting down her

full name and those of Fabia and Caspian, even Louisa, her relationship to Julius, his movements over the past few days.

"You're not his next of kin then? Is there someone else we could talk to? We don't actually have a named next of kin, but we know he has children."

"Can't you tell me what's happened? I'm as good as next of kin. He has a son, but he's at work, and his daughter is out for the day. We're not expecting her back until late this evening and I can't get hold of her. What's happened? Will you please tell me?"

"It's bad news I'm afraid. We can tell you but first we must ask if there is anyone you want us to call, to be here with you? Perhaps we should call Mr. Mortimer's son?"

"Well, he has appointments all morning, out in the middle of nowhere, so we won't be able to get hold of him until after lunch. It's okay for you to tell me, Julius wouldn't mind." She fiddled with her necklace, a single ruby on a thin gold chain that Caspian had given her.

"There's no easy way to say this Babette. I'm afraid Mr Mortimer has been found dead in the woods at Westbrook. We don't quite know the circumstances as yet. He was found by a woman walking her dog earlier this morning. His body has been taken to the mortuary for identification."

"No! No!" was all Babette could say, she had gone deathly pale and felt as though there was a huge lump in her throat that stopped her from talking.

"I appreciate this is very difficult. We need to know as much as possible about his whereabouts in the past few days. It would help us to understand what has happened, though at the moment it looks as if he died from natural causes, perhaps a heart attack. Does he suffer from heart trouble, or any other medical issues?"

Babette was visibly shaken, frantically fiddling with her necklace, "No, he's quite healthy, I think. Well, I wouldn't know, he doesn't tell us much, he keeps himself to himself. I know that sounds odd, but that's how he's been for years, it's just the way he is. The way he was. Oh my God!" She broke down and began to cry. "We haven't seen him for a few days," she said between gulps, "he often sleeps in the woods, he has a hut there. He likes it up there."

"Can I get you a glass of water my love? Or perhaps a cup of tea?" the WPC asked.

"No, no thank you. I can't believe this, it's such a shock," she blew her nose and wiped her eyes. "Are you sure it's him?"

"I'm afraid so. The woman who found him knows him quite well. He hasn't been formally identified, we'll need someone to do that as we have certain procedures to follow, but we are ninety nine percent sure. Do you think perhaps we should try calling his son? If he's out and not contactable is there someone we could leave a message with, for him to come home as soon as possible? Where does he work? Is it far?"

"He works at the architects on the business park, but he's out on appointments this morning. He was going to Jane Darling Farm and then to the aerodrome. We won't be able to get hold of him yet. I can't drive there. I don't have a car and I have to collect my daughter from school."

"Tomkins and Parker? Let's give the office a call, shall we? If they know his whereabouts, they might be able to send someone out to get him. Could PC Bastable use your telephone?"

"Yes, of course. It's in the hall, on the table."

"Thank you." PC Bastable stood, and tucking his notebook

back into his breast pocket, went to the hall, leaving WPC Dunn and Babette together in the sitting room. The WPC leaned across to Babette and put a reassuring hand on her arm.

"Are you okay Babette? I realise this has come as a shock to you. It's the worst part of our job this, and I'm sorry we're the bearers of bad news. Just let me know if there's anything you want or anything I can do. We'll stay with you until Caspian comes home, it's not a good time to be alone. Is there anyone else you'd like us to call?"

"No, I don't think so, there isn't anyone. There's no point in trying to get hold of Fabia, we'll tell her when she gets home tonight."

"Fabia is Mr. Mortimer's daughter, isn't she?"

"Yes, she'll be home later tonight. She's moving away, she's gone to look at a flat with her boyfriend. Will you tell Caspian on the phone or when he comes home?"

"We'll wait until he gets home. It's not a good idea to tell him over the phone if he has to drive home. Look, this is a big shock to you Babette, let me make you a cup of tea. A hot drink can help a little in these situations."

"That would be nice, thank you."

Poor, poor Babette; she was not close to Julius, no one could be, but he was a constant in her life and to be told that he was no longer alive was such a bombshell. Caspian and Fabia had yet to be told, and Elisabeth. It was all going to be very, very difficult.

* * *

Julius had not slept the night that Caspian and Babette came to him to tell him of their relationship. He had stayed curled in the armchair sobbing until the early hours of the morning and then gone quietly up to his room where he lay on the bed and tried to sleep. Instead he tossed and turned fitfully; again, and again he wept, a desperate man lost in a terrible maelstrom.

While it was still dark, he got up and drove to the woods, taking with him whiskey and brandy from the cupboard in his sitting room. He sat wrapped in a damp and holey blanket by the unlit fire and drank until finally, he crawled into his hut and collapsed into a deep sleep induced by alcohol and mental exhaustion.

When he awoke, just for a few brief seconds he felt calm, and then the anguish of the previous night pressed down upon him and a raging headache beat about his temples. His neck ached from the slumped position he had slept in and he wanted to eat. He opened a tin that was on the floor near the back of the hut and took out a handful of wholewheat biscuits, cramming them into his mouth; they were stale and dry, and he could barely chew. He had neither the impetus nor the energy to light the fire and boil water, so he washed the biscuits down with brandy. Julius was a tortured soul, his head heavy with drink and with distress. What could he do? Whatever could he do?

As he did not know what to do, he drank, and that is how he passed the day, sitting in the hut drinking, until once more he fell into a stupor on the floor. In the morning he ventured to the latrine, although his legs were weak, and he could barely get up the slope. On the way back to the hut he picked fungi to cook; he knew he needed to eat and to drink something other than alcohol, so he gathered twigs and small branches to light a fire. Stumbling back to the hut a sudden movement caught his eye and he turned his head towards the middle of the woods.

There it was again, the cloaked figure standing in the clearing where he'd watched deer feeding one evening in the spring. He narrowed his eyes to better focus; a branch slipped from his arms and he bent to retrieve it. When he looked up again the figure had gone. Julius was bewildered; was it ever there or had he imagined it? He was too exhausted to care.

By the middle of the day he was drunk again. He had eaten the fungi he'd cooked and had mopped the juices from the pan with a piece of stale bread he found in a carrier bag in the corner of his shed. Not bothering to boil the kettle he washed his meal down with gin mixed with water from the stream, drinking enough of it to send him into a deep slumber. When he awoke, he felt acute griping pains in his stomach and his bowels, and his throat was parched and sore. He stood to his feet and steadying himself against the thin trunk of a young ash tree, he vomited. He desperately needed to use the latrine and decided to try to get to the top of the woods. Overcome with sickness and very disorientated, he went not up along the side hedge as he usually did, but up through the middle of the woods, among the beech trees. Several times he stopped to vomit, and he feared that he would not be able to contain his bowels. The pain in his stomach had intensified and worked its way round to his lower back and it was such agony that he could not stand. He sank to his knees groaning and began to crawl very slowly, one hand clasping his stomach, the other clutching at the ground that was thick with decaying leaves and earth, his nails digging into the loam. He could not see properly; each time he lifted his head the wood span before him in a grey and cloudy blur. He tried to focus on his hand as he moved it on the ground but that too was fuzzy and shadowed. After a while he reached the colossal beech tree, the tree he admired most in the whole wood, and then hand, knee, hand, knee, hand, knee, he sluggishly crawled until he came to the mighty trunk and fell against it. His innards were burning, his head and heart thumping as his face, contorted in agony, scrapped the rough bark and sank to the rotting debris on the woodland floor.

* * *

Helena went across the field towards the woods, the long, wet grass swishing against her wellingtons as she walked. Maggie bounded ahead of her, now and then disappearing into the hedge, her whereabouts revealed by a fervent rustling and the cacophonous squawking of a pheasant disturbed from its sanctuary as it took clumsy flight into the grey November air. She had not been out for a couple of days because the weather had turned quite wintry with pelting rain and ferocious squalls that whipped around the treetops, the wind whistling at night like banshees. She was glad to wake that morning to see that it had subsided and calm was restored to the outside world; yet it was what she called a nothing day, still and dull with a strange, almost unearthly pervading quiet, the sky the colour of gun metal above the hills. She was a little disappointed as she'd been looking forward to a good walk since hearing the weather forecast on the radio the day before; they said it would be surprisingly warm and temperatures similar to those in early October when the South West still basked in the remains of an Indian summer. 'Not here,' she thought, 'we must have missed that.'

She turned at the top of the field to admire the view as she often did. It was a sight that she would never grow tired of, even at this forlorn time of year. Miles and miles of unspoilt countryside stretched on and on until it met the sky on the horizon; a patchwork of fields and wooded hillsides interspersed with farmsteads and old cottages. When she walked here at dusk, she could see the faint glow of lights from the houses in the near distance and she wondered who lived there and what they were doing. She imagined families sitting down to an early evening meal, elderly couples settling into favourite chairs with their lap trays to watch the six o'clock news, a plump spaniel curled up on the rug in front of the open fire.

When she reached the edge of the field she climbed over the stile and continued along the footpath then stepped across the ditch and went over the hedge into the woods. Helena wondered if the strong winds had brought down any branches or young trees, as it had uprooted the saplings at the edge of the copse that bordered her garden. Maggie scampered ahead of her, in and out of the undergrowth, nose to the ground, taking chase when she spotted a squirrel busy collecting food for the coming winter. Every now and then Helena called her back and she came obediently, tail wagging, pink tongue lolloping at the side of her mouth, white fangs exposed. Approaching the beech trees, the dog seemed to disappear out of sight; it was so hard to see her amongst the beech leaves that provided camouflage against her sandy brown coat. Helena was pleased to catch sight of her as she neared the biggest beech, the sentinel of the woods, where the dog was frantically pawing at the ground, sniffing and whimpering. "I hope she hasn't got a squirrel," Helena thought as she drew closer, and when she looked, she could see something lying at the foot of the wide trunk, though from that distance, without her glasses, she did not know what it was.

"What is it Maggie? What have you found?"

She froze, unable to speak when she was close enough to see clearly. At the foot of the enormous beech tree, covered with the leaves that the storms had shaken loose, lay a man. Only one arm and part of his face remained uncovered. At first, she thought, or hoped he must be sleeping or at the worst, unconscious, and she crept closer. She noticed the marble white hand, the pale grey skin of the face, the vomit stained beard, and she knew that it was Julius and that he was dead.

21

Louisa's Revelation

The autopsy revealed that Julius had died from amatoxin poisoning caused by ingestion of a particular mushroom; the Destroying Angel, *amanita virosa*. It also stated that due to the excessive amount of alcohol in his system even if he had received help within a few hours of eating the mushroom, it is unlikely that he would have survived.

* * *

It was late at night, on the day of Julius' funeral. Caspian, Babette and Louisa were sitting at the kitchen table talking; all were sad and solemn, and the conversation was interspersed with long and thoughtful silences during which each of them had their private reminiscences of Julius. They talked about holidays they'd had when Caspian and Fabia were children, and of weekend camping trips that Babette had joined them on with Nathan, the children complaining of the tediousness of long walks along coastal paths and over Dartmoor, struggling to keep up with the grown-ups, their legs aching and feet sore.

"We didn't know he ate wild mushrooms," said Babette. "He never mentioned it, but we're not surprised, it's just the sort of thing he'd do. We used to joke about him foraging for nuts and berries. It's so sad, he must have mistaken the poisonous ones for something else, it's easily done if you're not an expert. And well, he was drunk," she added.

"Well, there was a lot he never mentioned. That was Julius for you. He certainly liked to keep himself to himself," said Louisa. "He was always secretive, he wouldn't share any of his inner thoughts with anyone, not even me. It was always difficult for me to know how he was feeling about anything because he never seemed to show any emotion."

"We knew about the booze though; I feel terrible about that. We noticed he was drinking more than usual at home, but we had no idea how much, and we didn't know he was drinking like that in the woods. If we'd had any idea just how bad it was, we would have tried to help him."

"You mustn't blame yourself Babette. Even if you'd tried, I doubt if he would have let you help. He was often in denial you know, about a lot of things."

"But it's so sad, and what really hurts is that we'll never know why he reacted so strangely when we told him our plans. We wanted to talk to him about it, but he disappeared the next day and didn't come back, and now he's not here anymore, so we'll never know."

"What do you mean? Your plans?" Louisa put down her wine glass, fiddling with the stem, turning it round and round between her fingers. It had left a dark burgundy stain on the scrubbed pine tabletop that would not be easy to remove but it did not matter; such things, in this household, were not of primary concern.

Babette looked at Caspian, "You haven't told her?"

"No, I haven't. There's been a lot going on, hasn't there? I thought I'd get round to it before Mum went back." He paused, "Well let's tell her now? It seems as good a time as any, we're all here, Elisabeth's in bed sound asleep."

"Tell me what? What's this all about?"

"Our plans Mum, for the future," Caspian said and then he came straight out with it. "Babette and I are together now, we're a couple. It's not something we went into lightly, we've talked it over an awful lot, but I'm sure you know how it is, you can't help who you fall in love with. We had huge doubts because we were worried about what people would think, but we don't care anymore, if people want to gossip that's up to them. We're going to move away somewhere where no-one knows us, possibly America. I've been offered a job there."

Louisa was aghast. She stopped turning her glass, her face frozen. She had turned very pale. Babette took a deep breath, noting her negative reaction. This was not what she expected from Louisa who was always so liberal minded.

"You can't," stuttered Louisa, "It's not right. It's just not right. I don't know how you can sit there and talk about it so calmly, as if it doesn't matter. It does matter! You can't do this, do you understand? It has to stop."

"But Mum, why? Sure, it's a bit odd because we've grown up in the same household, but we aren't related by blood, are we? We aren't even cousins, that's a fact. So, no, quite frankly, I don't understand. I don't see what the problem is." He paused, "I didn't expect this from you Mum. Try to see it from our point of view - we're in love, we desperately want to be together and apart from what other people think, there is nothing to stop us."

"We've talked about it for weeks," added Babette. "We considered everything, how it would affect Elisabeth, absolutely everything. I'm sorry but I agree with Caspian, I'm surprised at your reaction. I didn't think you'd object, I thought you'd understand."

"Well I do object. You have to stop this. How long has it been going on?"

"We've had very strong feelings for each other for years, but it's only really developed over the last few months."

"A few months! Why the hell didn't anyone tell me! Why didn't you tell me before? Listen, you two, this cannot continue, it's completely wrong. You've got to stop it now."

"But Louisa, why? Like Caspian says, we're not even cousins. Why is it such a problem?"

Caspian was exasperated, "Mum, I don't get it. Why are you saying this? Is it that you don't approve because we've known each other since we were small, because we've grown up as though we're related? Is that it? Is that all it is? Because that doesn't matter to us!"

"No, it doesn't matter at all! We aren't related and we're both adults so we can do what we like," Babette was almost fuming, she could not believe Louisa's reaction.

Louisa had got up and was pacing from the table to the sink, words forming on her lips that she didn't know how to say, words that had to be measured somehow, not blurted out in the heat of the moment. She started to cry, very quietly, tugging her jacket tight around her small body, shielding her face with one hand. Babette watched her, looked from her to Caspian, back to Louisa; she also did not know what to say or do. Louisa who had always been so free thinking! It didn't make sense, it was hypocritical, and Babette was angry.

"Louisa, I'm sorry," she began, standing up and going to the other woman. "I'm sorry you don't approve, but I didn't expect this from you. Like Caspian says, is it just about convention? I can't believe that would bother you, you've never cared for that sort of thing, with your arty-farty ways. I'm shocked at your reaction, we both are."

"You're related by affinity," Louisa suddenly snapped.

"Not in the eyes of the law," Babette retorted. "We've read up on it, we're very well informed in that respect. And besides we're not talking about getting married, we just want to be together, as a family with Elisabeth. It's been pretty much like that for the last few years anyhow, it's just that we've grown closer."

"What did Julius say when you told him?"

Caspian shrugged, "He cried, if you must know. It was very upsetting; I've never seen him like that. I've never seen anyone like it. He behaved very strangely; it was like a wounded animal the way he cried."

Louisa looked at her son then quickly looked away, "Are you sleeping together?" Her eyes darted from her son to Babette as she became visibly more distraught. "Are you?" she demanded. "Tell me!"

"Mum, please! Don't embarrass us! We don't have to answer that question!"

"Well you must tell me because I need to know, it's very important!" She began to shake. "Oh God, why has it come to this? Why has it happened like this? We should have done something about it years ago!" she cried, raising her eyes to the ceiling.

"Mum, you're overreacting! You need to calm down! What's

the problem with two people falling in love? Don't you want us to be happy?"

"Is it me?" Babette asked, tears streaming down her cheeks, smudging her mascara. "Am I not what you wanted for Caspian?"

"Oh Babette, if only you knew!" the older woman cried. She blew her nose and turned to face them.

"Babette, I love you, of course I do, I always have done. But no, I don't want this for him, it's not you! I don't want this for either of you. Just promise me it will stop now, and we don't have to speak another word about it."

"No, Mum, we won't even consider it," said Caspian. He put his arm around Babette's shoulder and drew her to him, her tears quickly staining his white shirt.

Louisa was now very distressed, "Please listen to me! Just believe me, you cannot do this!"

"But you're not saying anything that makes sense! Why should we listen to you? You're reacting purely on the basis of convention, that's all. Well to hell with convention! I'll say it again, Babette and I are not related, there is no reason why we can't be together. We are staying together and that's it."

"Oh my God, Caspian, if only you knew!" Louisa began, wiping her nose again.

"Knew what?" Babette and Caspian said together.

Louisa blew her nose and tried to compose herself for a moment, "Sit down, both of you, we all need to sit down, I need to tell you something."

The three of them sat down again at the table, the two women visibly upset, Caspian shaking. Louisa took a very deep breath.

"I am so sorry you two. I'm sorry for what I have to say, but you have to know. It's something I've known for a long time; I

266

told your father several times to tell you all. I wish I had done it now, then we wouldn't be in this terrible mess. I have to do this, I hate to, because of course I want you both to be happy, I love you both more than anything, but this is very important," she sobbed again and took a deep breath in.

"Mum, what the hell is it? You're just repeating yourself; you're not making any sense at all. Say what you have to say and be done with it."

Slowly, Louisa exhaled and then she began, "It was Julius' place to tell you this, especially you Babette, and he should have told you a long time ago. You have a right to know, especially now. Please believe that I love you very dearly, you mean the world to me, and as I said, I want you to be happy, but there is a very good reason why you cannot be together and why this relationship has to stop now," she looked down at her hands, fiddling with her handkerchief. "It's because..." she wrung her hands, over and over, tears rolled slowly down her face. She looked towards the window and then back at them; "Babette, Julius is your father."

The silence that fell upon the room was enormous, the shock colossal, as if the whole house had fallen down around them. Louisa looked long at Babette, and then to her son, "I'm so sorry, but now you know. I had to tell you. You understand that, surely? Julius is your father Babette. I begged him to tell you years ago."

The lovers were stunned. They had both turned white as a sheet and could neither move nor speak. It was as though a great iron weight had fallen on them. Babette felt that she could not breathe, her chest hurt and felt constricted; this was not happening, she was not hearing things correctly. It felt unreal, these people sitting here talking in this kitchen were someone else, she was behind them, somewhere else, watching.

The silence broke with her scream, long and painful, "No! No!" she cried, "That's a lie, it's a lie! It can't possibly be true! Why are you saying this Louisa? Why? It isn't true! It can't be, please tell me it's not true!"

Caspian still could not move, rooted to his chair, he was numb. He too felt disassociated from that room and all that had occurred. Babette was shivering, Louisa sobbed and said nothing.

"You lying bitch!" screamed Babette. She pushed her chair away and stood up, her legs trembling beneath her. As she ran to the door, Louisa caught her arm.

"Let go of me, Louisa, you nasty, spiteful bitch!" shouted Babette.

"Caspian, help me!" pleaded Louisa, "I need to explain!" Caspian somehow went to Babette, his legs heavy, his head aching. He ushered her back to her chair where he sat holding her. Babette was rocking and crying uncontrollably now, in huge sobs that wracked her entire body. Caspian remained, ashen, trembling, his eyes red rimmed, as if he too would start to cry at any minute.

Louisa began to explain: "When Caspian was very young, just a toddler, Julius had a brief affair with a woman. She was a dancer who was in town for a short time. He... he got her pregnant and she wanted to keep the baby, but she told Julius that she didn't love him, and she wanted nothing from him. Not long after, she moved away. I promise you, every word of this is true." She sniffed and broke off, crying, "The last thing I wanted to do is hurt either of you. This is breaking my heart, but you have to know. That woman was your mother,

Martha," she continued, looking at Babette; "She came here with a theatre group who were touring this part of the country. They were staying in town. Julius sometimes did extra jobs at weekends, doing a bit of carpentry and that, and he got work helping with the stage set; we needed the money, we were struggling financially because I'd given up my job, so we only had your Dad's income at the time. The work was only for a few weeks but that was long enough for him to get caught up with your mother. I didn't know anything about this until you came to live with us after Nathan died, I swear. Julius was very insistent that we look after you and at first, I didn't understand why. I must be honest, I had doubts at the time, and I hope you'll forgive me for that. I would never have let you go into care but part of me wasn't sure I wanted another child in the house. It was purely selfish, I felt that I didn't have enough of Julius' attention as a husband and that he wasn't much of a father to Caspian or Fabia, so I didn't understand why he was so keen to take you in. We argued about it a lot and eventually he told me that he was your father. He told me about the affair with Martha, and he said that when she told him she was pregnant she had already made her mind up to move on, there was nothing he could do about it. She left and that was it, he never heard from her again. It was by fluke that she met Nathan at a festival when you were small. Nathan was besotted with your mother, she meant the world to him and he was always telling us about her and her beautiful little daughter, showing us photographs, and all the time Julius said nothing. He kept it from me and from Nathan. Nathan never knew."

"But that doesn't make sense. How could that work with her being so closely associated with Dad?" asked Caspian. "We even went to their wedding!"

"Well it must have been very awkward, but they kept it quiet. Perhaps Julius was protecting his brother, he'd gone off the rails a bit. We didn't really see much of any of you until Martha ran off, but I can assure you Babette, right from the start Nathan took you on as his own, he insisted on adopting you when he married your mother. He loved you as his own daughter, he did everything for you, took you to school, got you dressed each morning, cooked your dinner each night. He loved you, he was a good father to you. Martha was not a good mother, all she seemed to care about was herself. It was Nathan who took care of you. He was a lovely man, really lovely. So kind-hearted, I often wished Julius was more like him. It was only when she left that we all became close, that's when you started coming to stay for weekends and we all had those holidays together."

"So all the time Dad could watch his daughter grow up thinking no-one knew," muttered Caspian.

"Exactly. From a safe distance. I suppose that's what he thought. And if Nathan hadn't died, perhaps we would never have known. I'm ashamed that Julius took this secret to the grave with him, I'll never forgive him for that. He should have told you long ago, and he should certainly have told you when you told him about your relationship."

"Why didn't you tell me?" demanded Babette, "You've known all these years, you could have told me. Why didn't you?"

"I know, I agree, I should have. I wish I did now, more than anything. I understand why you're angry with me Babette, I would feel the same in your shoes, but I felt it wasn't my place, and Julius didn't want me to tell you. He said that he would do it himself when the time was right. I wish to God I had told you! It would have been so much better if I had. Do you think it was my responsibility to tell you? Honestly? Do you really think that? I'll always regret that I didn't, but I know that's no consolation to you. I just felt that Julius should be the one to tell you. I urged him to, so many times, but he wouldn't. He said he'd tell you when it seemed right. I couldn't bear it any longer, living such a lie, that's why I left. I wrote to him several times, begging him to tell you. Elisabeth is his granddaughter for goodness sake, he should have told you?"

"That explains why she was the apple of his eye," mumbled Caspian, "why he forgot everyone else's birthdays but never hers." He sighed and leaned back in the chair, "What a fucking mess," he said, banging his fist on the table and then he too started to cry. "What a fucking mess!" He picked up a cup, threw it hard at the wall where it smashed, and then he went out of the room and out of the house, slamming the back door behind him.

* * *

The ensuing days were utterly miserable. November had at last settled down in thick drizzle, bringing fog with it that made the already shorter days seem darker. Louisa returned to France feeling weakened and upset, even her suitcase felt heavier and her feet seemed to drag upon the wet and slippery ground. Her revelations had of course thrown an entirely different light upon Caspian and Babette's future; for them now there could not be a future and they had dismally resigned themselves to this fact. They barely spoke, both of them repulsed by the knowledge that their relationship was incestuous, that they

271

were closely related by blood. They were knotted inside, angry with Julius, furious that he had never had the courage to tell them the truth in spite of seeing their closeness unfolding before his eyes and in spite of them telling him of their plans. If only he had gone about with his eyes and ears open instead of closed to everything but the small sylvan world he frequented.

Life continued; Babette got up each morning after Caspian had left for work and took Elisabeth to school, collecting her at half past three in the afternoon. She did not go to work and she told her employers that she was sick and needed time to come to terms with Julius' death. They were very understanding and told her to take the time she needed, that they would look forward to seeing her when she felt able to return, adding that she must let them know if there was anything they could do to help; they even sent flowers and a sympathy card, which Babette tore into little pieces.

Fabia grieved for her father, but she did not let this interfere with her plans. Neither Louisa, Caspian nor Babette told her of Louisa's horrifying revelation, and they allowed her to think that Babette was distraught at Julius' death, agreeing to tell her in the near future, when it became necessary. Before she'd left, Fabia had twice knocked on Babette's door in the evening wanting to offer her comfort, but Babette only shunned her.

Her mother's visit had to some extent repaired the damaged mother-daughter relationship, and Fabia drove her mother to the airport where they held each other tightly, arranging to visit one another soon. Sticking to her plans and looking forward to the happiness her future would bring, Fabia moved to Wiltshire with Sam and found work in the town.

Caspian spent more and more time at his office, returning home late at night when Babette and Elisabeth were in bed.

Gone was the calm and placid Caspian, replaced by a man who was gloomy and melancholy, who hardly spoke. He did not wish to see Babette; he could not face her even though he still felt that he could not live without her and had made no effort to move out. Part of him longed to talk to her and he desperately wanted to find a resolution of some sort.

If he heard her moving about upstairs, he waited until she had gone back to her room. To encounter her on the landing or anywhere else in the house would possess him of an anguish beyond measure. He wondered sometimes how she felt; he knew that the night Louisa had broken her silence she had also destroyed Babette, but he could not comfort her.

Babette was utterly bereft. What had happened was like some sort of monster that had eaten a huge hole inside her, as if now she had not the organs and tissues of a human being inside but a fathomless black pit that she was crumbling into. She tried to continue with her routine; she had to for Elisabeth's sake. Her daughter still had to go to school, she still needed attention, and when she asked why Babette looked so sad and why she had been crying, Babette told her that she was sad because Julius had died. When Elisabeth asked where Caspian was, Babette simply replied that he was very busy, that he had lots of work to do and had to stay late at the office.

Neither of them spent hours and hours thinking about what had happened. They felt so tortured by it all that they had pushed it into a far corner of their minds in the hope that they could somehow move on with their separate lives and forget that they had ever been close. They could never even be as brother and sister now, and they feared that they would carry this terrible thing around with them until something, some huge and dark event, forced it out, in a long groaning howl so

273

that it would disperse and be gone for good. It was something they would never speak or think of.

Only Babette had thought in the early days after Louisa returned to France, that what if Julius had not died? What would have happened then? She and Caspian would have gone on planning a life together, loving one another, until Louisa learned the extent of their relationship. Elisabeth would have been caught up in a happy but false world that would one day be shattered. Better that it had happened now whilst she was young, but what next, Babette did not know. She did not know how long she would walk about with this emptiness inside of her or how she would ever shake off the despair that had descended upon her.

* * *

It was half past nine at night. Caspian was standing in front of the window in his office, his hands clasped behind his head. The only light came from the lamp on his desk. He could see the lights over at the farm cottage, and much further, those of the next village; other than that, he saw only his reflection. He was unshaven and looked weary, with dark circles beneath his eyes. He was emotionally exhausted, and the recent events were something he did not know how to work his way through. He felt that he was imprisoned by towering walls that hid the sky and kept him in darkness and he could not see any way out; no turning back, no going forward, just day after day of emptiness, nothingness. It could not continue, and he found that he was back in a familiar situation; once again he was desperate to avoid Babette. He thought the right thing to do was to shun her as he tried to do earlier in the year when he was seeing Laura, but still there was a part of him that knew he could not live without her.

A thought flashed into his mind and lifted his spirits a little. 9.30pm. It would now be mid-afternoon in Chicago. Jared Cole would be in his office, perhaps with a team of architects discussing the Michigan development they would be starting on next spring. Caspian went and sat at his desk, took a very deep breath, then exhaled and picked up the phone. He dialled Jared's number and waited for him to answer; it rang five times before he heard the now familiar voice.

"Jared Cole, hello."

"Jared, it's Caspian Mortimer."

"Caspian! Great to hear from you! How are things? We're looking forward to coming to the UK next week. Have you decided what you want to do? Do you have some good news for me?"

"Yes, I have. I'd like to accept your offer. I'd like to join you as soon as possible."

About the Author

Jayne Everard is a qualified journalist and proofreader; she has her own copywriting/content writing business and has had several magazine features and poems published over the last 30 years. She lives in Somerset with her husband and two sons. The Loved & The Lost is her debut novel.